Fatal Deceit

Tim Bacon

Clink
Street

Published by Clink Street Publishing 2022

Copyright © 2022

First edition.

ISBNs:
978-1-914498-72-5 Paperback
978-1-914498-73-2 Ebook

This book is dedicated to my wife Romina, my sons Alex and Daniel, and my daughter Ella. You are all my driving force.

Chapter 1

Craig lay motionless as his breathing and heart rate began to slow, perspiration covering his body. With his head buried in the pillow he could feel Lucy's long dark hair on his cheek as she breathed deeply onto his shoulder. After a minute he pulled himself up gently, he kissed her and climbed off the bed. As he got up, Lucy immediately closed her knees together and pulled the sheet over her naked body. He looked back in perfect time to have another glance at her breasts and crossed the bedroom towards the door. Lucy watched him walk away and admired his toned tattooed body and noticed the fresh scratches on is back and butt cheeks. She let out a sigh and rolled her eyes thinking about the great sex they had just had and after a few seconds remembered the text message she received but had not opened. She reached for her handbag on the floor, revealing a floral tattoo on her lower back, picked out her phone and opened the text message. The bliss instantly turned to guilt as she read the message.

By the time Craig had freshened up, Lucy was fully clothed. He entered the bedroom naked, and she hugged him and ran her hands from his upper legs up to his lean shoulders grasping his butt cheeks on the way. 'Got to go love,' she said gently before kissing his lips repeatedly.

The walk of shame was just under a mile. Whilst walking, looking uncomfortable in high heels, short leather skirt and crop top, she opened her purse and put on the engagement ring which she had removed at the start of the night before. Feeling anxious as she entered the road where she lived with her fiancé, she took a deep breath. It was near 10 am and people were out washing their cars, cutting their grass and children were playing. She approached the block of apartments and pressed the button on the intercom. There was no answer, so she walked around the back and saw that Tyrone was cleaning out his pride and joy 4- wheel drive truck. He was six feet tall, keen bodybuilder and rugby player with a mohawk hair style. He wore a tight vest to show as much muscle as possible and had a perfectly trimmed beard.

She sheepishly approached the truck and caught a glance of herself in the side mirror. Oh fuck! She thought, as she noticed a love bite on her neck. She tapped Tyrone on the back, and immediately turned to the side to prevent him from seeing that side of her neck.

'What time do you call this?' he asked loudly with a look of anger on his face, staring her in the eye.

'Sorry love I had too much to drink. Not like you never do it! I told you I was staying at Sarah's house anyway!' she turned away and entered the door, which was wedged open, up the stairs and into the flat. She went straight into the bathroom and into the shower, trying to think of a plan. As she was washing her hair, she did not notice the bathroom door opening. Tyrone stood and looked at her. At first, he was hoping to make the peace and join her in the shower. As he was stood admiring her sexy naked body, he noticed. His face changed to a grim, angry expression and a deep frown etched his forehead. He shouted, 'What the fuck is that on your neck?' Who have you been shagging you fucking slapper!'

She spun round firstly alarmed and then trying to dilute the situation. 'Shut up! It was Sarah fucking about! Don't you ever call me a slapper!'

He raised his hand and slapped her hard across her right cheek with such force that she fell against the wall and landed in a heap on the floor of the cubicle, almost unconscious moaning in pain. He then grabbed her wet hair in a tight grip of his left hand and lifted her off the floor as she screamed in pain. He punched her in the side of her jaw with his right fist instantly breaking it and threw her onto the bed. She cried hysterically as her hair was almost ripped out with the strength of his grip. He pushed her over onto her back, grabbed her throat with his left hand and raised his right fist which could easily end her life if he hit her again with his strength. 'Who was it?' he asked through his gritting teeth.

She could hardly put words together and tried to deny it as her jaw had been broken. Her eyes were vacant, and she was taking quick shallow breaths as terror and extreme pain set in. She was shaking all over and was still wet, cold, and naked. He calmed slightly but had a cold stare. He released his grip on her neck and unbuttoned his jeans. As he began to have sex with her, she was falling unconscious, but he had no interest in how she felt as he had his way, and when he had finished, he left the room abruptly, slamming the door.

The V8 truck drove out of the courtyard at speed and Tyrone drove straight to the gym. He had a change of clothes, shower gel and towel with him and had no intention of returning to the flat until extremely late. He trained hard and following a shower admired the results of his work as he dried himself in front of the mirror. There were other muscular men in the changing area, but he was the biggest, and most men were cautious around him. Particularly today as his facial expression was far more menacing than usual and his actions were erratic. No one dared get near him.

After Lucy left, Craig put shorts and a t- shirt on and watched television. The usual Saturday morning programmes were on which he found boring, so he watched a Jason Bourne movie for the fifth time. He ate cold baked beans straight from the tin with a spoon and not bothering to take the empty tin to the bin, left it beside the sofa. Even when he got up and went into the kitchen to make a coffee, he left the tin, along with last night's pizza box in the lounge.

He was hoping for a text from Lucy at some point because although he had different women regularly in his flat, he enjoyed Lucy's company and really enjoyed the sex they had. The message alert came, he picked up his mobile and it was his mate from MMA, Sam.

'How was the shag you dirty fucker?'

He replied, 'Not bad, coming out tonight?'

'Yep, about 7.00.'

'OK cheers dick head.'

Chapter 2

Saturday night, mid- June. Jack had finished work at midday for the premium rates overtime and had showered, watched *Final Score* and was ready to meet up with Pete. They met in a bar in the centre of Bristol and were preparing for a long night of drinking. It was 7 pm and the bars in the city centre were quiet with a few seasoned day- time drinkers, half- way through their last pints of cloudy cider before staggering home.

Jack had been working in the engineering workshop since he left school and had served his apprenticeship there. He was a regular at the gym but was not a body builder, he just liked to keep his fitness level up. He was no good at football or rugby, although he enjoyed watching sport. He recently split with a girl his own age, 22, following a turbulent and manipulative relationship. He was not bitter or saddened by the split, more relieved it was over.

Pete was a carpenter and was athletically built but had bad acne when he was a teenager, and the scars were prominent. They had been friends for a couple of years and went out every other week when both were available. Pete had never had a long-term relationship but had a good sense of humour and was never short of female attention. Jack was now single, so he was a regular at the pubs and clubs in town. He only went out on weekends and always had the company of work mates or other friends. He was enjoying single life and the benefits of freedom, although back living with his Mum had brought its limitations. Pete had his own apartment, and it was a short taxi ride from the town centre, as was Jack's Mum's house.

So, where shall we go then?' asked Jack and downed the final third of his lager in one take.

'King Street? There is always plenty to look at down there, my mate Craig pulled in there last night. He's a scaffolder I work with occasionally.'

They made their way through the old part of the town, along the river where a floating restaurant was preparing for a busy night and turned right into King Street. They entered the first pub and ordered a couple of pints and some vodka chasers. They lent with their elbows resting on the bar and commented on women of all shapes and sizes passing by. Then faced the bar, counted to three and both downed their chasers and slammed the glasses down almost simultaneously. They turned to each other, laughed, and carried on sipping their pints and admiring the view of a group of well-dressed attractive ladies who had just entered the bar loudly.

Meanwhile, Craig and Sam met in a bar on king Street bang on seven, dressed up in designer gear. Slightly rough looking but they were both good looking and super fit. They had a few drinks and chatted up as many girls as they could. Some more guys entered the bar, and they all knew each other from previous nights out.

Tyrone had been out all afternoon after his training session, not wanting to go back to the apartment where he left Lucy barely alive. He chose to put her in the back of his mind as he downed pints of cider with two guys from his rugby team. Every bar he approached, the door security would move to one side, and he would walk past unchallenged. He had a reputation for taking them out of the game for refusing entry. He walked into a lively bar, bought a round of drinks, and stood with his mates, chatting about the rugby. The time was 9.30pm and the bar was lively. Sam shouted over to Craig. 'Tell us about that bird last night then!'

'Juicy Lucy mate. Dark hair, nice tits, a tattoo above her ass, good shag. What more do you want to know?'

Tyrone heard him describing his fiancé. Every muscle in his body tensed up and he did not hesitate. He walked straight over to Craig and slammed his hammer like fist into his left cheek. Craig did not see it coming. The punch sent him across the bar, and he hit the floor hard. Years of military and martial arts training kicked in and he got straight to his feet and launched himself at the big guy, kicking him clean in the nuts and following up with several fast punches to the head and body, one of which broke his nose and sent blood shooting across both their clothes. They continued to fight for a minute or two, Craig at this point still had no idea why he was targeted. He ducked out of the way of another hefty awkward punch and as he prepared for a counter punch the leg of a barstool struck him hard, at full swing across the right side of his head. At that instant he saw a white flash, then darkness.

Jack and Pete were chatting with the drunken ladies at the bar and although Jack was the better looking of the two, it was Pete, with his way with words who was receiving most of the attention. Jack looked like a young Eric Cantona with a chiselled face and deep hypnotic eyes. He was a thinker and could hold a good conversation with anyone, but Pete seemed to have the ability to make anyone laugh.

They left the bar after an hour and the ladies took turns kissing them before wandering off in the opposite direction to the guys. 'There's a music venue down here, that should be good.' Pete said as he stumbled down the step onto the cobbled street. As they approached the bar, less than 50 yards from the previous one, there were screams and shouts as a fight was just starting. From the outside it looked as if the entire bar was fighting but it was only six to eight men, some heavily built and some smaller, faster. The guys walked quickly on and made their way to the next bar.

It was busy, but not too busy to get served quickly. They stood at the bar and looked around for talent and both were quite drunk by then. As Jack glanced round, he noticed a girl he went to primary school with and had not seen since. She was fair haired and looked after her appearance. She was naturally beautiful and very well dressed. His initial thought was 'no chance.' Pete noticed that he had looked over at her several times and suggested that he goes over. As Jack denied it, Shelley looked across and recognised Jack. She dismissed the over- dressed man with the fake smile who had been chatting her up for the last half hour with cheesy jokes and made her way through the crowd. 'Is it Jack?' she said nervously.

'Shelley! I was wondering if it was you! How are you?'

Pete backed himself away as he knew Jack was keen, and they already knew each other. Within minutes, Pete had Shelley's friends in stitches of laughter and one girl was showing interest.

Jack and Shelley were getting on very well and remembering old friends from primary school. 'Did you hear about Geoff Taylor?' Jack said with a serious look on his face.

'No? What about him?' she asked curiously.

'He was at his army base in Germany and was found dead in his bunk. He had got pissed and swallowed his tongue in his sleep.'

'Oh my god that's terrible!' Shelley said. 'My brother came out of the army last year. Can you remember Craig?'

'Yes, vaguely, wasn't he always in trouble in school? I thought he was hilarious with his messing around.'

'That's him, he hasn't changed a bit. He's a scaffolder now and likes mixed martial arts. Still lovely but a bit crazy as you can imagine.

Lucy came to her senses an hour after Tyrone had left. She was freezing cold and naked on the bed, and in excruciating pain. Her head was pumping, and her jaw would not move. She slowly raised herself off the bed and got dressed. Taking a glance into the mirror, her face was swollen, and the bruising was beginning to show. She was trying to suppress her emotions and had made up her mind. She stood on a chair and reached above the wardrobe to pull down the suitcase. When she raised one foot and the chair tipped sending her crashing to the ground. She was unhurt and got straight up, back on the chair and carefully pulled the suitcase until it bypassed her and landed loudly on the bed.

Coughing after inhaling some dust from the top of the suitcase, she unzipped and removed the bikini, swim shorts and European plug adapter and throwing them on the floor. She grabbed all her clothes and hanging clothes from the wardrobe and crudely shoved them into the case, then into the bathroom where she grabbed all her toiletries and again shoved them into the case. Passport, driving license, a few family pictures were shoved into a back-pack. She paused and remembered a secret stash of money which Tyrone tried to hide from her under the bed side cabinet. A thousand pounds, minus roughly 50 she had previously stolen. She thought he would return home any minute, so she was growing increasingly anxious. Although mid-June, she put on a big winter coat and pulled the collars up so to hide her bruised, swollen face. Wearing large sun-glasses she left the apartment, down the stairs and straight to her car with her head down. She remembered the previous day filling the Mini Cooper with petrol, so she didn't have to do it over the weekend. After placing the suit-case and back-pack onto the back seat she drove off at speed.

Her parent's house was not an option. Lucy hated to be proved wrong and her parents had warned her about Tyrone and his history of womanising and violence. Shane, her dad, was a member of the same rugby club and saw first-hand how arrogant he was. Lucy decided to drive to Exeter to her auntie and uncle's house. They were the people she could talk to about anything and would not pass judgement. After her grandmother died, she stayed there for a week and was distressed when she had to leave. That was two years previously and she longed to go back but was dating Tyrone by then who was proving to be controlling.

She entered the M5 at Avonmouth and the traffic was at a stand-still. There was an accident near Clevedon and down to one lane this had a tail back up to Cribbs causeway, where she entered the M5. Still suppressing her emotions, she started feeling faint, as she had not eaten all day and it was approaching 4pm. The shock of the physical trauma was beginning to affect her, and she was shaking. She took the left-hand lane and exited the motorway at the next junction and into the services. Driving into the petrol filling station she picked up a bar of chocolate, bottled water, and a large coffee from the machine. The attendant looked at her as she paid by card and asked if she was ok. 'I'm fine thanks' she replied, without being able to move her jaw, turned away and exited the shop. She stumbled slightly as she crossed the forecourt and into the car. She opened the chocolate bar wrapping but could not eat it, so she took a sip of coffee which spilt onto her chin and scolded her mouth. She swore and started crying with her head in her hands to try to shield her face from the people filling their cars and vans up, but one guy noticed and gently knocked on the window 'Are you ok love?'

She lifted her head, stared straight ahead, and drove off at speed.

Chapter 3

Jack and Shelley left the bar together, both trying hard to act slightly more sober than they were. It was around 11.30 and the city centre was busy with groups of drunken women staggering home, a stag party carrying the stag with vomit dripping from his chin, men urinating in office doorways and the odd couple arguing loudly, but not making much sense. After walking for five- minutes they reached the taxi rank. Jack said how good it was to see her again and she said similar. They exchanged numbers on their mobiles and Jack being the gentleman offered the first taxi to her. As he did Shelley heard her message alert. Her face dropped, and her facial colour seemed to fade. Looking vacant with anxiety she said to Jack 'Craig has been rushed to hospital!' She looked around whilst thinking of what to do. She looked at Jack and said, 'I need to get to the hospital!' Her breathing was deep and fast, and she was stroking her hair. The taxi driver at this point was becoming impatient. She apologised and climbed into the back and said, 'Bristol Royal Infirmary please.' She briefly waved at Jack and the taxi pulled away.

On arrival to the emergency department reception, Shelley said 'Craig Mercer was taken in earlier. He's my brother.' The receptionist typed for a few seconds and said 'He's still being assessed by the surgeon down the corridor, room B24 on the left. The waiting room for relatives will be open.'

She walked quickly down the corridor and entered the waiting room. She saw Sam sat in the corner with a black eye and lacerated knuckles. 'What happened? Where is he?' with a tear falling from her eye. Sam explained that he had been attacked by some bloke, was fighting with him and one of his mates smashed a stool over his head.

Craig remained unconscious and the doctors were examining an MRI scan which had been taken. There was bleeding on the brain and pressure was building. The doctors and surgeons on duty all agreed to carry out emergency surgery and was arranging the theatre by phone. The porters wheeled him in and within minutes they began surgery. One of the nurses walked into the waiting room. Sam stood up and patted Shelley on the shoulder. She stood up and introduced herself as Craig's sister. The nurse raised her eyebrows and said, 'He has a fracture to his skull, and there is bleeding on the brain. He is having emergency surgery at the moment. That's all I can tell you at this stage. I will keep you informed and come and see you after the surgery.' Shelley could barely hold back the tears. She reached for her phone and called her mum. It was late; therefore, the call went straight to answer phone. She waited patiently and after the tone said 'Mum, call me back as soon as you get this! Craig is in hospital, it's serious!'

An hour passed and Shelley had been in tears for the whole time, asking Sam questions about the person who did the damage and why he thinks Craig was targeted. The nurse entered the waiting room with pursed lips. Shelley and Sam stood up. The nurse said, 'The surgery had successfully removed the swelling and haemorrhage and he is in recovery'.

Shelley asked, 'He will recover, won't he?'

'He has been incredibly lucky, and the next few days are critical. He will remain in a medically-induced coma until the doctors are satisfied that he is stable enough to regain consciousness. We are doing all we can, but he may or may not be the same person when he regains consciousness.'

Tyrone and his mates left the bar as soon as the barstool incident ended the fight. They walked together and commented on how good a fighter Craig had been, and that if Terry hadn't hit him from behind with the stool, Tyrone would have been in trouble. Tyrone dismissed this and said he was in control. He knew that this was not the case and felt relieved that Terry had ended the fight and affectively saved him from humiliation. He would never admit that.

They walked together and at the end of the road went their separate ways. Tyrone was dreading going home as he was beginning to physically relax and come to terms with the day and night he had. He was feeling low and almost guilty at what he had done to Lucy and seeing Craig unconscious on the floor with blood dripping from his ear. He felt stressed and wondered if there would be consequences but knew the security and was sure that the CCTV would be tampered with before the police arrived.

This was not the case, and the police arrived at the same time as the paramedics. They asked around for witnesses, but no-one was coming up in fear of Tyrone and his mates finding out. Sam gave a vague statement but was carrying out first aid on Craig at the time so just gave his details. The police officer went into the back office and caught the main security guard scrolling back over the footage in a view to delete the start of the fight. He turned and saw the officer and stopped in his tracks. He knew it would be seen as perverting the course of justice if caught tampering with potential evidence. The officer, PC Paul Johnston, examined the footage and saw Tyrone walk briskly across the bar and punch Craig. He examined the full fight to the moment when the stool struck Craig. The person who swung the stool had his back to the camera and his identity was not obtainable. Johnston recognised Tyrone and asked security if they knew him. They all denied ever seeing him before, but Johnston knew they were hiding the truth in fear of reprisal.

Tyrone was approaching home. He felt ready to try and make it work with Lucy, apologise for hitting her and put the events of the last couple of days behind them. He opened the door to the apartment and walked in. He glanced around and headed into the bedroom, expecting Lucy to be asleep, he was going to hug her and say sorry. The bedroom was dark and there were clothes on the floor and the adjoining bathroom door was left open letting a faint beam of light into the bedroom. He could see the bed was empty so went into the lounge and turned on the light. He then realised that Lucy had gone. He stood, staring at the empty sofa feeling anxious, saddened, and heavy with guilt. He went back into the bedroom, switched on the light, revealing the wardrobe doors open, the suit-case gone and all her clothes rails and shelves empty. He held his head and sat on the bed. Moving his hands down to his face and noticing blood all over his shirt, wincing as he touched his broken nose. He laid down on the bed with all his clothes and shoes on and closed his eyes.

PC Johnston had organised a warrant for Tyrone's arrest and within an hour a group of ten officers surrounded the apartment block. Silently, Johnston in standard uniform including a stab vest and two officers in full riot gear went up the stairs to the apartment door. Johnston whispered to the others to stand out of site as he rang the doorbell. Tyrone woke and initially thought Lucy had returned home. He walked to the door but slowed down as he approached. He felt something was wrong. Lucy has a key to the apartment, so she would just walk in. Who could this be at this time of night? He silently approached the door and peered through the spy hole where a tall stern looking police officer wearing a flat hat stood listening intently. Whilst Tyrone was looking, the officer banged hard on the door and shouted 'Open up! Police!'

Tyrone jumped back at the loud banging and realised he had no choice. He opened the door and Johnston stared at him. 'Tyrone O'Mally?'

'Yes, can I help you?' Tyrone asked, planning his escape.

'I am arresting you on suspicion of assault. You have the right to remain' Tyrone landed his fist hard into Johnston's stomach, following through with a devastating punch to the face. The two officers in full riot gear suddenly appeared and blasted him with pepper spray, wrestled him to the ground and cuffed his hands together behind his back. One held his head down whilst sitting on his legs to prevent him from attempting to run off, the other attended the injured PC Johnston and pressed his radio button. 'Officer down, requiring urgent medical assistance! All officers move in, suspect restrained.'

Chapter 4

Lucy arrived at the farm at 10pm. There was a car outside which she didn't recognise. She could see her Auntie Theresa through the kitchen window holding a wine glass chatting to another lady curiously as she saw the headlights approaching up the drive. Lucy's emotions were over-boiling and the pain had grown more intense as she turned off the car engine. As she opened the car door and climbed out, the front door of the house swung open and Uncle Chris was standing there, looking intensely at the person standing at the car, crying her heart out. He instantly realised it was his Niece and walked at speed over to her saying 'Lucy! What is the matter?'

She stumbled and fell into his arms as she cried 'He hit me.'

Chris supported her and took her indoors, sitting her on a chair in the kitchen. Her auntie Theresa took one look at her face and gasped. 'Oh, Lucy darling! What happened? You need to get to hospital!'

Their friends appeared at the kitchen door 'everything alright?' Patrick said, knowing that it was a silly question.

It was clear that the social get-together was over, so they called a cab. 'Is there anything we can do Chris?' Patrick asked as he downed the last of the scotch from his glass.

'No mate, sorry about this, Lucy, our niece has got into a bit of trouble again. I will call you tomorrow mate.'

Within 5 minutes Patrick and his wife had gone. Lucy told her auntie everything apart from sleeping with Craig, cheating on Tyrone, and steeling the money, practically lying about everything apart from Tyrone abusing her. Chris's eyes were growing more furious with every comment. Theresa and Chris were in their mid-fifties and were well spoken with a successful business running their organic farm. They had no children, as their daughter died at the age of 8 from meningitis 15 years ago. Kelly would have been 23, two years older than Lucy. Lucy had many memories of Kelly and still often thought about her. They were not close as Lucy always lived in Bristol and Kelly and her parents near Exeter. But when they were together, they always enjoyed each other's company. Chris and Theresa loved Lucy unconditionally, which they were both aware that the loss of their daughter was the real reason. Lucy could never replace Kelly but could offer some distraction and they were able to offload some love and attention.

'In the morning I will take you to hospital. Your jaw looks broken love.' Chris demanded. 'In the meantime, get some rest. The spare room is always ready for you, I will call your Mum in the morning.'

'No. please don't tell her! She will hate the fact that I came here instead of there! I will call her tomorrow and tell her I'm fine and staying with Sarah.'

'OK, love, don't worry. Come on, I'll take you up,' Theresa helped her off the chair and up to the spare room.

Chris couldn't sleep. The spare room door was slightly open, and he walked past silently and paused to glance at Lucy, checking she was ok. He was tall and muscular but a gentleman and very loving towards his family, particularly Lucy who looked like his late daughter. His sister would be furious at the thought of her daughter going there instead of to her, Lucy was right. Chris was thinking all night what to do as revenge for hurting is beloved Niece. Drinking far too much scotch he paced the floor, walked up stairs, checked on Lucy, back down, upstairs again, all night. He eventually fell asleep at 3.30am in a chair and woke at 6.30am with a dry mouth, thumping headache, nausea, and tinnitus driving him mad. Rubbing his bloodshot, blue eyes and his cropped, sore head, he immediately went up the stairs and saw that Lucy was sound asleep still, looking comfortable. This was enough to put his mind at ease and he went down the stairs and took some pain-killers and a large glass of water. He went into his office and opened his emails. He ignored all the items in the inbox and clicked on the compose icon.

Jim, Tyrone has done it again. Been a naughty boy and hurt Lucy. She doesn't want anyone to know as she's scared. Really pissed off with this prick mate, can you call me?

All the best,

Chris.'

Jim was a police sergeant based in Bristol and a close friend to Chris. They get together a few times each year with a group of university friends in each-other's towns. They all help each other out and have international links, and there are many different backgrounds between the individuals including police, solicitors, construction consultants, doctors and MP-s. The ball was in motion, just a waiting game now.

Three weeks passed, and Jack had not heard from Shelley. He assumed she was not interested but by the way the night ended that she had other concerns, and that relationships were the last thing on her mind. He was right.

It was a Wednesday evening and he had just finished his dinner. Loading the dishwasher up as his mum sat to watch

TV his mobile rang. He saw Shelley's name appear on the screen and answered it with a surprised but gleeful 'Hello!'

'Hello Jack, how are you? Sorry I haven't been in touch, just that Craig was in a bad way in hospital. How are you?'

'Fine Shelley! Great to hear from you. How's Craig?'

'He's on the mend, still in hospital but the doctors say he can go home in a week or so. He was badly done over in a bar on King Street. A barstool was smashed over his head, and it nearly killed him. They got the prick that did it though, apparently, he had a go at a copper as well. They refused him bail and remanded him in custody until the trial. Total prick.'

They arranged to meet up and the following night they sat in a gastro pub in the centre of Bristol and had a long chat over a meal and a couple of bottles of wine. Jack tried hard not to get caught looking at her low-cut top revealing her cleavage. She looked sexy but not tarty. She made an effort, but she already looked good, her hair seemed to always fall into place with minimal input. Not much make-up and minimal jewellery as she had some items stolen in the past, so she only wore a single chain in town which didn't mean much to her. Jack was also low-maintenance when came to appearance. He put on some jeans and a shirt with the first few buttons undone, gelled his hair up, and that was it. He piled on some after shave on this occasion which proved too much as Shelley was struggling with her sinuses with the strong, but nice smell of cologne. They talked for hours with no hint of embarrassing silence.

Neither wanted the night to end. They were talking, laughing, and looking into each-other's eyes. Shelley somehow forgot the stress of Craig's injuries and the presentation she was doing in front of the directors in the morning. She rarely went out on a week- night but she was busy all weekend preparing the flat for Craig to return home. She had organised a carer and was planning to clean the place from top to bottom having visited after Craig's incident and saw the state of the place.

Jack suggested that they share a cab, and Shelley agreed. It was 10 pm and they both had work in the morning. From time to time, Shelley would remember that she had a busy day ahead and her face would sink. She was a Project Support Administrator for a construction company who were based in the city centre. She caught a bus every morning which took 20 minutes from her house which she rented, shared with two friends to keep the cost down.

The cab arrived and Shelley greeted the driver and asked for Chessels, a trendy 1900's housing estate two miles from the town centre. With a nod the driver pulled away. Jack looked pensive. How would he get into her place and finish the night off in style, without disrespecting her? Shelley said, 'Just pull over here please.' The cab went on ten metres where there was a gap in the parked cars and pulled in. Shelley reached for her purse, but Jack had already lurched forward and said to the driver 'No worries mate I'll get this when you drop me off.' Shelley glanced at Jack and said to the driver 'No need to wait thanks, here's 20 quid, that should cover it.' They exited the cab on the near side and Shelley took Jack's hand and led him into the front door. As the door closed, she turned to Jack, took him lovingly in both arms, kissing him slowly and tenderly. Jack responded and could feel her body pressed against him. He was feeling more relaxed and enjoying it more than he thought he would. Shelley stopped, looked longingly into his eyes, and led him upstairs. They went into her room which was very tidy and still had lines on the carpet form the vacuum cleaner, which Jack noticed. She turned to Jack and said 'Make yourself at home, I'll be back in two-minutes. Do you want a night cap?'

'Ok, whatever you're having.'

She left the room, and Jack was not sure what to do. He looked around and admired how organised it was and the bed which had been immaculately dressed like a high-class hotel. Five-minutes later he heard her coming back up the stairs. Checking his breath, he sat rather awkwardly on the bed as she entered the room with a bottle of white wine and two-glasses, dressed in a negligee and not much else. She smiled at him and said 'When I said make yourself comfortable, I meant it. Relax.' She poured the wine and left the glasses on the chest of drawers, sitting down on the bed, taking Jack with both arms around his shoulders and kissing him, laying him down on the bed. As she held him, he ran his right hand up her back slowly and onto the back of her neck as he slowly led backwards on to the bed, feet still on the floor. She raised one leg onto is thigh as she continued kissing and unbuttoning his shirt.

The morning arrived far too soon. They both had no more than three-hours sleep and they couldn't leave it any longer to get up. The bus to Jack's house came on time and gave him enough time to quickly shower and head off to work. Shelley got to the office on time and set up the meeting room with projector and her lap-top and the day began. Shelley sat and went through the PowerPoint slides one last time before the board of directors, senior managers and commercial managers entered the room. The first to arrive was an arrogant project manager who always looked her up and down when he thought no-one was noticing. She wore a blue dress to the knees which was classy but not over-sexy so not to give the wrong impression. 'Morning Dave,' she politely said and lowered her eyes back to the screen.

'Hi gorgeous' he said walking past and making a point of looking at her cleavage with a smug, appreciative grin, raising his eye-brows at the sight. The meeting went well, and all thanked her for her input and professionalism in chairing the meeting for the first time. She felt pleased with herself and was finalising the meeting minutes as all the delegates left the board room. Dave came up and sat on the table next to her, uncomfortably close. 'Really good presentation Shell. I must say you look nice today.'

'Thanks Dave, see you soon,' Shelley replied, not taking her eyes from her laptop screen on purpose, thinking, 'You really don't know who you're messing with, you idiot!'

He could see in her eyes that she was not interested so he faked a mobile phone call and left the room, pretending to speak to someone in an overconfident manner. Shelley glanced over the top of her lap-top, slowly shook her head and carried on working.

She finished up and as she was posting her lap-top into the bag, the managing director re-entered the room. 'Shelley, that was an excellent piece of work. We have a site visit for you next week. You'll need some kit to take with you.'

Shelley knew exactly what was required and nodded with pursed lips as she left the office and walked to the bus stop. As soon as she sat on the bus, she sent a text to Jack '*How was your day? X*'

Within minutes Jack replied '*Fine, bit tired. How was the presentation? X* '

The conversation went on for an hour and neither had eaten. Jack signed off saying '*See you Saturday. X*'

Jack finished work early and drove straight home, had a snack and a shower. He was looking forward to seeing Shelley and having a few drinks. Mum was away so he made sure the house was clean, particularly his room with fresh bed linen, no dirty dishes, or clothes on the floor. The wardrobe was in a state of desperation and everything from the floor was rammed in, with the doors barely holding closed. Checking the football results and grooming himself again, he called a taxi which arrived within 15 minutes. 6.40. Perfect. He got out at the front door of Shelley's house, and she quickly answered. She greeted him with a big smile and a gentle hug and kiss. She looked fantastic in a summer dress slightly off the shoulder and just above her knees. The taxi driver watched her walk down the path and found it hard to look away as she approached the cab. He looked away just in time before he was likely to be noticed as they climbed into the back.

They arrived at the restaurant early so they sat at the bar and ordered some drinks. Jack was doing most of the talking but Shelley was responding and not making him feel awkward. Twenty-minutes later the waiter led them to their table and gave them both a menu and a drinks list. They ordered their meals five minutes later and decided to share a bottle of house white wine. Shelley said she was sorry for being quiet, as she had been cleaning out Craig's flat all day and it was worse than she thought. She chose not to mention that she found some white powder in a plastic package which she was sure was cocaine or something harder. This was playing on her mind as the care worker was going to have access to all areas of the flat, so she took it home. This was new territory for her as she chose never to be involved with drugs. She was worried that someone would find them, the consequences, who would find them, was she being followed from Craig's? All these thoughts were running through her head, and she was trying to enjoy a date with someone she really liked, almost loved. He was such a gentleman but also a lad, a football fan, someone she would like to be with. She was able to calm her thoughts down and after a couple of glasses of Sauvignon Blanc, started to relax and talk more. She was aware of every person who walked in the restaurant, and she was aware of her surroundings maybe much more than she should. She was certainly more intensely observant than most people, but she never let it show. She appeared to be focussed on Jack and hardly looked away. She noticed one of the bar staff slicing lemons, which was behind Jack and about ten-metres away. She shuddered at the same split second he cut deeply into his thumb. She felt it before he did and rubbed her left thumb onto her index finger in empathy but carried on talking to Jack about the presentation.

Without appearing to move her eyes, she said 'You'll never guess who just walked in!' in a loud whisper.

'Who?' Jack asked, wondering how she noticed, as she was looking at him or the wine the whole time.

'The guy from that DIY series on TV. Nick something? He is over there at the bar,' She discreetly pointed to her left.

Jack slowly looked around and said 'So it is! How did you see him? You hardly looked away from the table.'

'I just notice things going on around me I suppose, some of my friends say that I'm ridiculously observant, I don't notice it myself.'

They finished the meal and Jack paid the bill. Shelley said, 'Next time I'm buying.'

Jack replied with 'I don't give to receive, don't worry about it.'

They went to a bar a few hundred meters away and sat on barstools. As they sipped their drinks, three guys walked in and stood next to them. They were all over six-feet tall and well built, toned, and fit looking. They were stood next to Shelley and Jack started looking uncomfortable as they checked her out. Shelley kept her eyes on Jack and that side of the bar as the guys grew ever closer and louder. One had a mohawk hair style and was particularly coarse with words, stating loudly that he was now single and up for it. He was fixing eyes on Jack now and again deliberately trying to intimidate. Jack was trying not to show that it was working and trying not to show Shelley that he was bothered by this guy who was very menacing, and had eyes all over Shelley, deliberately brushing up against her occasionally. Shelley was in full control of her emotions and confidently turned to this guy and said, 'Touch me again and you will regret it.'

Tyrone smirked as he raised his left hand and went to place it on her shoulder as he said, 'You going to get your boyfriend to beat me up love?'

As his hand landed on her shoulder, she took his little finger and with a sharp hand movement cracked it outwards breaking the knuckle. As she did this, she hooked her ankle around the back of his calf and struck his chin with the palm of her left hand hard enough to force his teeth together, sending him crashing head- first into the corner of a hardwood clad column. She hardly left the barstool as she dealt with Tyrone and remained seated as she waited for a reaction from his friends. No one present was aware that Tyrone was one of the guys who nearly killed her brother recently. They looked at Tyrone on the floor and looked sheepishly at the gorgeous young lady who unbelievably did the damage, almost knocking Tyrone unconscious, hardly moving.

Security came over and Tyrone stood up and shouted, 'Fucking psycho bitch!' as he nursed his broken finger and the back of his head which were both, equally as excruciating. He felt totally humiliated as he walked with his head down out of the bar and headed towards the hospital. He knew he couldn't react as he had been granted bail that day and had to keep out of trouble. His friends walked behind and glanced back shaking their heads. Tyrone had grassed up Terry in a view to save himself from prosecution clearing his name for Craig's injuries, but he was still facing trial for hitting a police officer and he knew he could be facing a jail sentence. He was barred from the rugby club as a result.

The security guard stayed and watched the humiliated body builders leave and turned to Shelley. 'Well played Shell! How are you doing?'

Shelley replied 'Great thanks, this is Jack. Jack, this is Neil. We train together.'

Jack was still shocked at what he just witnessed. How could someone this beautiful do so much damage to a bloody big guy like that? He suddenly felt inadequate and slightly out of place as Shelley and Neil caught up, talking about instructors, dojos and tournaments. His thoughts were racing and not sure if he liked it. He felt the adrenaline drain from his body and slouched on his stool, leaning on the bar with a bad posture, his expression appeared lost and like a child being told off.

In reality, Shelley was after a guy who would step up to the mark and take control. A guy who was not bothered or intimidated by her karate skills and would be able to take the lead in a relationship. She wanted normality in one part of her life, at least. Jack was perfect for this role as he was, in all the right ways, a lad. Someone who would be attentive and a good boyfriend but would go off with his friends now and again, get pissed and enjoy himself but always be there. She wanted normality above all the karate training and the expectation and reputation it brings. In the future, a real family.

Jack was quiet. He hardly said a word following the incident. When he did, his voice was soft and deep. 'Well, that was unexpected, where did you learn all that stuff?'

'I'm the assistant instructor at a Shotokan karate club. I have been in karate since I was six. I achieved my 3rd Dan last year. But I don't dwell on it, only when a prick like that pisses me off. Are you ok Jack? You seem a bit down. Shall we go back to yours?'

'Yes OK, I'll get a cab, No I'm fine, just a bit shocked.'

The cab pulled up outside Jack's house and drove off. They went inside and Jack was still thinking about the incident and still quite surprised that Shelley was a martial arts expert. Still not sure how he felt about it, for several reasons. But she was gorgeous and had a great personality, they had a lot in common and got on well. He decided to try and relax and enjoy her company and in the back of his mind wondered if it would last, hoping it would.

Shelley sat on the sofa looking at Jack with pursed lips and a slight grin. Her eye-brows were raised and head slightly tilted. 'Sorry Jack, I didn't want you to be put off by this, I wish that jerk hadn't been there tonight. I just want you to be yourself for me. It's just a hobby you know, I'm not an alien or some mad fighter. I'm just the same as anyone else really.'

Jack half smiled and sat next to her. 'Just a bit shocked, that's all, I've never done karate or anything like that before, I wouldn't mind trying though. Look how flexible I am.' He said as he got up and attempted to do the splits, with a painful look on his face.

They both burst out laughing and the night continued. The sex was even better than the first time and they tried different positions. They fell sleep in each-other's arms around 2am and had no intention of waking up early. They were both very tired and slept until 11am.

Jack came up to the bedroom with two mugs of tea and said 'good morning' gently as he put Shelley's tea down on the bedside cabinet next to her. She opened her eyes and smiled as she looked up at him. 'Hi gorgeous,' she said. She didn't move and Jack walked to the other side of the bed and peeled the covers back revealing her beautiful curves and her perfect bum. He was almost instantly aroused once again and spooned her with his semi-erect penis touching her lower back. She liked the thought of him feeling horny so turned around and hugged him whilst gently rubbing her thigh up his. Within minutes they were having sex, and it felt better than ever. Shelley was very vocal and looked into his eyes as he reached climax. They were both falling deeply in love, and it was written all over their faces. But neither dare say anything in fear that it would scare the other one off.

Chapter 5

Tyrone woke up after leaning on his broken hand. He had his fingers strapped together and it was helping keep the small finger from straying to the outside. Badly swollen and painful, the bruising was beginning to show around the outside of his hand. He also had a lump on the back of his head. He felt humiliated and his friends didn't stop mocking him for the rest of the evening, which he didn't respond well to. He wasn't used to being subject to this and was usually the one dishing it out. The apartment was a mess, as Lucy was the one who usually cleaned up and did the washing, ironing, and cooking. He sent her a text reading, 'Where are you? I'm sorry.' There was no answer. He tried to call but it went straight to voice mail. He picked up his clothes from the floor and pushed them into the washing machine. He had never used it before but had seen Lucy load it up. He put two tabs inside and closed the door, pressed the on button, nothing happened except a screen lit up which seemed complicated. Not sure what he pressed but it started, which was good enough for him.

A couple of hours passed, and the spin came to a stop. He opened the door to find his white shirt a grey-blue colour and his t-shirt shrunk. The temperature on the display read 95 degrees. He swore and threw his shirt across the kitchen, catching is broken finger, and knocking his coffee cup off the side. He crouched onto the floor, head in hands and groaned. He sat on the floor for a couple of minutes staring forward until he slowly got up. He was calm by then and slowly and carefully cleaned the apartment and vacuumed the floors. Another attempt at using the washing machine went better with the temperature down slightly and whites only. Not wanting to be seen, he decided to wait until late evening to go shopping to a local garage which sold the basics. Struggling to change gear with his left hand strapped up he drove down the street. A police car was at the end of the road between parked cars. As he passed, the head-lights came on and followed him to the end of the road. He was aware, but knowing he was fully legal and had not been drinking, he knew if he was pulled over, he would be alright. The police car followed him right up to the garage and carried on as he pulled into the forecourt. Picking up a few cheap microwave meals and some milk, he put the bag onto the passenger seat and drove off. Forgetting to indicate and accelerating down the road, a blue flashing light suddenly appeared behind him, head lights full beam flashing. He pulled over and the police car pulled in behind him. The officer got out and walked up to Tyrone's door. 'Can you get out of the vehicle please sir?'

Tyrone climbed out of the truck and followed the officer to the rear.

'Is this your vehicle sir?'

'Yes.'

'Tyrone O'Mally?'

'Yes, is there a problem officer?'

'You were not wearing your seat-belt sir. You were also speeding. This road has a limit of 30 miles per hour, you reached 45. I'm glad I stopped you when I did otherwise you may have reached 70.' His tone was sarcastic and smug, but Tyrone knew that he had to be on his best behaviour. The officer deliberately became uncomfortably close to Tyrone as he spoke, invading his body space, with his head tilted back so he was looking down his nose at him straight into his eyes. Tyrone was very uncomfortable with this and could not look the officer in the eye, trying to look anywhere else. As they spoke, a white transit passed, the horn sounded, and the three men shouted 'Tyrone, you fucking loser! Woo hoo!'

The police officer seemed to enjoy it as he pulled out a pad from his pocket.

The officer wrote the ticket and told Tyrone to expect a fine through the post within 2 weeks. He drove off slowly and as he lost sight of the police car shouted, 'Fucking pig bastard!' at the top of his voice. As he arrived home, a car left the rear of the apartment block and drove off in the opposite direction passing Tyrone at speed. He didn't recognise the car, a Ford Focus, and thought they may get pulled over as well and grinned as he indicated and pulled into the parking area. He parked the truck, picked up his bag of ready meals and as he turned to enter the communal door, noticed his kitchen window had been smashed. He was in a state of disbelief as the last 24 hours had been a series of bad luck. He went upstairs and straight to the kitchen. Glass everywhere and a cricket ball on the floor with the word 'prick' carved into the skin. He considered calling the police, but they probably wouldn't respond as his name was known to them and after being charged with ABH on a police officer, would make excuses why not to carry out an investigation. Wedging a sheet of ply from the garage over the window, he ate a microwave meal, drunk a can of cider and went to bed, trying to put the recent events to the back of his mind and attempting to sleep.

Monday morning. Tyrone got up at six and had a shower.

He had to be on site for 7.30 so didn't have long. Still in pain, he locked the apartment door and walked down the stairs. As he left the communal door, he stopped. His body sank as his eyes fixed on his truck and his mouth fell open. A pick-axe had been left having been smashed through the cab roof, stuck with the pointed blade half- way through the metal and the lining bulging underneath. He was at boiling point but had to get to work. He was already close to losing his job having been remanded in custody for weeks. He climbed onto the back of the truck and with effort was just able to pull the pick- axe out of the roof. His thoughts were running wild as he drove the 20 miles to the housing project where he was a machine operator. Who was doing these things to him? Was it Lucy? Surely, she wouldn't have the bottle to do it. He was thinking had he upset anyone else, who might have the bottle to do these things to him but could only think it was Lucy or one of her friends. He pulled up at the contractors' car park and climbed out of the truck, walked the 100 yards to the site entrance and signed in. walking straight to the canteen there were several guys in their high vis vests and hard hats. 'Morning,' he said as he made eye contact with the foreman.

'Morning Ty, had a nice holiday?' Ken said with a sarcastic tone looking down on Tyrone, being slightly taller than him. 'Hope you're up for it, you got some catching up to do. I was just about ready to replace you. Plenty of operators about now.'

Tyrone knew this and there was less work than qualified operators about during this recession. He couldn't risk losing this job, as he was now alone in his apartment and had no-one to share the bills with. Especially now he had a kitchen window to re glaze, the truck to repair and a fine, and possible imprisonment to deal with. Signing for the key to the 20-tonne excavator, he walked past the site office to the machine, hard hat in hand and high vis vest tied at the ends. He knew the site manager would be watching as he passed, and knew he didn't like him, as he was always pushing the boundaries. Sure enough, there was a knock on the office window and the manager shouted, 'Put your hat on!' Tyrone slowly and annoyingly put on his hard hat the wrong way around, without showing any signs of acknowledging the site manager's request. Winding up the site manager was something he had always done and could not break the habit. Wherever he worked he would do it, particularly regarding health and safety. As he sat in the cab, he realised he must try and stop upsetting people and try to adhere to the site rules. He knew he would struggle with it but thought he should at least try.

Chapter 6

After three weeks Lucy had almost made a full recovery and felt on top of the world. She was helping out on the farm, getting all her meals for nothing and even getting out in Exeter now and again on the weekends. She was looking for a job, as she was getting fed up with getting covered in mud every day. She was a hair-dresser and had worked as a temp when she was living in Bristol and was mainly covering for staff holidays, although she knew she was better at her job than most of the staff she worked with. Her attitude let her down every time she had a temporary appointment as she would be quite arrogant towards the other staff.

She arrived at 10am sharp at a well-established salon in the centre of Exeter. She had a good feeling about this one, and the manager greeted her with a firm but welcoming hand- shake. They sat in the back office which was immaculate with files all in numeric order and a desk top computer with a Lady Gaga screen saver.

After the interview, which was more like a social chat, the manager asked when she could start. Lucy was visibly delighted and said, 'Whenever you want me!'

The manager said, 'Obviously the trial period is three months, would you like to start this coming Monday?'

'Great! See you then!'

It was Thursday and it gave her enough time to pick up some new clothes and have a rest over the weekend before she started. He parents were coming to visit on Saturday, which was going to be awkward, as she hadn't seen them for months but chose to move in with her Auntie and Uncle following separating from Tyrone. She went shopping and bought a trouser suit which felt comfortable but smart and some other clothes to wear when she went out into town.

Later that day she returned to the farm and shouted, 'I got the job!' as she dropped her bags and waved her arms in the air in the kitchen.

'Oh, that's great news dear! When do you start?' asked Theresa.

'Monday! I have just picked up some clothes, look!' she showed Theresa her new clothes and took them upstairs. Uncle Chris was out seeing to the farm so hadn't seen her, but noticed her car parked by the house. He was just finishing for the day and parked the truck in the yard before going in to have a shower. Noticing that Lucy was in the shower he decided to lie down on the bed until she had finished as the shower cubicle in the en-suite was a little cramped for him and he was always knocking his elbows on the glass doors. He believed that one day he would demolish the whole cubicle being so clumsy. She left the bathroom and Chris said, 'Well done getting the job love.'

She looked through the open door and said, 'Thanks Chris' with her hair wrapped in a towel and a robe barely covering her body. Chris didn't notice as he always considered her as a daughter and never looked at her with any recognition of how she looked, even though she was very attractive. Lucy, however, had not had sex since Tyrone abused her whilst she was barely conscious, which she couldn't remember. She could remember the night before, having spent a lovely night with Craig, but could not remember his name, just the sex. She had needs and was going out that night in hope of meeting someone. Logging on to her favourite dating website, she noticed a good-looking guy who had expressed interest in her profile picture. He was in Exeter, and they arranged to meet up in a bar just off Cathedral Square.

Arriving five minutes late on purpose, she went to the bar and noticed James walk towards her and introduce himself. He was there on business and was staying at the hotel next door, the Royal Clarence. An old building which didn't interest Lucy, she liked modern things and would not be bothered if they decided to demolish the old building and put up a shopping centre or trendy apartments in its place. They went outside for a smoke and got on fine. Lucy noticed that he was muscular, and she was attracted to him. They finished their cigarettes and threw them into a bin full of sand. Lucy didn't notice a gust of wind as she dropped hers and it blew the cigarette into the bar, smouldering on the carpet.

Returning to their bench seat in the corner of the bar, Lucy placed her hand gently onto his thigh and stroked it looking into his eyes. They began kissing and he turned his body to face her as her hand slowly reached the top of his thigh, glancing across his penis and onto his other thigh. He rolled his eyes as this happened and enjoyed it so, that he couldn't physically hide it with a prominent bulge in the front of his jeans. 'Would you like to come to the hotel?' he asked in his well-spoken, slightly London accent.

'Maybe,' she replied with a sparkle in her eyes. 'What's in it for me?'

'Come and see for yourself,' James said. They finished their drinks and left the bar, which was adjoining the Royal Clarence Hotel next door. They entered the hotel room on the second floor and awkwardly sat on the bed looking everywhere but at each other. Lucy made the first move, placing her arm around his shoulder, pulling him close and gently kissing him. They kissed passionately for a minute or two as she massaged the back of his neck. Suddenly he broke off the kiss and said, 'I can't do this.'

She looked confused and hurt. 'What's up?'

'Sorry, I'm in a relationship. I haven't been happy for a while and I have been looking for a way to get out, but not sure if I can actually go through with it.'

Lucy sat thinking for a few minutes as he talked about his girlfriend and the problems they had, which to her seemed ridiculously tame compared to what she had gone through with Tyrone. She considered trying to make it happen but decided not to, as he seemed weak, which she was not attracted to, also being the 'other woman' didn't appeal to her. She kissed him on the cheek and left the room. She walked out onto Cathedral Square, flagged down a passing taxi and went back to the farm.

As people were leaving the bar, no-one noticed the cigarette as the door opened disappear under a bench seat which had an old newspaper stuffed crudely under. As the door repeatedly opened, the air would blow under the bench and the fire had started, unnoticed for a few minutes, until thick smoke and some flames appeared from the sides of the bench seat, which was made of very old, brittle oak. By the time it was noticed by an elderly man who had been drinking cider most of the day, the flames had spread to the wall panelling and out of reasonable control. The smoke alarm went off and soon after the full alarm was in full voice, evacuating the bar. Two-minutes later the entire ground floor was engulfed in flames, with glass breaking under the heat and pressure and smoke bellowing high into the night sky. The Clarence Hotel was evacuated, and James stood outside with a look of horror as most of the hotel, including his room was in flames. Ten minutes later and the entire hotel was engulfed in flames and the fire service were trying to contain the blaze as it intensified. The heat from the fire was so intense that the hotel residents were almost backed up to the cathedral.

The following morning Lucy was woken at eight by Theresa. She opened the bedroom door and said 'I'm off into Exeter to do some shopping with some friends. Heard the news? The Clarence burned down last night.'

'Really?' said Lucy bolting upright in the bed 'How did that happen? Was anyone hurt?'

'Apparently not. They all got out and no-one was hurt. Miracle really, anyway Chris is gone to Taunton and Callum is coming in to pick up the keys to the tractor. I'll leave them on the kitchen table if you can give them to him, he will be here about ten.' Theresa looked surprised at the interest that Lucy was showing about the fire.

Callum was a 24-year-old local farm hand who helped on the weekends. He was lean, almost skinny and Lucy had seen him from time to time whilst helping. She got on ok with him and they made each other laugh although hardly knowing each other.

Theresa left the house five-minutes later and Lucy had a shower. She went down- stairs in a short negligee and nothing else, made a coffee and waited. 9.50 and the door- bell rang. Lucy checked herself out in the mirror and answered the door pretending to be half asleep. 'Hi Callum, come on in.' He nodded his head and smiled as he walked in and took off his boots. 'Do you want a coffee before you start work?'

Callum said 'Ok' as she walked past him. He was admiring her legs as she walked towards the kitchen and could almost see through the tight negligee which he liked, a lot. He couldn't remember the last time he had sex and he was loving seeing her dressed like this and could see she was wearing nothing underneath, leaving little to the imagination. He was slightly trembling with excitement as he sat on a stool at the breakfast bar, still checking her out. She could see his reflection through in the kitchen window and wore a slight knowing grin. She dropped a teaspoon on the floor on purpose, and turned side on to Callum as she bent over to pick it up, showing some of her butt cheek but not all, and slowly pulling her negligee back down as she said, 'Oops.'

He couldn't resist it. 'Nice bum!' he said smiling at her.

'Thanks Callum' she said as she turned her head and looked at him with a smile. 'You like?' as she lifted her negligee and mooned at him and quickly dropped it back down.

'Oh, wow!' he said. 'Gorgeous! Let's have another look!' he said as his eyes almost popped out of his head.

She walked over and straddled him as she gently put her arms around his shoulders and kissed him gently on the lips. 'Coming up-stairs?'

She took his hand and led the way. As she walked up- stairs in front of him, he pulled up her negligee and admired her tattoo and her slightly round, but firm bum. He was flying high and as they entered the bedroom; he almost ripped his t-shirt as he removed it. She turned around and within a second, his button flies were undone, and she slowly pulled his jeans down. She was impressed with his size and laid on the bed still wearing her negligee. He kicked off his jeans and as he climbed onto the bed asked if she had any condoms.

She said quietly 'I'm on the pill.'

He looked at her with excited eyes and started slowly making love to her. An hour passed and after the third time Callum lay next to Lucy exhausted. She was on her side facing him stroking his chest. 'I need to get some work done I suppose' he said, and Lucy agreed as she lifted herself off the bed and said 'That was lovely. We must do it again sometime.'

'Definitely,' he said as he got dressed.

Chapter 7

Friday night and Tyrone stayed in watching telly until he finished a bottle of cider. He went to bed and almost straight to sleep. He was in a deep sleep about 2am and was dreaming about Lucy. Their first holiday together drinking Raki in a Greek taverna watching the sunset. Finding a deserted beach and spending the day sunbathing naked and chasing each other around, making love in the sea.

His chest suddenly felt tight, and his breathing laboured which woke him up abruptly. As he opened his eyes there was a dark figure over him. He tried to shout but his mouth was taped up, his wrists and ankles zip tied to the bed. The man was wearing black jeans, a mainly beige camouflage jacket and a balaclava. He was holding a hand-held gun with a silencer pointing it straight towards his forehead. Tyrone started to panic, thinking his life was over. His breathing shallow and rapid, he was trying to break his hands loose, but it was no good. His eyes were full of terror, and he was making a muffled humming sound which would be loud screams if not taped up. He felt a warm glow as he felt his bladder emptying and the assassin had one of his military black boots on his chest which was restricting his breathing even more. The assassin moved the pistol to the left of Tyrone's head and discharged a single shot which was still loud but quiet enough not to wake up the neighbours. A cloud of pillow feathers flew upwards, and the assassin removed his foot and walked out of the room. Tyrone was petrified and couldn't move. His pulse was racing, breathing was very fast, and he was shaking violently all over. Chris concealed the pistol and drove straight back to Exeter without stopping.

An hour later he had calmed down. He started working on freeing his hands, particularly his right hand which was stronger. As he struggled to break the zip tie it was cutting into his wrist. He eventually broke the tie and worked on the left. He remembered that he had a pair of nail clippers in the drawer next to the bed. He could just reach the drawer with is ankles still tied to the bed. He reached into the drawer and after a few seconds the clippers were in his hand. Still shaking he started to snip bit by bit at the zip tie on his left wrist, then dropped the clippers onto the pillow, then as he moved his head to grab them, they fell on to the mattress. He was just able to grab them and within a few seconds his left wrist was free, then his ankles.

He got off the bed, bunched up the wet sheets, put them straight into the washing machine along with his boxers and put them on a hot wash. He paced the floor wondering who he had upset enough to threaten his life! Surely it wasn't Lucy? She wouldn't have the bottle... would she? He remembered Lucy's Auntie and Uncle in Exeter and tried to remember the address although he had only been there once. He would go down there and see her to try to put things right. Even if they wouldn't get back together just to put an end to all this grief. Even if it was going to cost money, he would do anything to stop the threats, anything.

Craig was in therapy where he was slowly working towards being able to walk again. The nurse was encouraging him, and he was taking very short steps for the first time. He had a slim grin on his face and a determined look in his eyes. As the session ended, he sat in his wheel-chair and Lucy entered the room. 'How did it go?' she asked as she stooped down and kissed Craig on the cheek.

'I took a few steps!' he said in a drunk like tone. His speech had improved, and he was making slight progress every day. Lucy was very supportive and encouraging by nature. She mentioned Terry who had been arrested for GBH and the trial was due the following week. 'I will pick you up at nine on Tuesday, that should give us plenty of time to get to the magistrates.'

Craig's face dropped when she was talking about the incident, he was trying to forget the whole thing whilst concentrating on his recovery.

They arrived at the Magistrates' Court with 20 minutes to spare. As Shelley pushed the wheelchair through the doors, they were greeted by Sam and two other friends who were there at the night of the incident. They all took it in turns to greet Craig with a hand-shake and smile. Craig was almost tearful seeing his mates again and was asking them all how they were. The doors to the magistrates were just wide enough for the wheelchair to get through. They entered and Shelley put the brakes on as she sat next to Craig. As they waited, people were slowly entering the courtroom and Shelley noticed a man enter and quickly sit down at the back, collars up and head down. She recognised him instantly and was shocked as she turned to face the front wide eyed not sure what to think or do. Tyrone glanced up just as she looked back, and their eyes met. He saw Craig in the wheelchair, Shelley's hand on his and Shelley looking rather menacing straight at him. 'Excuse me,' she said as she got up and marched towards Tyrone. 'What the fuck are you doing here you fucking prick?' she asked loudly.

'None of your business bitch!' he said smugly. She glanced

at his hand which was still taped up and sniggered as she slowly walked back and sat down with Craig. 'What was that all about?' as he glanced back. He noticed Tyrone at the back and thought he recognised him vaguely but couldn't remember where from. Tyrone instantly recognised Craig and looked down awkwardly and realised the damage that had been done by the barstool, wondering if the damage was permanent.

Shelley explained to Craig and Sam what happened when she was out with Jack and how she sorted him out.

Sam looked back and saw Tyrone looking sheepish and awkward in the back. 'That's the bloke who started it in the first place! He came over and punched you in the bar, and you started fighting him before that other bloke hit you with the stool!'

Shelley looked back over her shoulder and stared coldly at Tyrone. 'What's his name?' she asked quietly.

Sam replied 'Tyrone O'Mally. He plays rugby for the same team as I used to before I started training with you two.'

Shelley sent a text discreetly.

'When am I going to meet Jack then? Seems like a decent bloke.' Craig asked Shelley.

'I'll pick you up Thursday if you like. We can go out and meet him for a drink. He's out with friends on Saturday so we're going out together Friday.'

The magistrate entered the room and then the suspect was escorted in hand cuffed to two guards.

'Is your name Terry Francis Jeffries, of 30 Callington Road Bristol BS3 4SW?'

'Yes.'

'You are charged with grievous bodily harm with intent to endanger life. Do you plead guilty or not guilty?'

'Not guilty.'

As the name and address were read out, Sam was writing the details on a piece of paper and glancing at his friends. It didn't matter about the trial to him, he just wanted the details of the guy who did the damage.

Chapter 8

Lucy was trying hard to get on with everyone in the salon but each day she was relieved to get back to the farm. She was not used to having to be this friendly and was struggling. It had been two weeks since her encounter with Callum and hadn't heard from him. It was Friday evening, and she was going into town with some work-mates who she was pretending to like. After getting ready, Chris offered her a lift and commented on how good she looked, joking about fighting off the local blokes.

Meeting her group in a trendy bar in the town centre, she started on the cocktails and bought a round of tequila slammers for the group. They were all thankful and wondering where the money was coming from, as the salon didn't pay well.

'You only live once! Enjoy!'

They moved on and went to a bar with loud music and disco lights. Jigging around whilst ordering more drinks enjoying the fact that most of the guys in the bar were watching them in their short skirts and mini dresses, hair immaculate and plastered in make-up. As Lucy was dancing and chatting, she noticed one of the door men refusing entry to someone and they were reaching into their jackets for their rubber batons. She slowly walked over to see what was going on and suddenly gasped and turned away in shock. It was

Tyrone. He was shouting at the security staff saying 'You don't know who you're fucking with! I'm coming back later with all my mates! You're all fucking dead!'

Lucy went straight into the toilet and sat in the cubicle shaking and crying. Tracy came into the toilet and said 'Lucy, are you alright?'

Lucy opened the door still crying and shaking. She was drunk and would normally not open up to someone she had only known for two weeks and was trying to keep an emotional distance from. 'Oh my god! What's up?' she said as she put her arm around her.

'My ex was outside, he's after me, he's going to kill me!' she said as she sobbed loudly, eye liner running down her face. She tried to control herself, but the anxiety was overwhelming her. The tension was all over her face as she stared at the door shaking as it swung open. Another woman walked in, glanced at Lucy and her friend and disappeared into a cubicle. Lucy looked away with slight relief and started to wipe the eye lined off her cheeks as she started to compose herself. 'I need to get home!' she said without looking at Tracy who was confused, asking loads of questions. 'Are you able to ask the bar staff to get me a taxi? I will stay here until it arrives.' She said as she looked at herself, in the mirror struggling to hold back the tears, wiping her face. Tracy left the toilet and asked the bar staff to order the taxi. She was confused at the way Lucy was with her. Demanding, abrupt, not opening up to her. She started becoming resentful but as the door man came over and told her the taxi was outside, she thanked him and went back to the toilet. Lucy was still holding back her emotions and Tracy walked in and said, 'The taxi is here Lucy' with no emotion.

'Thanks Tracy, sorry about this, I will explain on Monday. I hope I haven't ruined your evening.' She said with a false look of sympathy on her face. She left the toilet looking nervous. As she walked past the door staff she sheepishly looked left and right and quickly ducked into the taxi.

The following morning, she walked through the farmyard over to Chris. He was always busy, but every time Lucy approached would stop what he was doing. 'Hi, how was last night? I heard you come in quite early for you, it couldn't have been that good!' he said with a slight laugh.

'Tyrone was in town.' She said with a worried look. 'He was trying to get into the bar we were in but was refused entry. He had a go at the bouncers and walked off. I thought it would be best to come straight home. I don't think he saw me luckily.'

Chris looked serious. He put down the tools he was holding and leant against the work bench. 'Does he know you are here?'

'I haven't spoken to him or replied to his messages, but he probably assumed I would be here.'

'Right,' he said calmly. He pursed his lips and hugged Lucy. 'Don't worry love, I'll make sure he is dealt with.'

'I don't want you to get into trouble!' she said concerned.

'I won't get into trouble love.'

She looked at him, smiled, kissed him on the cheek and walked back to the house.

Chris watched her enter the back door and as soon as she left his sight he reached for his mobile phone. 'Brian, I'm coming over. See you in half an hour.'

Tyrone woke up and had breakfast in the guest house. It was nearly midday, and he was ready to try to find the farm where he assumed Lucy was staying. He had a hangover, but it wasn't too bad. As he left the guest house the rain was just starting and was irritating him. He climbed into his truck and noticed a Subaru Impreza parked in the corner of the car park full of guys, music blasting. As he drove out of the car park, the car followed him. He assumed it was coincidental and they just happened to be leaving the car park at the same time. He drove out of town and onto a country road. The car was still behind but two cars back at this point. Tyrone was getting slightly concerned at this point but was stubborn and still believed that he was hard enough to take them all on. He pulled into a lay by and the car pulled in behind. As he removed his seatbelt, the sun- roof opened on the Subaru and a fierce looking guy appeared holding a sawn- off shot gun, pointing it straight at Tyrone. 'SHIT,' he shouted and drove off at speed, the Subaru speeding up behind him. He drove fast for two miles and as he negoti- ated a bend in the road the tyres barely gripped the road, but the Subaru had no issues with traction, and they were very close behind. Up ahead there was a truck blocking the road and a lorry stopped on the other side, totally block- ing both lanes. Tyrone noticed a small lane to the left and took it at speed, thinking of going off road to shake off the chasing car. He drove at speed down the lane looking to exit into a field if he could find an open gate, the Subaru right behind. There was a sharp right- hand bend ahead and struggling to stay on the road he took it at speed, looking in his rear- view mirror. The Subaru seemed to slow down. Still hard on the accelerator, his eyes looked forward again. There was a large tractor with a bull- dozer blade attached to the front. Too late. The impact was so great that the truck came to an immediate stop from 40 mph. Tyrone had not put his seatbelt back on from the lay by and flew through the windscreen and landed on the bonnet of the truck.

The Subaru turned and drove off slowly and a large man with greasy hair and a beard appeared from a field. He climbed into the tractor and bull dosed the truck, along with Tyrone's lifeless body into a fresh deep hole in a field a few meters away. Within a few minutes the hole was filled, and no evidence of the incident was visible.

Chapter 9

'Has the jury reached a verdict?'

'Yes, your honour.'

'How do you find the defendant?'

'Guilty as charged your honour.'

There was a sigh of relief and Shelley looked at Craig with glee and punched the air.

'Terry Francis Jeffries, I sentence you to two years imprisonment.'

They left the courtroom at 12.30 and went straight to a nearby bar. Sam and Shelley sat with Craig and discussed the civil claim which could result in thousands of pounds compensation. 'That Tyrone O'Mally didn't turn up for his witness statement then?'

'No. he was also due to stand trial for hitting a copper last week but didn't turn up to that either. A warrant is now out for his arrest. Hopefully he will go down for a long stretch with that other twat,' said Sam then took a sip of his pint.

Craig was drinking water and wheeled himself into the centre of the bar. He unfastened his seatbelt and slowly raised himself off his chair. With effort he walked, slowly back to the table to a rapturous applause from his friends. Shelley was slightly emotional but did not show it, just acclamation for the progress Craig had made. As she sat back down, she picked up her phone. There was a message from Jack. 'How was the trial? Call me when you have a minute. Xxx.'

Shelley raised herself from her chair and headed for the door, noticing two men walking past the window of the bar towards the entrance, recognising them instantly. They were friends of Terry Jeffries who had just been sent down. She recognised then from the courtroom. She turned her back as the connection to Jack's ringtone started. Jack answered after a few seconds and Shelley was in a quiet corner of the bar side on to the rugby players who had swaggered towards the bar, clocking Craig and his mates sat on the opposite side.

'Hi love, he got two years. Great, isn't it?' she said quietly.

'Great! One less lunatic to worry about.' Jack said. 'Will I see you tomorrow? I'll cook at home if you like?'

'Yes ok, sounds lovely. What time do you want me over?' at this point Shelley sounded vague. The guys were staring straight at Craig and his friends. It was looking very much like it was about to kick off.

'About six. Is that ok? Everything alright Shelley?'

'Yes fine. six it is. See you then love you.' She pressed end call, keeping the phone to her ear, and pretending to be still talking sat where she was, observing from a distance. Craig noticed that the guys were paying them too much attention and was getting worried. He was unable, for the first time since he was a young child to defend himself. Up until lately he had been right up for fighting, even provoking it when someone upset him.

Sam was resilient. He boisterously walked up to the bar and waited for the bar man to come over. The rugby players were surprised at the young bloke who was singing along to 'Angels' by Robbie Williams loudly. He ordered the drinks and the bar man put them on a tray. Four pints of lager, half a pint of iced water and a pinot grigio for Shelley, who was sat pretending to talk on the phone, observing. As he turned with the tray of drinks, one of the guys stuck out his foot and tripped Sam, not quite enough, as his reactions were quicker than the average man, kickboxing had paid off. He turned back round, calmly placed the tray back on the bar and without turning round, side-kicked the guy next to him hard into the side of his knee. He collapsed onto the floor and Sam stamped on his stomach, looking directly at the next man, who backed off instantly, seeing his mate doubled up on the floor, struggling to breath. He helped him up and they all left the bar.

Shelley walked over and congratulated Sam on his skills. They all sat back down with Craig and the drinking and chatting continued. Shelley got up after half an hour and called Jack back, knowing that he would be disappointed about hot the last phone call ended. The call rang off and went to voice mail. 'Hi love, sorry about that, it was kicking off in the bar with some guys who were mates with Terry Jeffries. Call you later, love you.'

They left the bar a few hours later and headed for the taxi rank in the centre of Bristol. Shelley went with Craig and helped him into his flat. They sat together watching TV for another hour and Shelley helped him into bed, undressing him after helping him in the toilet. Craig looked her in the eye. 'What would I do without you Shell?' his eyes welling up and bottom lip shaking.

She dismissed the comment with 'Oh, don't be silly, you're my bro! I love you!' as she hugged him. She laid next to him, and they both stared at the ceiling. 'This has been a nightmare few months for you, hasn't it? I'll always be here for you Craig, you know that. I don't need thanks or anything, after all; you have always helped me, haven't you?'

Shelley's phone rang. As soon as she saw Jack's name on the screen she answered. 'Hi love.'

'Sorry I didn't call you back earlier, are you ok?'

'Yes love, some jerk tried to have a go at Sam, so he sorted him out. I'm at Craig's just helping him out tonight until the carer comes in the morning. I'm looking forward to dinner tomorrow, what are we having?' Shelley asked as she sat up.

'Is Chilli Con Carne, ok? There's enough for Craig if he's interested.'

She looked at Craig who heard the offer and with a smile, raised his right thumb. 'Great, if you're sure?'

'Yes of course! See you about six!'

Shelley wheeled Craig up to the front door at 6.05, apologising for being late as she kissed Jack on the lips with a short but intimate hug. 'Jack, Craig, Craig, Jack.' She said with a broad smile.

'Good to finally meet you mate.' Craig said with his eyebrows raised and grasping his hand in a friendly way.

'Likewise, Craig. Looking well mate. How are things?'

'Good. The twat that did the damage got two-years for GBH, and one of his mates got a kicking yesterday by my mate. Good times!'

Shelley laughed. 'He started it though, we went to the pub after the trial and a couple of his mates followed us from a distance. They were mainly after that Tyrone bloke. Remember that bloke who I had to take out that time in the bar?'

'How could I forget?'

'Yeah. He was called in as a witness but did not show up. He was also facing trial for hitting a copper, he didn't show for that either. I'm sure those guys were after him but thought they would have a go at us instead. Bad mistake.' She smiled and took Jack's hand.

All evening Craig and Jack got on really well. At the end of the night, Shelley drove Craig home. 'Well? What do you think of him?'

'Really nice bloke Shell! Absolute gentleman!'

Shelley put him to bed and headed straight back to Jack's house as arranged. As she arrived Jack greeted her with a glass of white wine, her first drink of the evening. They sat together on the sofa and Shelley told him all about the trial, Tyrone not turning up, hearing that a warrant was issued for his arrest and how Craig had progressed health-wise. She was quite emotional, and it showed. Not trying to hide the tears she hugged Jack and sobbed loudly. It had been a difficult time for her, but she had held it together for the sake of Craig and their family. Also, a new, very close relationship she had found with Jack. The night passed and they woke up together around 9.30 am. Somehow Jack felt even closer to her after the display of raw emotion. He was head over heels in love with her, but still worried that she didn't feel the same.

They sat opposite each other at the breakfast table, poached eggs, and toast with a pot of tea. Jack cleared the plates and loaded them into the dish washer under the watchful, loving eyes of Shelley. He sat back down to finish his tea. She took both his hands and looking him straight into his eyes and said, 'I really love you, Jack.'

He inhaled deeply and exhaled slowly with his mouth wide open. Looking back into her eyes he said, 'I love you too!'

'Shall we book a holiday together for next summer? Somewhere hot maybe. Greece? Spain?' she said with an excited tone.

'I'd love that! What about Craig?'

'No, just us two!' they both laughed and sat for another hour planning their future.

Jack picked Pete up and drove to a race-track near Chippenham. They had organised a track day to drive for three hours on time trials and have a few drinks after. Jack was full of energy and enthusiasm about everything.

'How's it going with Shelley then mate?'

'Great! We're planning a holiday together in the summer, She's fantastic!'

Jack was telling Pete all about the court case, the time Shelley sorted out some twat in a bar and the fact that she was a karate expert, when their names were called.

Following a safety briefing they put on their protective suits and picked helmets out. Taking the piss out of each other they walked over to two sporty-looking hatches and had a briefing from the staff. Pete went first for a couple of practice laps. Jack followed a minute later but almost caught up with Pete which impressed the co- driver.

'OK guys, time for some timed laps,' one of the staff said. 'Who's first?'

'I'll go first, is that ok Jack?' Pete asked looking nervous.

'Go on then, this might take a while mate, I'll get some sleep while I'm waiting.' Jack said as he turned to the member of staff, who smiled back.

Pete revved up the car. The co-driver said loudly 'Three Two One Go!' and he released the clutch, spinning the wheels as he accelerated off.

Jack looked impressed with the start, but knew Pete was not a fast driver so wasn't concerned about beating him.

Ten minutes later Jack manoeuvred his car to the start line and heard Pete's car enter the pit lane.

'Three Two One Go!' they were off. Jack made it to full revs before changing gear, making full use of the engine power. The co-driver was wide eyed at this point and as they negotiated the first bend, he was holding on to the handle as Jack took the bend right on the limits of the car's capacity using the best line possible, then accelerating out of the corner as if he was a formula one driver or at least a professional racer of some sort. This form continued for the remaining three laps, and when they finished, the co-driver was actually relieved it was over, having pushed the car to the limits and endured the fastest laps he had ever experienced from an amateur driver.

Jack was the clear winner and Pete tried every excuse going blaming the car, wet weather and the co-driver, but when all failed admitted defeat. They drove back to Pete's, parked up and headed into town to finish the day off in style. Saturday night was always busy and there were plenty of people to talk to and most of their mates were out. Towards the end of the night, they met Shelley and a few of her mates in a bar on King Street, not far from the one they first started seeing each other, and the same bar where Craig sustained his injuries. Shelley felt uncomfortable but did not show it, and they all got on well. Pete spent a whole hour talking to Kerry, one of Shelley's best friends.

'Have you seen those adverts about adopting snow leopards? If you pay £2 per month, they send you a news- letter every now and again, and a stuffed leopard!'

Kerry almost fell off her stool laughing, loud enough that almost everyone in the bar could hear them as the music was quiet for a few seconds. They eventually left the bar, Pete and Kerry exchanging numbers and arranging meeting for a drink the following Tuesday night.

PC Johnston was trying to gain entry to the apartment where Tyrone had been living. He had been knocking at the door for a few minutes and had two riot police with him. He had a warrant and authority to force entry if required. He decided to use the permit and kicked the door a few times until the frame split, and the door swung open. Unsure of what he was going to be faced with, he paused, listening intently and slowly entered the apartment, stepping on all the mail which hadn't been cleared for days. The officers took a door each and as they entered each room, batons ready, checked behind the door and proceeded into the room. Still keeping quiet, listening out for each other, they all entered the lounge and Johnston said 'Clear.' As they left the apartment and crudely secured it, a lady in her early sixties was outside. 'Hi, I'm Tyrone O'Mally's mum. Is he home?' she said looking concerned at the thought of riot police leaving the apartment.

Johnston stopped in his tracks. 'Do you know where we can find him?'

'No, I haven't seen him for weeks. He hasn't answered his phone or anything, I'm getting worried. Is he in trouble?'

'Can I take your name please?'

'Sharon O'Mally.' She produced her driving license and Johnston glanced at it.

'We have a warrant out for his arrest for not appearing for a trial. Are you able to come to the station? Just for an informal chat?' Johnston said with a persuasive tone.

'Well, I don't have much to tell you I'm afraid, he hasn't contacted me for weeks as I said. He came over to say he'd split up with his fiancée back in June, but I have hardly spoken to him since, three, maybe four weeks ago. He hasn't even been to the rugby club for ages either apparently.'

'His fiancée; did she live here as well?' Johnston asked.

'Yes, she did. Lucy Gardiner her name was, he said she left him for someone else, he was devastated.'

'Have you any idea where she might be?'

'Not really, she had family in Devon, Exeter way. But her parents live in Horfield, Bristol.'

The officers went back to the station. Johnston said to the sergeant 'This could turn into a missing person's enquiry.' As he looked up Lucy Gardiner, he found that she had minor offences to her name, shoplifting, class C drug possession and some minor motoring offences. Her dad had been a semi-professional rugby player and was now a coach, and Tyrone had been a member of the same club.

That evening Johnston went to the rugby club to ask a few questions. He knew a few of the regulars so gained easy access to the bar. It was Friday evening, and the regulars were turning up in their work clothes, mainly builders covered in dust and cement. One or two scaffolders were in, who were easily recognised by the rust stains on their clothes and the right shoulder of their t-shirts virtually non- existent with orange-stained shoulder muscles showing through.

Ordering a large cola, he stood at the bar chatting to an old mate. 'Have you seen Tyrone O'Mally lately?'

'No!' Steve said. 'Won't be seeing that prick in here any-more! He stitched up one of the lads after a fight in a bar. He's not welcome here.' Steve did not know that Paul Johnston was a police officer, thinking that he was in construction. 'He caused a load of trouble, one of his mates waded in to help him out and he got 2 years for GBH. O'Mally was released without charge for naming him. Fucking prick.'

Johnston went into the toilet and as he left the bar, a young guy went over to Steve. 'What's the old bill doing in here?'

'Where?'

'That bloke you're talking to, he's a copper.'

As Johnston returned to the bar the atmosphere was different, cold. He felt eyes on him from all areas and suddenly felt uncomfortable. He stood next to Steve, finished his cola and said 'Right, see you again Steve, good to catch up.'

Steve shook his hand lightly, with a suspicious, pensive look on his face. Johnston left the bar, walked down the corridor and exited the building. As he was walking towards the car across the dark car park, he heard the doors burst open and Steve appeared, 'Paul!' he shouted as he walked quickly over.

Johnston was ready for whatever was going to happen with all his senses on high alert, glancing around for any-one else who may be around.'Yes mate.'

'Just a quick one, I know you're in the force, if I can help in any way, here's my number.' Steve handed over a business card. With an element of relief Johnston took it and looked at it briefly.

'I appreciate that mate, I would just like to find O'Mally. I obviously can't talk about it but if you hear anything here's my number.' Johnston wrote his number on a note pad he had in his pocket tore the sheet off and handed it over. 'Thanks Steve, see you again mate.' Shaking his hand.

Chapter 10

Lucy met up with Callum for a drink in Exeter town centre. She walked past the ruins of the fire damaged Royal Clarence Hotel and remembered the night spent in the bar next door where her date failed to come up with the goods and as a result, she found herself in bed with Callum the following morning, which was nice, but he wasn't the one, just some bloke who had a bit of money and fairly good in bed. She was planning to fleece him.

This was to be the third time they got together since their morning encounter, and she led him to believe that she was falling for him. He was very keen and thought she was gorgeous. He loved having sex with her and was willing to do whatever it took to get her back into bed at every opportunity. He liked her personality also, slightly mad but clever. He did not realise how clever. She had not spent any money on any of the dates they had been on. She would make up for it with sex, or sexual acts and he was falling for it every time.

'So, how has your week been Cal?'

'Fine, I worked at your farm for two days, then over at Shaun's. We had a job to do on Saturday, but it all went well.'

'What sort of job? On a farm?'

'Kind of, yes. I won't go into it, but it all worked out.'

'Go on! Tell me! We don't keep secrets, do we?'

This persuasion lasted for a few minutes and Lucy looked disappointed when Callum stopped talking knowing the possible implications of too many people finding out of the manoeuvre which killed Tyrone, someone he would never have dream of linking to Lucy. She decided to try another approach. She would get him drunk and get him talking. She was not used to men not opening- up to her and she had ways of making them talk to her.

Just before eleven and the bar was closing. Lucy had bought a couple of rounds and with them some Jägerbombs. This should do the trick, she thought. She was pretending to get pissed and was faking slurred speech and swaying on her stool. He was not faking it, he was totally smashed, not knowing if he was able to perform in bed. They had arranged to have a meal, but Lucy decided to get him pissed to get information out of him.

'So, what did you get up to on Saturday morning then?' she said. 'We met later in the afternoon, and I could tell you were tense.'

'Nothing, I went to work at Shaun's farm and then came to meet you.'

'You lying fucker!' she said smiling 'You were up to something. I could tell. If you're seeing someone else, tell me.' Her smile receding as she said it.

'No, nothing like that!' he exclaimed as he sat up straight. 'No, we had to do a favour for someone, a big one. It's all sorted and that's it. I can't tell you.' His speech was starting to fail him with the mixture of cider and spirits which Lucy had gently forced him to drink. 'At the end of the day people shouldn't mess with the locals. There was this guy and one of the main players in town wanted him to disappear, so we made it happen. I don't even know who it was or anything. I was just one of the drivers.'

Lucy had managed to bleed the whole story from him after ten-minutes and showed no emotion as it became clear that it was Tyrone who had fallen victim to the local mafia. 'You can trust me Cal, I wouldn't tell anyone.' She said kissing him on the cheek.

They walked the mile or so to Callum's house, him stopping to piss in a bush half-way home and trying to grope her bum after, with her gently refusing him sex in an alley way. They went to bed after Lucy helped him after puking in the toilet and she turned her back on him, checking the room out while he was snoring next to her. Expensive trainers, a sports car outside, a house worth double of what her apartment in Bristol was worth, she had hit the jackpot. But she had found out that Tyrone could be dead as a result of upsetting her uncle Chris. She knew he was well connected, but this was power. She already worshipped her uncle but at the same time felt guilty about partly causing the death of Tyrone. But also feeling that how he treated people including her, Tyrone probably deserved it.

Callum woke up with a splitting headache. Lucy had left the room and was making coffee and toast. She entered the bedroom and put the tray of toast and coffee on the table and climbed back into bed, kissing Callum on the cheek. He responded with a strained smile but looked ill. She ran her hand down his body and down the side of his thigh, across his knees, and slowly up the other thigh and glanced across his penis, which responded instantly. She wasted no time and climbed on, inserting him into her and enjoying him as much as possible, not knowing how long it was to last. Because he had been drinking and was still slightly numb, he was able to hold out until she had a very vocal orgasm. As she collapsed onto the bed he climbed between her open legs and started guiding himself in with his right hand, as she said softly 'No.'

He didn't hear, or chose not to, or thought she was joking as he carried on and within a minute had climaxed intensely. She just lay there and silently looked at the ceiling, knowing she had him. That she had the power. Thinking how she would use it. She quietly got up, went into the bathroom. He was almost asleep on the bed as she came back in and dressed. She left and drove back to the farm without speaking a word to him.

Chapter 11

Following some vague leads, Johnston entered the high-ways department and having introduced himself studied the CCTV of the area of Bristol where Tyrone had lived. It took hours and it was clear that he had driven to Exeter on a certain day, as the truck owned by him stopped appearing after a certain date. He checked a CCTV location on the M5 South and discovered shortly after the moment the truck left Bristol was captured on cameras right down to the Exeter junction.

Johnston reported to his Sergeant, Matt Bailey. 'Do you want me to follow this up Sarge?'

'Yes, I do Paul. Report back every two days, there's a useful civilian contact in the area, and report to Sergeant Brian Chapple at Exeter Central.' He handed Johnston a folder and turned back and sat at his desk.

'Thanks, Sarge.'

Plain clothed, Johnston headed down to Exeter and stopped at the services in Taunton. As he left the toilets, he heard a security guard shout at a group of 20-somethings who were shouting and laughing as they walked out of the main exit, barging through the crowds with no regard for anyone else. Stopping the overweight, stressed guard, he asked what was going on, displaying his warrant card.

'They just stole from the shop and have thrown food all over the place in the restaurant!'

Johnston was still in the Avon and Somerset Constabulary area so was able to take action. He ran over to the group, and slowed down as they entered the car, a Mitsubishi Shogun. As the driver climbed in, he reached and snatched the keys from his hand and asked them all to step out of the car. Surprised but resistant and not knowing who this tall stern looking guy was, they all disembarked and surrounded Johnston, in a view to intimidating him. They were loud and as they started pushing him around. One of them was particularly muscular and moved in to grab Johnston who threw both his arms upwards which struck the guy's forearms and forced them up and outwards. The guy still had slight forward momentum which Johnston used as he raised his knee and struck hard into the stomach which badly winded him. As he crouched with a loud grunt, Johnston struck him on the back of the neck with his right palm which sent him face down onto the tarmac. To his left another lean, angry looking guy came in with a haymaker which was likely to be harmful, but Johnston was fast, and he blocked the punch and countered with a sharp jab which crippled his knees and a stream of blood immediately fell from his nose. He turned to the other two and stepped towards them, he was ready for anything at this point and had the upper hand having taken out the meanest looking two of the gang. The remaining two raised their hands and said 'Ok, Ok! We don't want any trouble!' At this point Johnston revealed his warrant card.

Five minutes later all four men were cleaning the restaurant with mops and cleaning cloths having given back the chocolate bars they had stolen and all placing £50 each into the 'Help for Heroes' charity box.

An hour later, Johnston reported to Exeter Central

Constabulary and introduced himself to Sergeant Chapple. A slightly overweight loud- mouthed man with a northern accent, originally from Greater Manchester, who made a point of looking down his nose to everyone. 'I want to be informed of every single item of this case and any progress made. I have not heard of this Tyrone O'Mally character so if he's on my patch I want to be the first to know. Understood?' Chapple demanded.

'Of course, Sarge.' Johnston said as he left the office. He made his way out of town onto a country road, following his sat nav to Court Farm. He slowly turned and entered the drive up to the farm-house, noticing a black Mini Cooper parked to the right, looking like it hadn't been cleaned for a long time, and tyres worn almost to the canvas. He climbed out of his Ford Focus and knocked on the front door. It was just after 5.30 pm and getting dark. The door opened a minute later, and Lucy stood and admired the lean tall stern looking man. 'Hi, can I help you?' she said with half a smile.

'Is it Lucy?'

'Yes, why?' she said, not sure what to expect, wondering how he knew her name.

'My name is Paul Johnston from Bristol CID. I have a warrant out for the arrest of Tyrone O'Mally, and I believe you used to live with him in Bristol. Do you know where I can find him by any chance?'

'No, sorry, we split up a few months ago and moved down here with my auntie and uncle. I haven't seen him since and quite frankly don't want to, He beat me up and I walked out. Do you want to come in?' Lucy hid her nerves well as Johnston entered the hallway and wiped his feet on the door-mat. They sat at the breakfast bar and Lucy put two cups of coffee on place mats. 'What has he done this time? He was always in trouble, either at work or he had hit someone. He was a bully.' She realised that she was talking in past tense and began to correct herself. 'Is he not still living in our apartment then?'

'Sorry but I'm limited to what I am able to tell you, but it is an assault charge against a police officer, and not appearing in court for his trial. I have reason to believe he is in the Exeter area, as his truck was spotted on CCTV. There is no evidence of him returning to Bristol, or even on the M5 north since, so he may still be in this area.'

'Oh right.' Lucy said, faking a concerned look on her face.

Johnston was attuned to fake expressions and, as convincing as she thought she was, he was fully aware, but chose not to mention it yet. Chris pulled up the drive, bypassed the house and parked his truck in the farm-yard. As he turned off the engine, he ended the call he had on hands free and with a pensive look, entered the rear door of the farmhouse straight into the kitchen to be faced with Johnston and Lucy sharing a joke with two empty coffee mugs in front of them.

'Hi. You must be Paul Johnston,' he said as he held his hand out.

Johnston stood up and shook his hand. 'How do you know who I am?' he asked with uncomfortable surprise, and a fake smile.

'Oh, just local gossip, don't worry about it. Do you want another coffee?' Chris said looking straight into his eyes, in a friendly way with an underlying warning.

'No, I must get going, but thanks anyway mate.' He said his goodbyes and headed down the drive in the dark, turning right onto the single carriageway. Deep in thought as he hadn't spoken to anyone apart from the police staff until reaching the farm-house. How did that farmer know who he was?

Chapter 12

Jack looked agitated as he entered Shelley's flat. It was 6.30 and he was early, by about an hour. Shelley noticed straight away that something was wrong but was on the phone to Social Security who was informing her that Craig was walking unaided and that the funding was being cut, because he was able to care for himself now.

Ending the call, she walked into the lounge and greeted Jack with a kiss and a hug, she asked what was wrong.

'Redundancies are coming. I haven't been told anything yet, but they said there is uncertainty with Brexit and the supply chain has escalated their prices.'

'Try not to worry about it love, you've been there for years. It would cost them a fortune to make you redundant.'

Jack was wearing jogging trousers and a t-shirt, Shelley was in her karate suit held together with a black belt which was worn out so it was more white than black. 'Time to go,' she said with an element of excitement.

Jack looked concerned but intrigued. He was about to attend his first karate lesson and Shelley was one of the instructors. They arrived at the dojo, a community centre, at 7.20. Entering the hall, Shelley stepped to one side, placed her hands on the outsides of her thighs, and bowed as she entered. Jack watched as others did the same, so he did.

There were over 20 people in the room, some stood chatting, some were practicing moves, and some were stretching their legs with side splits and box splits.

Following introducing Jack to the main instructor, they all lined up in grade order and the lesson began. A hard warm up followed by stretching which Jack struggled with, then some basic punches and kicks. The black belts were training at the far end of the room and Shelley was teaching them a kata. Whilst taking a break he was mesmerised by the complexity of the kata and techniques which Shelley was teaching. At the end of the lesson, they all sat quietly and meditated for a minute before bowing to the instructors and then it was over. Shelley walked over to Jack and asked how it was for him.

'Amazing! Complicated but really enjoyable!' he said, wiping the sweat from his forehead.

'Neil, this is Jack, we met that night in your club'. Jack recognised the bouncer from the night that Shelley dealt with the bodybuilder who was trying it on in front of him.

'Hi mate, how are you? Good to see you again'. Neil said with a friendly smile.

'I'm good thanks mate, this is my first time in martial arts, I really enjoyed it!'

'Great. We'll be seeing more of you then.' Neil said with a hand on his shoulder. 'Shelley, can I have a word?'

They went to the other side of the hall and spoke quietly. Shelley returned with a pensive look on her face and asked Jack if he was ready to leave.

Jack started the car and as they drove off, he asked 'Everything ok Shell?'

'Mmm kind of, you know that guy who I sorted out that night when he tried it on? Well rumour has it that he's dead. Keep it to yourself though, at the moment he's just missing.'

Jack looked alarmed. 'Really? A bit over the top, isn't it? What sort of shit are you into Shelley?'

'You don't think I did it do you? I had nothing to do with it. Cut the attitude, it's just a rumour. Some guy in Exeter who is close mates with Neil heard about it. I shouldn't have told you; I didn't know you were going to get all weird about it.'

They didn't speak for the remaining 25 minutes of the journey and Jack hated it. Shelley just stared out of the passenger window. When they arrived at Shelley's she released her seatbelt and opened the door. 'Coming in?'

'OK' Jack said, and they entered and went straight up stairs. Shelley sat on the bed and Jack sat next to her. 'Can I trust you, Jack?'

'Of course, you can I was just confused. Was the guy the one who turned up in court as well? You said you had words with him.'

'Yes, it was but I swear I haven't seen him since. I don't know what happened to him, I swear. I heard he didn't turn up for his hearing for hitting a copper, that's all I know. We hear a lot of what goes on because...' Shelley stopped talking and stood up. 'Do you want a drink? I have a bottle of wine.'

'Yes please, but first, what were you saying?'

Shelley left the room and closed the door. She shouldn't tell Jack the whole story, but she loved him and felt she could trust him. Also knowing the implications of him telling anyone else. She took longer than usual to return to the room and when she opened the door, Jack was stood up with his jacket on, looking like he was leaving, 'I want to know what's going on. What am I getting involved with?' He said looking stern and assertive.

Shelley just stood and looked at him with a blank expression. She was used to not showing emotion or feelings, with the martial arts training, and being the only young lady in the office and having to deal with senior management, and all the gang stuff which she was very good at. Inside she was burning up. Most other women would melt at this point, or at least show some emotion. Maybe that's what Jack wanted. Some show of emotion and her to show that she did care if he walked out. She just stood and looked, with a glass of wine in each hand.

'Are you going to tell me or not?' he said, hating this situation but not sure if he was able to walk out. He kept asking himself 'Should I stay?' But he felt he had to know what all this was, and what kind of life he was likely to lead if he stayed with her, and the implications of leaving.

'I'm not directly involved Jack, but there are certain things I am unable to tell you. We are well connected and hear all sorts of things happening all over Europe. Our parents were involved, now we are. That's all you need to know. I don't want you to walk out, but that's your decision. You're not getting into anything Jack, but let's say you will be well looked after if you stay with me.' she put the wine glasses on the chest of drawers and stood looking at Jack. She was beginning to show emotion with her eyes welling up and her eye-brows slightly raised. She loved him with all her heart and inside she was desperate for him to understand.

Jack stepped over to her and offered a hug, and she accepted with a passionate embrace, a tear from each eye forming wet patches on his soft-shell jacket. 'Do you want to sleep here?' she asked with her fingers secretly crossed.

'OK, but I need to leave early in the morning because we have a union briefing in the morning before work.'

'Better make the most of tonight then, hadn't we?' she said followed by a deep sigh and half of a smile. She unzipped his jacket and gently, slowly removed it, with a sweep of his lean shoulders and arms. She continued slowly until he was stood naked in the middle of the room. He didn't realise the curtains were open and the light was on, she knew and found it amusing. There were houses opposite and they were often outside having a smoke. She handed him his glass of wine and said, 'Don't move.' She gathered up is clothes behind him, opened the bedroom window and dropped them all onto the decking below, closed the window and the curtains and stripped naked. 'You can turn around now' she said in a sexy voice. Jack turned around and laughed at what he guessed she had done.

'If you try to leave now, you will have to go down the stairs naked and get your clothes from the garden.' They both laughed and hugged, still emotional but so deeply in love. 'Lie down on your front.'

He obliged and she began to massage his back. He was in ecstasy as she seemed to know every single muscle in his back and was able to identify every tender one which was aching. She was enjoying it as much as he was stroking his toned muscular body. She massaged his legs and feet and asked him to turn over. Straddling him as she worked on his upper arms, he was led with his eyes closed and breathing deeply. He was trying to control it, but he was physically aroused. She was also excited and as she raised herself onto her knees, he opened his eyes and was faced with her perfect naked body with her hand guiding him into her.

'I've had to come off the pill because they were upsetting my stomach, so we need to be careful.'

Chapter 13

Lucy chose not to act on the rape allegation she had master-minded, but decided it was over with Callum. She had not told him yet and was keeping him hanging on in case she changed her mind. Following the recent news from Callum and the visit from the CID officer, she thought she should go back to the apartment.

Sunday morning and the traffic was bad on the M5, as there were road works and an accident near Weston-super-Mare. When she eventually made it to the Clevedon junction, she started moving at speed and then the nerves took over. She hadn't been near Bristol for six months or more, not even to see her parents. Social media had kept her in contact with her friends in the area and her parents had visited a couple of times.

The weather was cold, as Christmas was only two weeks away and the wind was blistering. She climbed out of the car and looked at the first-floor apartment for a few seconds nervously, noticing the kitchen window was clad with a timber panel, broken glass still visible on the outside. She took a deep breath and walked into the communal door, up the stairs and pushed her key into the lock. The stress was etched on her face as she didn't know what she was going to be faced with, asking herself, 'What if Callum was wrong, and Tyrone is in the flat? What if he committed suicide in there?'

She slowly pushed the door open, noticing that the frame had been crudely repaired after it had been forced at some point. Pushing the door over a mountain of mail, she noticed a mouldy smell and stepped over the mail that had not been pushed over by the opening door. It was cold in the apartment and felt damp as it had not been lived in for a long time. Looking around, she started feeling emotional. She thought about the day they first moved in and how excited she was, and how much she loved Tyrone back then. How could things have got so bad between them? Why did she have to be unfaithful? Why was he always unfaithful? What if they were loyal to each other and how different it all could have been?

Wiping a tear away, she picked up a pile of mail and started sorting through them trying to identify any urgent or important ones. There were several from the Crown Prosecution Service, one from the Inland Revenue and the usual ones from the bank etc. most were addressed to Tyrone, as she had redirected her mail to the farm-house. There were one or two which had slipped through to the apartment, but none were important.

Lucy started to open the CPS letters and was surprised as she read that a warrant was out for his arrest for not appearing at his hearing for GBH to a police officer. As she opened a letter from the bank, there was a knock at the door. She felt her heart jump and she began to tremble, almost jumping to her feet. She looked through a gap in the curtains and noticed a short stocky man talking to a CB radio looking straight at her. He was dressed in blue jeans and a black leather jacket. He looked menacing and clearly noticed her looking out of the window. She approached the entrance door and looked through the spy hole and instantly recognised PC Johnston with a CB close to his ear. He knocked loudly again which made Lucy jump backwards. She said nervously 'Who is it?'

'Paul Johnston. Do you have a minute please Lucy?'

Lucy opened the door and said 'Hi! You scared me to death! What can I do for you?'

'Lucy Gardiner! Good to see you again. Do you mind if we have a little chat?'

Lucy looked startled. 'I was just leaving. Can this wait? Have you found Tyrone yet?' she asked with her eye-brows raised.

'I was just passing and saw your car outside, wondering if you had any more information on his whereabouts?' Johnston was trying to keep his eyes up to her face as she was wearing a tight top which hugged her breasts. She looked worse for wear but still attractive. He could smell alcohol on her breath and last night's perfume. 'This place could do with a clean.'

'Yes, it could, are you volunteering?' she asked with a smile.

He laughed. 'No way! Are you free tomorrow lunch time? Maybe we could meet up for a chat. Informal, off the record, don't worry, well what do you think?'

Lucy thought for a moment, how could she get out of it, but it may be interesting. And he was gorgeous. 'OK, how about 12.30 at the coffee shop on Park Street?'

'See you then.' Johnston left.

Lucy spent the rest of the day cleaning the apartment and washing the bed linen. She planned to stay there for a while. That night she arranged to meet some friends in town, so she had a shower and was ready for 7.30. Kerry was someone she knew from the rugby club as she was also in a relationship with one of the players. They regularly met up at the club and went out together in town. Lucy was looking forward to catching up.

'Hi Lucy!' Kerry said hugging her.

'How are you? It's been ages!' Lucy replied. They spent an hour catching up with the local gossip and Kerry told her all about her new man, Pete.

Lucy explained, without revealing the full truth that Tyrone had hit her, and he had since vanished. Kerry knew that she had family in Exeter, and some were involved with illegal activity, but she thought it best not to mention it. She knew what Lucy was capable of.

'Hi Shell, what time shall I pick you up?' Jack spoke in an upbeat, almost excited voice.

'Come round whenever you like love!' Shelley instantly felt warm as she spoke to him, especially hearing his tone of voice. She knew he had been called into a meeting that day with the senior managers and judging by his voice, it went well.

Jack arrived at seven and as Shelley opened the door, he kissed her lovingly on the lips. They sat in the kitchen diner and Shelley poured them both a glass of wine. 'So, tell me about your day.'

Jack lent forward on his chair, elbows on the table so he was closer to Shelley. 'I've been offered a management post.'

'Wow! That's fantastic! You have been worried that you were going to lose your job, then this! Brilliant news!' Shelley grasped his hands and smiled lovingly at him. Come on, it's Friday night. Let's go out and celebrate.'

They took a taxi into town and met Pete and Kerry in the usual bar. It was a good foursome and they all seemed to enjoy each-others company. Jack was telling Pete about his job and Shelley and Kerry were getting to know each other. eleven, and the bar was in full capacity and bar staff at full stretch. People were getting agitated as service was taking too long, but generally the mood was good. Kerry turned around having been patted on the shoulder. 'Lucy! Shelley,

I'd like you to meet my friend. She's just come back from staying in Exeter for far too long.'

'Hi Lucy, welcome back to the best city on earth. So, were you working down there then?'

'No. Well I did get a job while I was there for a few months. I split up with my fiancé, so I stayed with family for a while until things settled down. It was always only going to be short term.'

Shelley instantly figured out who she was and knew all about her. She showed no emotion and carried on, not asking any more questions because she already knew all she wanted to.

Kerry turned back to Lucy. 'How did you get on with that copper you were meeting on Monday?'

'Oh, he cancelled. Something urgent came up. Shame really, he was hot.' Lucy said, checking out Pete from behind, noticing he had a nice bum. Aren't you going to introduce me then?'

Pete turned around and raised his eye-brows at the sight of Lucy in a low-cut top with amazing breasts. 'Hi! Pleased to meet you both.'

Lucy looked him in the eyes and laughed. She liked what she saw, and he also made her laugh. Everyone else present noticed the mutual attraction and felt awkward. As the night wore on, at some point, Lucy managed to give Pete a piece of paper with her mobile number written on with a kiss at the bottom. It was done discretely but Shelley noticed. She never missed anything. Kerry laughed it off but knew that there was an obvious attraction between them. She was bothered by it but not particularly upset, as Pete was funny, but he was quite shallow. She was probably going to end it soon anyway, as she was still getting over breaking up with her long-term boyfriend from the rugby club.

Without making a point of looking over, Shelley noticed

a group of men at the other side of the bar. They caught her eye because some of them looked like trouble. She pulled out her mobile and started composing a text. Within seconds, the doorman had appeared and nodded at Shelley. Minutes later, sure enough there was a fight. It was quickly dispersed by the bouncers thanks to Shelley's observation of the situation. 'Thanks Shelley, free drinks for the rest of the night.' Aaron said.

Aaron was the head doorman on this shift and was friends with Craig. 'How is he?'

'He's fine thanks, getting about a lot easier now, I'll tell him I saw you, take care Aaron'. She kissed him on the cheek, and he disappeared into the crowd.

'So, who is Craig then?' Lucy asked, genuinely not knowing it was the guy she slept with which caused all the trouble.

'My brother. He was done over earlier this year. Apparently, he slept with the wrong slapper.' Shelley could not resist the comment, but Lucy just nodded and carried on jigging to the music, not understanding what Shelley had said.

Jack was drunk to the stage where he couldn't speak clearly. Some guy, also drunk pushed past, almost knocking him over. Jack swayed and shouted over 'Fucking prick!'

The guy turned around and clumsily jabbed Jack with his right fist striking his left cheek. Jack's head jolted back but no damage was done, just anger. Jack replied with a clumsy punch and the guy backed off holding his nose. Jack was relieved but failed to notice four of the guy's mates rush over. By the time Jack landed the punch, Shelley had put her drink down and made her way through the crowd, noticing four or more men from the other guy's group marching over towards Jack. Barging past Jack, she stared at the first one, who tried to dismiss her. As he tried to get past her to get to Jack, she placed her had on the right side of his face and slammed her elbow into his jaw. His legs buckled but it wasn't enough force to break his jaw, enough though, to stun him on his feet. A split second later she swivelled to her right and with the palm of her hand vertically striking the second man under the chin, sending him backwards onto the floor, but not with force. The other two men backed off with hands in the air. Grasping Jack's hand, they left the bar and she nodded to the doormen as they attended the scene.

Lucy was in awe of Shelley and asked Pete how they knew each other. Whilst their conversation went on, Kerry left the bar glancing back at Pete and Lucy and walked off alone. Pete saw her leave but was not bothered, knowing it was going nowhere. Sometime later, Lucy turned her head, and then looked at Pete and said, 'Looks like all our friends are gone, what do you want to do?'

They left the bar together and straight to Lucy's apartment. As they pulled in and paid the taxi, Pete noticed the broken window. 'What happened there?'

'My ex got into a bit of trouble, and someone threw a brick through it. He's gone now so I won't get any more hassle.'

'Gone where?' Pete asked.

'No idea. Don't worry he's not coming back.' Lucy unbuttoned her coat and slipped it off before she entered the communal door. As she walked up the stairs, she was fully aware of Pete behind her checking her out, so she made a point of putting on a show with her tight dress, gently swaying her hips with every step.

Chapter 14

Unshaven and looking scruffy, Johnston entered the sports bar in Exeter town centre at 6.30 pm. Discretely glancing around he noticed a farm hand leaning against the bar with a pint of rough cider. Johnston made his way across and stood next to him and when the barman came over ordered a lager.

Callum looked at him with friendly eyes. 'Hi mate, haven't seen you here before, are you a local?'

'No mate, I have just moved into the area. What's your name?'

'Callum. Yours?'

'Steve. Pleased to meet you. What's the score round here then? Anything I should know?'

'No, not really mate, just like anywhere really, there are some people you don't fuck with, others not to worry about.'

'That's true, I come from Bristol. I know all about gangs, guns, drugs and all that crap, there's one gang in particular that seemed to even have the police under control.' Johnston said convincingly. 'Fancy a game of pool?'

'Sure. I'll get a round in and then I'll have some change.' Callum waved a tenner at the barman and ordered the drinks whilst Johnston set up the pool table.

Callum brought the drinks over and chalked a cue,

having lost the toss. Johnston decided to break, and the evening continued.

It seemed that they had been evenly matched all night playing pool and drinking pint for pint, but Johnston was on duty and was playing a game. Knowing that Callum was getting more intoxicated, Johnston could handle standard strength lager all night, and keep his wits about him. He was also very good at pool and was always the best when in the Paras. At 10.30 the time was right to ask a few questions.

'So, are there any major gangs to look out for around here mate?'

'Yes, I'm in it myself. We have coppers, solicitors and all sorts involved. I shouldn't talk about it really.'

After half an hour of gentle questions Johnston had heard all about Tyrone being buried, he just needed to establish the location. By this time Callum was almost unable to speak after ten or more pints of rough cider and a few shots to top them off.

'There's this lane off the A361 near Tiverton called Badgers Brook. That's where it happened, a nasty accident that was.' As Callum slurred his speech, the barman was watching and listening as he pretended to do something under the counter with a serious look on his face. Johnston looked unimpressed with what he heard but inside he was storing all the information.

'I need a piss.' Johnston left the bar and headed into the toilet. Quickly relieving himself he darted out of the back door of the bar, and to the hotel. He went straight to bed as he needed to be fresh for the morning with all the information he had received.

Meantime, the barman made a phone call. 'Brian, Dennis here, Callum has broken silence. Badly.'

The following morning, Chris was working on the farm erecting temporary fencing for cattle segregation. At eleven he called Callum. 'Morning mate, can you work tonight please? I have a cow about to calve down, and I still have fencing to put up. I will pay extra.'

'Yes mate, I will be there for eight.' Callum said, in a gruff voice, still nursing a hangover.

Seven pm and Chris was lining the back of the truck with polythene. It had a typical rear fibreglass enclosure over the rear with a hydraulic glazed hatch at the rear with a twist lock. He places a pile of one meter timber fence posts behind the cab and closed the tailgate and hatch. At 7:45 Callum pulled up in his Subaru. 'Hi boss, what are we doing?'

'Hi Callum, jump in mate, we need to go down to the bottom field and out up some fencing mate.'

Theresa was in the kitchen with Lucy. They were small-talking whilst waiting as the cottage pie was cooking in the oven. Lucy poured a glass of wine for each of them and sat at the breakfast bar, ignoring the fact that Callum was around, and that he had purposely tried to catch her attention as he walked past the kitchen window.

Chris drove down the farm track with Callum next to him still stinking of booze but looking keen to work, as the money would be good. They reached the bottom field, and to a remote location where a broken section of fencing had been removed. There was a roll of wire mesh, a neatly stacked pile of timber and a bag of fixings on a small pallet next to where Chris pulled up.

They both climbed out of the cab and Chris looked like he was aching and stiff as he walked slowly to the back of the truck. 'Can you jump in and pass out the posts please mate?'

'Sure.' Callum answered, and with one hand on the tailgate, he jumped onto the truck with ease, crouching down took a few steps forward into the truck and grabbed two lengths of timber. As he turned, Chris produced a pistol from the inside of his coat, pointed it at Callum's head and with one squeeze of the trigger it was over.

As Theresa was removing the cottage pie from the oven, she heard the shot. She paused, glanced up, and carried on having let out a deep sigh. Lucy looked up from her trashy magazine. 'What was that a gunshot?'

'No, probably nothing.' Theresa replied, knowing exactly what it was.

Chris wrapped the body in the polythene sheeting in the back of the truck and sealed the package tightly using almost a whole role of gaffer tape and sat on the tailgate, rolled a cigarette and waited until 10:30 until he received a text from Theresa confirming that Lucy was in bed, asleep. He drove the truck back to the yard, secured it in a barn and then the Subaru was picked up by a local scrap merchant, and gang member.

Shelley was not impressed with the fact that Jack got into a fight, and she had to step in to help out. She made a point of not saying a word for the entire journey by taxi to her house. Jack felt bad about it but had too much to drink to think too much.

They arrived at Shelley's and Jack handed the driver £20 and said keep the change. Lucy then said to the driver 'Here's another tenner, can you drop Jack off at 152 Kingsdown Road please?'

Jack looked at her with shock and disbelief and sat back down. Shelley kissed him on the cheek and left the cab closing the door firmly walked up the steps and entered the shared house. The taxi driver looked awkward as they drove to Jack's house. As they arrived Jack said, 'Thanks mate' and climbed out. As the taxi drove off, he staggered slightly as he walked up the path into his mum's house. Still not quite comprehending how Shelley had dumped him in the taxi he went into the kitchen and poured himself a glass of vodka. He lent against the kitchen worktop and sipped the vodka slowly, his thoughts unclear, he was very drunk at this point. He lifted his elbow off the worktop and stood upright for a second, then his right knee gave way as his balance failed and he crashed head- first into the cooker, cutting his eye badly and knocking himself unconscious. He remained on the kitchen floor for the night, in a pool of blood.

His mum woke up at 6.30 as usual and having gone to the toilet made her way down the stairs to make a cup of tea. 'Jack!' she shouted as she reached the bottom of the stairs and saw him on the floor. She had first aid training and instinctively checked for a pulse and breathing as she wiped the blood from the side of his head with a tea towel. She could feel that he had a good pulse and was breathing but noticed a deep cut above his eye which she attended to. She called an ambulance and it arrived 15 minutes later. As the paramedic arrived Jack started to regain consciousness and looked ill, in pain and confused.

They spent the day in hospital. The scan revealed no hae-morrhaging within the brain and no long-term damage. The bruising was severe, and Jack had stitches above his eye, but his sight was not affected. Although he was starting to feel better physically, he was emotionally drained with the thought of splitting up with Shelley. He was beginning to remember the events of the previous night and the way Shelley left him in the taxi. He felt terrible. He reached into his pocket for his phone, but it wasn't there. He looked at his Mum who was reading a two-month-old magazine and asked, 'Where's my phone Mum?'

'I don't know love. It wasn't on you when I found you.'

Jack began to worry. He tried to reassure himself that the phone was on the kitchen side, but it didn't help. 'When can we go home?' he asked when the nurse went past.

'Just waiting for the consultant to see you and then you should be on your way,' she said with a polite smile.

It felt like hours, but the consultant took 20 minutes to get around to Jack. Following some tests, he confirmed that he was fine to be discharged and that a follow-up appointment will be sent through the post.

The taxi pulled up outside the house and Jack was impatient getting inside. He went straight into the kitchen and to his relief the phone was on the floor. He picked it up to find the screen shattered and it wasn't working. He knew that he no longer had Shelley's number as he hadn't saved it anywhere else.

He started filling up the mop bucket with hot water and detergent as his Mum opened the mail. She looked up and said 'Love don't worry, I'll do that! Sit down!'

'I insist.' He said carrying on, thinking about Shelley. What if she had tried to contact him? Why did she dump him? It was only a scuffle. What should he do? Contact her? Go to her house?

Chapter 15

Pete had been trying to contact Jack all day to tell him all about the night before and also to mention the night he had spent with Lucy. They enjoyed a night of sex, had a few hours' sleep and started again in the morning. He eventually left her apartment at 3 pm and spent the rest of the day resting. They planned to meet the following Saturday night on their own and he was looking forward to it.

He heard a car pull up outside and opened the door to Jack. 'What the fuck happened to you?' he said looking at Jack's face, which was black on one side above the cheekbone, and a dressing above his right eye.

They went in and Jack told Pete the whole story. He was regretful talking about the fight and he no longer had Shelley's number. 'I don't know what to do mate. I love her and now it looks like it's over. My phone is dead so I don't know if she has tried to call or text me.' he wasn't in tears but could easily have been.

Pete was a good listener and put his hand on Jack's shoulder. 'I'm sure it will work out mate, one way or another.'

They arranged a track day at the same circuit as before, for the following Saturday. Jack felt slightly better and decided to cool it off regarding Shelley and see if she would contact him. After all, it was her who ended it.

Monday morning and Jack considered calling in sick from work, but he had just been promoted so made the effort. Still feeling down about splitting with Shelley, and still slightly in pain, he arrived at work and headed for the canteen for the usual coffee before the shift started.

He soon became tired of telling everyone about it and felt impatient with all of his team but made it through the day, and the remaining week.

Friday night and there was a live band in his local, so he went along. He thought it best not to go into town as most security guards probably wouldn't let him in to their bars because of his facial injuries. In the pub there were many of his old school mates. The bruising had gone down and just a slight black eye and the stitches were healing. He looked better, but had visibly lost weight, and was looking off-colour. He enjoyed the music, punk and new wave covers. He had a few beers but not too many as he was being cautious. It was nice not to be in town on a Friday night and no taxi home. He had a new phone and was messing about with it all night, figuring out how to use it.

After the track day with Pete, Jack went straight home and stayed in. He had a training course for two weeks in London and he was on an early train on Monday. He had a six pack of lager, watched a movie and went to bed.

Shelley had sent numerous messages to Jack asking to meet up. The first message was sent an hour after she left him in the taxi. 'I'm sorry Jack, can we meet up in the morning? Love you xxx.' Not receiving a response all week, Shelley was very upset. Trying to get on with her week and coming to terms with the fact that Jack had not responded to her messages. The last one she sent was on Friday night. 'Jack, I understand you not wanting to see me again. All the best for the future. X'

Shelley stayed in all weekend, not feeling up to going out.

She was considering her future alone and trying to convince herself that men are too much trouble. She missed Jack, and was thinking of him constantly, realising how much she loved him, but he hadn't responded. She was convinced it was over and he was not interested. Thinking he had deeper issues with her, probably with the fact that she was involved with a group of bouncers. Maybe he felt emasculated with the fact that she was a karate expert. He may have felt intimidated by her group of friends. She blamed herself for it all, particularly the way she had treated him in the taxi, sending him home alone. 'What have I done?' she said out loud with her head in her hands, sat on her bed in her pyjamas. She started crying and couldn't stop. She cried herself to sleep and woke up feeling worse, as she had drunk a small bottle of vodka the night before, which added to her deep emotions. She felt better after a shower, three coffees and some toast, and drove to Craig's. She let herself in, kissed Craig and carried on the Sunday ritual of cleaning the flat and cooking roast dinner for them both. Craig was a good distraction as he was funny, and a good listener. Craig loved her and appreciated the fact that she came around and did so much for her. 'Shell, he will come around, don't worry. Why don't you go around his house? He might have lost his phone or something.'

'No, he was very careful with his phone. I know that I've messed up, I fucked it right up. It's all my fault and I will just have to live with it'.

Monday evening, Lucy was applying for jobs online and her mobile rang. 'Hi Uncle Chris!' she said with a smile.

'Hi love, I'm in Bristol for a couple of days. Can I stay at yours?'

'Yeah of course you can. Do you mind the sofa?'

'Of course not darling, that's fine.' Chris was there within half an hour, and with just a small bag with bare essentials in, but the bag looked heavy. Lucy greeted him with a hug and kissed his cheek. He responded by holding her tight and kissing her forehead.

'So, what brings you to Bristol then?' Lucy asked, pouring two glasses of red wine.

'Just business, I'm meeting a load of guys tomorrow night in an Italian restaurant on Corn Street, then on to a few bars.'

Chris was very good at hiding his feelings, but Lucy knew him inside out. Something was wrong, she could tell. They sat in the lounge, and she told him about Pete, and the fight that broke out in the bar a couple of weeks ago. Chris didn't say much, but just listened.

There was a knock at the door and they both got up. Lucy casually strolled out of the lounge and went to open the door. She peered through the spy hole and froze. It was one of the rugby boys. She turned around thinking of what to do. As she turned, Chris gently pushed her shoulder to one side and flung the door open, pointing a handheld pistol straight forward. 'FUCK OFF, YOU FUCKING SCUMBAG!' he shouted, and the guy jumped back in shock and ran down the stairs. He got into his car and drove off at speed. Chris was pacing the floor. 'Come back to Exeter Lucy, in case they come back. Just for a week or so.' Lucy agreed to go back the following day after visiting her parents.

Chris left for the evening to meet up with the friends. He took a taxi to Corn Street and waited next to The Needles. Shelley appeared and they walked together down St. Stephen's Street and up an alley and a key fob let them into a secured entrance to some flats. Chris pulled the pistol from his jacket, with the silencer attached, and Shelley did the same. They took the stairs to the first floor to flat 112, and the waited silently for the timed hallway lights to go out. Shelley inserted the key and with one turn there was a delicate click, and the door opened, and they slowly and silently entered the flat, Chris closing the door behind him. There was a faint light coming from the bedroom on the left and Shelley tried the door, which opened revealing the target. He was stinking of alcohol and clearly unconscious from a heavy session, which made the hit easy. Chris stood one side and Shelley the other, training their pistols at the target, and then Shelley switched on the light, which woke up the overweight accountant, who had ripped off the firm, and started mouthing off about it. He immediately screamed as he sat up and shouted 'Wait!' which was his last word. Shelley and Chris both shot at the same time. The noise was little more than the clap of hands, but the devastating rounds caused brains and blood to decorate the wall behind.

They both left the flat and calmly walked away, shook hands and went separate ways.

Jack was ready for two weeks in London. He had his suit-case next to the front door and a back-pack with his laptop, a jacket and some food inside. At 3.30pm on the Sunday the taxi driver sounded the horn outside. 'Bye Mum' Jack said and stooped down kissing her on the cheek.

'Take care love,' she said and waved as the taxi pulled away.

The weather was warm, and Jack arrived in Paddington at 6 pm. He took the tube to Kings Cross and checked into a hotel which was pre-booked. London was busy as usual. and he decided to stay in the hotel for dinner. The training course was in a building on St Pancras Square which was about half a mile away, so he set his alarm for seven.

In the morning he headed down Pentonville Road past the Poor School Academy and found the venue in between St Pancras and Kings Cross stations. The first day of train-ing was more of an introduction to the weeks ahead. The management course seemed interesting to Jack, but his mind was on Shelley. He missed texting her three or more times per day and calling her in the evening if not meeting up with her.

End of the first day and he showered in the hotel and met up with a couple of guys from the course. Darren was in his 30s and married with two kids. He was a mechanic whose company was expanding, and he was asked to become a manager. Sue had just become a human resources manager after her boss retired. She was 27 and slightly over-weight. They met in a bar near Kings Cross Station and had a light meal and a few drinks. Jack was not his usual lively self and was trying hard to be friendly and put his relationship trouble behind him. He was struggling but no one noticed.

Jack was back in the hotel by 10.30 and had a beer in the bar on his own. There were the odd couple of guys in the bar who were probably builders working in the area and some guys on their own on their laptops. Jack was not tired and was bored so he decided to go for a walk. He turned left out of the hotel entrance and walked down Pentonville Road and past Kings Cross Station. He carried on walking until be reached Gower Street. He turned left and just carried on walking. Thinking about Shelley and their whole relationship, he remembered when she first revealed her martial arts skills and how intimidated and emasculated, he felt. He also thought about how much he enjoyed her company and the sex they both enjoyed so much. Shelley was everything he wanted in a woman and more. But he was also worried that she was in deep with a gang, or a mafia type thing which really concerned him. The night that she left him in the taxi kept playing on his mind. Why did she just send him away like that? It was just one night that went slightly wrong. He knew he shouldn't have hit the guy who pushed him, but these things happen every so often.

Before he knew it, he was on Parliament Square. He had walked for miles, and it was mid-night. The tubes had stopped, and he had about four miles to walk back to the hotel. He got a map up on his phone and started heading back. Arriving at the hotel at 1 am he went straight to bed. Still unable to sleep, he sat on his laptop and listened to music on YouTube until he eventually drifted off.

The rest of the first week was pretty boring until the Friday afternoon when they all got off early and went out in Covent Garden together. Jack was staying in London for the whole two weeks in the hotel as he had no reason to go home. They started drinking at 3 pm and carried on all night. Sue was getting closer to Jack as the evening went on. He failed to notice and just chatted to everyone blissfully unaware.

They flagged down a cab and dropped Darren off first. Sue said to Jack 'I'm staying at the Premier Inn on Euston Road. Where are you staying?'

'A small hotel just down Pentonville Road.'

'Coming in for a last drink?' She asked, with a smile.

'OK, great.'

Chapter 16

Johnston was at Exeter Station with Sergeant Brian Chapple. He had written a report and was reading it out. Chapple's office door was closed, and he was listening to the report, glancing over Johnston's shoulder to ensure no one was listening in. When Johnston had finished reading the report, Chapple took it and locked it in his desk drawer. Johnston looked surprised, but he was keen to crack on.

'I have a JCB and a group of officers meeting us tomorrow at Badger's Lane at 12.30. Don't be late.'

Johnston arrived exactly 12.30 and there was a roadblock with two officers supervising at the entrance to Badgers Lane. He showed his warrant card, and they moved the cones to let him drive through. The excavator was in the field in the spot Johnston had pointed out, where there was a patch of land where nothing had grown. There were two police cars and six officers standing by. Chapple emerged from his car and entered the field standing next to Johnston.

'Carry on,' he said, swinging his right hand and pointing to the patch of ground.

After half hour the hole was three meters deep and just as wide. The bucket appeared to hit something metal and got stuck. The operator managed to free the bucket within seconds and Johnston leant over to look. He took a picture with his mobile phone and as he did, looking uncomfortable in an ill-fitting police uniform, Chris kicked him hard in the back and Johnston fell awkwardly into the excavation. As he landed, Chapple reached into his jacket and produced a pistol. All the officers turned around apart from the machine operator who watched everything and appeared to enjoy it. Chapple shot Johnston in the back of his head. Then aimed carefully and shot his mobile phone. Two officers including Chris, went over to Chris's truck, opened the back and pulled out the body of Callum which was still wrapped in polythene. They struggled with the package and dropped it clumsily into the hole. The operator revved up the machine and began filling the hole.

Chapple called everyone in close. 'Gather round. See what happens when someone gets gobby? We all need to keep our mouths firmly closed. That was a waste of a bloody good copper. I feel bad about all this, but you all understand that he had to be sorted, don't you? Anyway, get those uniforms off and load them into my car. I need to get these back in the nick before someone notices they are missing.'

The second week of the training course was better. It was uncomfortable, as Jack turned down sex with Sue, but they got through it and still spoke politely. On the Wednesday they finished early, and Jack decided to take a tube to Marble Arch and take a walk around Hyde Park. As he emerged from the tube station there were more sirens than usual, and people looked concerned. He carried on walking into Hyde Park. As he was approaching the Serpentine, his mobile rang. 'Hi mum, are you OK?'

'Yes, love you? There has been a terrorist attack in Westminster! I knew you were in London, so I needed to call you!'

'I'm fine Mum. Any other news?'

'Well, actually there is. Shelley popped in the other day, she said she wanted to see you.'

Jack stopped walking and stood there on the cycle path.

'She looks like she has lost weight. Not that she had much to lose mind, but she didn't look well. Her eyes were dark, and she looked pale. She came in for a coffee. Lovely girl that. I told her about your accident and that you lost your phone. I said I didn't have your new number because I wasn't sure if you wanted me to give it out.'

'I thought she was not interested in me anymore.'

'Well, she came around asking for you so she must be love'.

Jack was deep in thought following the conversation. He sat on a bench and just stared at the Serpentine. He was asking himself if he wanted to get involved with Shelley again after the last few months. After an hour he phoned his mum back and she read out her number.

He went into a bar near the BT Tower and had a few beers, everyone was watching the news about the attack on Westminster Bridge. He plucked up the courage and called Shelley.

'Hello.'

It was so good to hear her voice. Jack could hardly talk. 'Hi Shell, It's Jack.'

'Hello Jack! How are you? I heard about you having an accident, are you ok?' Shelley said, her heart pounding and holding back the tears.

The conversation lasted for a whole hour, and they arranged to meet up.

Saturday evening and Jack was getting ready to meet Shelley. He had bought a new shirt and put on some smart jeans. He felt good but nervous. He wanted it to work but he had to get things off his chest. There were terms, and he wasn't sure if she would like them.

He got to the bar half an hour early and had a pint whilst waiting, constantly grooming himself in the mirror behind the bar.

Shelley arrived right on time at seven as planned. She wore a tight- fitting mini dress and as she walked through the bar, every man, and most women looked at her. She looked stunning. She walked straight to Jack, who stood up from his stool and they hugged each other for a couple of minutes. Stopped and looked at each other and hugged again.

The night went perfectly, and Jack explained how he was feeling. Shelley said she would always be involved in the firm but agreed to take a back seat.

They stayed in Shelley's house and Jack noticed she had lost weight, and that he was now out of shape. She told him to be careful as she was not on the pill. It felt different sleeping together. Nice but different. They had both been through an emotional roller coaster and it seemed that their feelings for each other had changed.

They woke up early in the morning and they were both quiet but still enjoying being together. Neither could work out why they weren't talking much, and they felt slightly uncomfortable with it. They both wanted it to work out, but it seemed that it was going to be harder than just being together. It was going to take work from both of them.

Shelley raised her head off the pillow, turned to Jack and said 'I have a mate with an apartment in Barcelona. We might be able to use it on the cheap if you want to? I'm sure it will be available in June. Flights will be reasonable if we book early!' She was hoping for a positive reaction as she was feeling uncomfortable with the quietness.

'Sounds great!' Jack said unconvincingly. He was feeling the same as her but couldn't seem to shake off the quietness. The more he tried the worse it seemed to get. 'Shall we book it now? Otherwise, we might make excuses with work commitments and stuff. He smiled as he said it and immediately Shelley was in high spirits.

She picked up her phone and called a friend. 'Hi Joe! How are you doing? Is the apartment free in June? Sure. Great! How much do I owe you? Are you sure? Ok, See you then. Bye!'

Jack sat up while Shelley had the phone conversation. 'Well?'

'All booked! All we need are flights! I'm meeting him on Monday night to seal the deal.'

'Do you want me to come?'

'No, don't worry. It's a favour for a favour thing.'

Jack looked at her disapprovingly. 'Tell me about the favour.'

At first, Shelley looked like she was about to say 'none of your business', like a parent scorning a child. But instantly changed her attitude and said 'I'm sorting out his accreditation with a safe builder governing body. I'm doing it for a favour so he kind of owes me one already. He's one of our contractors.' She dismissed her feelings of Jack policing her and felt better for explaining herself knowing that she was in the right, and no gang stuff was going on for a change. She seemed to convince him but knew the apartment was owned by the mob and only managed by Joe.

Chapter 17

Lucy reached into her hand-bag and realised that her purse was empty. She had not had consistent work since leaving Exeter months ago except a few private jobs, hairdressing in Bristol for friends. She had upset a few people in Exeter and knew she would not get any private work whilst she was there. She went to the cash point and the balance was low, showing less that £300. She had an over-draft of £500 but this was a short-term fix which she rarely used. Working out what to do as she walked through the centre of town, she noticed there was a sign up in the salon she used to work at 'staff wanted, apply within'. She thought about it but decided she didn't like having a boss or having to work within a team. She needed to get back to Bristol, but she was waiting for Uncle Chris to give her the all-clear. She knew he would sort things out as he always did.

Chris was out on the farm herding some cows in for milking. He was working alone, as there was no one to help him, and he was now working longer hours. He had been working the farm since 6am and it was now 9.30pm. He was quite short tempered by now and small things were setting him off. The ground was soft, and walking was hard work especially when the cows had been there first, churning the mud going through the gate into the next field. Chris was walking behind, slowly following the last few cows through the gate. His right foot got trapped in the mud, where a small tree branch had been trampled into the mud. He fell forward but his foot remained flat in the mud, hitting the side of his head on the ground, into a stone. He heard a crack and with excruciating pain he had snapped his ankle, face in the mud. It was April, and still cold. He was unable to move apart from turning his head to one side so he could breathe. He reached for his phone in his trouser pocket but couldn't find it. Then he remembered it was in the truck. He knew he was in trouble, so he started shouting 'Help!' knowing that he was a good 600 yards from the house.

The cold started to affect him, and he was shivering, soaking wet and covered in mud. The pain was getting worse, and his ankle was swollen, and blood was still oozing from his head into the mud. He managed to get to his knees but was unable to walk as the pain was intense. He was dizzy and feeling nauseous. He was not sure where he was, and his vision was failing.

It was 10 pm and the temperature was dropping fast. Theresa was getting worried as Chris was always in the house by 9.30. Knowing that he had no help this week she dismissed it but kept it at the back of her mind. At 10.20 she went upstairs and opened Lucy's bedroom door. 'Hi love, Chris isn't back yet and not answering his phone. I'm going out to see where he is. Are you coming?'

'OK, I'll get dressed,' Lucy said reluctantly.

Each of them had a torch and made their way out to the first field. They could hear the cows in the distance, so they headed in that direction, Theresa knowing he was tending to them earlier. As they approached the field Lucy shone her torch across the field and noticed a figure led on the ground. She instantly panicked and ran over, almost leaving Theresa behind. Chris was unresponsive, but there was shallow breathing. He was covered in mud and his head had been bleeding which had stopped by then. Theresa was crying as she called the ambulance and took off her coat to put over him. Within ten minutes a rapid response unit was there and started to stabilise him. She was talking loudly to him, but he was barely conscious. The paramedics arrived and Chris was taken in, and Theresa stayed with him. After an hour in hospital, he was taken into intensive care. Theresa was asking questions to the staff, but they were reluctant to answer, as they were unsure at this stage of the severity of his injuries.

Lucy stayed up all night and sat in the lounge watching TV with her phone on charge next to her. At 7.30 am the phone rang. 'Hi Lucy' Theresa sounded subdued, tired and upset. 'It's bad news love' she said and was noticeably holding back the tears 'I'm afraid Uncle Chris passed away at 6.30 this morning.'

Lucy dropped to her knees and screamed. Chris had been her hero, her body-guard and her mentor all her life. She was devastated. How could he be gone? He was fit, strong and healthy. She loved him with all her heart, far more than any lover that passed through her life.

The second instalment of management training was booked in London and Jack was kind of looking forward to it. He didn't mind being away from home from time to time as it broke the routine. Especially in central London, near Kings Cross, it was always lively there, and he was getting to know some of the other students. As he sat opposite Shelley at a coffee shop on the corner of Union Street in central Bristol. He told her about the two-weeks training which was scheduled to finish on a Tuesday which was three-days before their trip to Barcelona. 'I will miss you Jack.' She said with sad eyes.

As she said it her phone rang. She reached into her bag

and looked at the screen before answering it. 'Hi Craig, are you ok?' Her face slowly dropped and after a few seconds she stood up and said 'Oh. Right.' The conversation lasted another minute as she walked out of the coffee shop, then returned with a concerned look on her face.

'What's up?' Jack asked.

'One of the main guys in Devon died last night. A heart attack apparently, anyway, don't worry, it won't interfere with our day.' She said clutching his hands, on top of the table.

Chapter 18

The day of the funeral and scores of people were approaching the crematorium. Lucy was wearing a classy black dress and was trying not to cry as she completed her make up. Her mum was already downstairs with the rest of the family and was urging to quiz Lucy about why she was staying in Exeter and didn't think to tell her. In fact, not telling her most things about her life. She suppressed the feelings and focussed on the day ahead.

The hearse arrived with two black limousines, both with six seats. The funeral directors gathered the flowers and placed them solemnly on the coffin and the floral letters reading CHRIS alongside the coffin. Theresa and Lucy climbed into the first limo with her mum and dad.

As they arrived at the crematorium, there seemed to be a couple of hundred people there, but the chief mourners hardly noticed, as the tears were flowing like white wine.

It felt like the service only lasted a few minutes, but it lasted an hour. With Lucy making her emotional speech, breaking down twice, and limping through to the end with her mum's hand on her shoulder. They left the crematorium at the rear and into the garden where the flowers and tributes were displayed. It was then that they realised how many people turned up. Lucy felt overwhelmed with both grief and gratitude that all her beloved uncle's friends and family there. She knew or recognised about 50 people. As she was hugging people she knew, a familiar face caught her eye. Shelley made eye contact and politely nodded with pursed lips and a sympathetic look on her face. Lucy made her way through the crowd, kissing and hugging more family members and eventually made it to Shelley. 'Hi Shelley, thanks for coming along! Did you know Uncle Chris?'

'Yes Lucy. So sorry for your loss, I know how close you were to him.' Shelley said hugging her insincerely. 'You have met Craig before, haven't you?' she said as Craig approached with a confident look.

Lucy turned to her right and came face to face with Craig. He was looking dapper in a black suit and black tie. Under that he wore a light grey shirt, and his hair was immaculately cut. He had put on some weight since their encounter but held it well, with more muscle and very little fat.

'Oh, hi Craig!' Lucy said with a look of admiration.

Over half of the people who attended the funeral turned up at the wake. The main restaurant area of Jury's hotel near the centre of Exeter was packed with mourners and drinks were flowing. It was 3.30 pm and Lucy had already downed four glasses of red wine, which tasted remotely better than the chardonnay which was the house white. Shelley and Craig stood together and chatted to the odd member of the firm as they passed and introduced themselves. Every member of the firm knew them, but they did not know all their names which felt quite good, but equally as embarrassing. Lucy came over, slightly off balance. 'So how are you, Craig?'

'Getting there, haven't been right since that fiancée of yours fucked me up last year.' He said with half a smile.

Lucy looked uncomfortable. 'I'm so sorry that happened, I thought he had chilled out a bit but clearly I was wrong.'

she looked at Craig longingly, hoping for him to accept her apology. He did.

'It's ok, the main thing is I'm on the mend. I owe it all to Shelley though, she has been there for me the whole time.' he said as he put his arm around his sister and slightly pulling her close and adjusting his walking cane. At this point Lucy noticed that Jack wasn't there, and that Shelley was drinking mineral water.

'So, where's Jack?'

'He's on a training course in London. He's back on Tuesday, then we go off to Spain for a week.' Shelley said with a glimpse of humanity.

'Oh, that's nice! I've always wanted to go there. Can I get you two some drinks?'

'I'm OK thanks I'm driving,' said Shelley.

'OK, I'll have a Stella. Thanks Lucy.' Craig said.

It was approaching 8.30pm and Lucy had been drinking red wine like it was the last night on earth. Shelley had driven back to Bristol and Craig had arranged to stay at a firm member's house. He had finished seven pints of strong lager by then and was starting to struggle with the quantity of liquid and gas he was taking on, with his stomach feeing heavy and bloated. There was a group of men and women around his age who had come together, including Lucy and were planning the rest of the evening. A girl called Molly piped up looking like she had invented electricity. 'There is a party at the sandstone in Exmouth tonight! Members only but I know the door staff!'

Within half an hour they were in two MPV taxis heading for the party. As they approached, the door staff looked firm, as if they were going to refuse entry to all of them. There were ten of them in total, including Lucy who reluctantly travelled in the second taxi, as she wanted to go with Craig in the first. She knew all the other girls were interested in him. As they debussed the first taxi, Craig climbed out and immediately placed his walking cane firmly onto the ground to assist his exit from the cab. He was aware that his balance was failing, as he hadn't eaten much all day and Stella was quite strong, especially when consumed in high quantities in the daytime.

Molly walked up to the security, and they talked for a minute, then they appeared to approve of them all entering the party. As Craig approached, the black security guard on the left of the entrance looked at him and opened his mouth. 'Hello mate!' he said loudly. 'How are you, my man?' He took a couple of steps and carefully hugged Craig, being cautious not to put him off balance or touch his cane.

'Hi Garfield, I'm getting there, thanks mate. You OK?' Craig asked, confidently. They were from the same gang in school in Bristol, and Garfield heard all about the incident which almost killed him having been on the kickboxing circuit. The night continued.

Chapter 19

Sunday had been a drag for Jack. He had sat in a lecture room all day and the weather in London was great. All he, and the other eight students wanted to do was to sit in Hyde Park with a few cans of lager and watch the world go by. At 2.30 pm their wishes were granted, and the lecturer decided enough was enough for a Sunday and as he broke the news, everyone sat up and sighed.

They arranged to meet at a bar near Paddington and have a couple before heading for a supermarket, then on to Hyde Park. The weather was great, about 28C and a very light wind. They all sat on the grass, and Jo, a guy from Newcastle had an iPad, and was playing the new Liam Gallagher album. Jack was talking to him and there were many other conversations going on, mainly about Maslow's hierarchy of needs theory and other management models which were being drummed into them. Jack had drunk one pint of Heineken at the bar in Paddington, and he was half-way through his can of lager and suddenly he was struggling to focus. As if he was drunk. He tried to shrug it off, as Jo was telling him about his girlfriend. It was getting worse, and Jo asked if he was ok. 'No mate I don't feel well. My head is spinning!' Jack said, starting to feel worried, and increasingly nauseous.

Within a few minutes, he was vomiting uncontrollably and could not move his head from the grass. The whole party was trying to comfort him, and eventually a paramedic turned up. His pulse was ok, and they had established that he was not having a stroke, or a seizure. But could not determine what the problem was.

As he arrived in A&E, it was confirmed that there was a long wait, as there had been a multi vehicle accident on the north circular earlier. Every time Jack moved his head he vomited. He was empty of food and liquid by that time, and was discharging small quantities of stomach lining, but the heaving was intense. He had never felt that ill in his life. The doctor examined him and administered an anti-sickness drug into his arm. 'You have labyrinthitis. You need to see your GP when you get back to Bristol to discuss further treatment.'

Jack was woken up at 6.30 am and told to leave hospital, as there was no room. He could hardly stand up and was struggling to walk. Not knowing where he was, where he was staying or how he was going to get home. He asked a nurse which hospital he was in and she confirmed it as the University hospital near Euston. Jack staggered to the nearest tube station and asked a member of staff how to get to Kings Cross. As the Asian man in the transport for London uniform spoke, Jack was unable to comprehend what he was saying as he tried hard not to vomit.

With little or no balance, he made his way onto the escalators, grasping hard onto the rubber handrails and the escalator descended underground. As the escalator platforms levelled out and disappeared under the stainless-steel plate, Jack failed to respond by stepping off and fell forward striking his left elbow hard on the floor, then the left side of his head, but no injury, just a bruise on his elbow. He was helped onto his feet by two men. 'Do you need first aid mate?' one asked in a cockney accent.

'No thanks, I have just left hospital and my medication hasn't kicked in yet, thanks for your help guys.' Jack said gratefully, and then he leant against the tiled wall of the platform. There were approximately fifty school children on the platform being spoken to firmly by three or four teachers. The kids seemed loud, and it was affecting Jack's ability to think. He staggered onto the first train and people were looking at him with judgemental eyes as if he was a drunk. Two stops later he exited the train and made his way to the hotel. He went straight to sleep and was only woken by the housekeeper who didn't even knock but sounded shocked to see the naked man laid faced downwards snoring loudly with a litter bin next to him. She was a big girl and appreciated seeing a fit naked man but chose to keep it to herself, quietly closing the door with a small, closed mouth grin. She was more pleased about getting off early, not having to clean the room.

The morning after the funeral. Lucy slowly started regaining consciousness, but it was a slow process. As her sight was coming into play, it was equally being blinded by intense light. She could hear seagulls and her head was banging with pain. As she came around, she noticed she was covered in a tartan blanket, and without it was naked. She looked to her right and there was Craig laid next to her with his back to her, also naked. She could feel that they had been having sex recently and started to try to remember how it all happened.

Their clothes were scattered around the vicinity and Craig's walking cane was stuck upright in the pebbles. There was a camp-fire burnt out and dog walkers were whistling and throwing sticks for their spaniels and retrievers, looking at them knowing that they were naked under the blanket. Lucy sat up and noticed that the sea was about 30 meters away. Calm, but still rough enough to make noise on the pebble beach.

An hour later Craig and Lucy were sat in a coffee shop supporting their heads and drinking cappuccinos and tap water, piecing together how they managed to find themselves naked on a beach at 9.30am with dog walkers and whoever else seeing them. As they approached the coffee shop, they noticed a sign which confirmed that the beach they woke up on was a designated naturist beach, which made it slightly more acceptable that people may have seen them naked, as it may be no surprise to them. They were both relieved that they weren't on a family beach and not likely to be arrested or be faced with a Punch and Judy show.

Craig's phone rang. 'Hi Shell, you OK?'

'Hi Craig, fine. How was it?'

'Fine. What I remember of it! Had far too much to drink though.'

Shelley laughed. 'Do you have your meds?'

'No but I'm catching a train home later, so I'll take them when I get back'.

'OK, love you.' Shelley said and hung up.

Shelley hadn't heard from Jack the night before and although not worried it was on her mind. She knew he would be fine, but it was not like him. She arrived at work at 8 am sharp and with a coffee, sat at her desk and started working. At 10.30 her mobile rang. She finished typing her sentence and looked at the phone which had JACK XX displayed on the screen as an incoming call. 'Hi gorgeous! How's it going?'

Jack sounded like he had just woken up after two hours sleep, and a bottle of whiskey. 'Hi Shell, I'm not well. I collapsed yesterday and was rushed into hospital.' He continued to tell her all about it and felt quite emotional. He just wanted to come home but felt like he needed to go back to college. He did feel slightly better and was not vomiting anymore and could walk without falling over. He only had the remaining day and the next day left then he could go home, so he had decided to endure it. As he entered the lecture room everyone looked at him with concern and empathy. He sat down and pushed through the two days. He had never been more pleased with arriving home on the Tuesday night to his mum, and texting Shelley to arrange meeting up.

Jack still felt off balance when he arrived at the surgery and checked in with reception. After 15 minutes his name was called and he made his way to room 5, Dr Maarit Rahman. 'The dizziness is caused by an inner ear infection and a condition similar to labyrinthitis. I have booked an MRI scan to ensure nothing else is of concern. In the meantime, just be aware that your balance is impaired, and could feel worse if you catch a viral infection.

Shelley picked Jack up and helped him into the car. He was still visibly unwell, and his balance was badly affected by the illness. She sat in the driver's seat and before starting the engine sat and looked at Jack. 'We're not going.'

'What? Yes, we are. I'm OK, just a bit off balance that's all! We've been looking forward to this trip for months!' Jack said sternly.

'Are you sure?' Shelley asked, looking concerned.

'Yes! Absolutely!' Jack replied.

As they waited in the check in queue, Shelley reached into her handbag searching for her passport. She suddenly inhaled deeply, and her eyes widened as if standing bare foot on a Lego brick.

'What?' Jack asked with concern.

'I left my passport in the kitchen!' Shelley said worriedly.

Jack reached behind her and pulled her passport out of her back pocket, grinning as he held it up to her.

'Oh shit. That was a horrible feeling!' she said grasping the passport and rolling her eyes upwards. Jack saw the funny side and started laughing uncontrollably, whilst struggling to stand straight.

'At this rate they will refuse to let us on the flight with you laughing hysterically and not able to stand!' Shelley said smiling. 'You look pissed, and now you're acting pissed!' she said laughing.

Lucy arrived back at the farm- house at midday, to the disapproval of Theresa. They hardly spoke as Theresa was busy putting the farm on the market, and looking for a cottage to live in. The insurance company had confirmed a pay out and no mortgage or debts left to worry about, and the farm was going to be too much to handle. It was always Chris's interest, not necessary Teresa's. She just went along with it but didn't know enough about it to manage the up-keep.

Lucy went up and had a shower, thinking hard about what to do about a regular income. She was also thinking about Craig, as the night before was slowly coming back to her. The funeral, and Uncle Chris still laying heavily on her mind. She felt vulnerable without the protection of her beloved uncle. Her confidence was low, and she thought about all the people she had upset, knowing that she was protected. But not anymore. Chris was dead, Tyrone was too, and it was all her fault. Tyrone didn't really protect her, but she felt safe with him because most people feared him. She left the shower and dried herself, walked into her bedroom and the emotions took a hold. She sat on the bed and started to cry. Unable to control herself, she just sat and cried on the bed, loudly. Theresa was asleep in the lounge with the door closed, having shed a few tears herself after reading an old birthday card from Chris, with his distinctive handwriting, saying 'All my love, as always, Chris. Xxxx'.

Jack and Shelley arrived at the apartment block at 3 pm. They went up to the 5th floor and entered the key into the door, opened it and entered a basic but well-equipped apartment. They decided to go straight out and get some dinner as they hadn't eaten since the airport lounge, which was not very filling, but shockingly expensive. Arriving at a tapas type bar, they ordered a large white wine for Shelley and a pint of San Miguel for Jack. The food seemed to take ages, but they were excited to be away and having a good time in each-others' company. A few more drinks and the food arrived. They enjoyed it and ordered a last drink each before heading back to the apartment in a half drunk, but happy state. 'I'm having a quick shower.' Shelley said as she headed for the bathroom with some clothes and a shower bag.

Jack opened the sliding balcony door and stood enjoying the sea view as he pulled open a can of beer and took a sip as the initial foam release from the can tickled his nose. He took a deep breath and sighed as he thought how happy he was, and how life was treating him well. He still felt off balance, not helped by four beers, but felt alive with happiness and excitement for the future.

Shelley emerged from the bathroom in a negligee and helped herself to a glass of chilled white wine from the mini bar. Jack kissed her as he passed, heading for the bathroom. As he left the bathroom, Shelley was on the balcony with a glass of wine, leaning against the handrail. The wind had picked up slightly and her hair was swaying. The breeze was also lifting her negligee slightly, showing her perfect bum. Jack looked for a minute or two and admired her until he could resist no longer. He stripped naked and crept up behind her. Starting at her hips he ran his hands slowly and gently up her back. After gently squeezing her shoulders, he moved his hands slowly downwards and ran them the length of her spine and gently lifted her negligee. He repeated this a few times and then guided his erect penis into her from behind. She let out a sigh and arched her back downwards to allow full access. She trusted him to be careful as she was no longer on the pill, but she didn't really care. They made love for what felt like hours, but it was about 15 minutes. He ejected just in time and collapsed on the sun lounger. As he led down catching his breath, she sat on his lap and passionately hugged and kissed him.

On the third day, Shelley sat in the shade of the beach bar and waited for Jack to emerge from the sea. She had a glass of wine and some green olives and was reading the newspaper, not entirely interestedly as she had other things on her mind. Jack appeared next to her, out of breath following a long swim and drying himself off as he ordered a beer. They finished their drinks and headed to the apartment. Shelley didn't waste any time. As Jack entered the apartment, she followed him and as the door closed grabbed his shorts from behind and yanked them down. Jack smiled and turned around to find her on her knees, pulling him close and instantly giving him oral. They transferred to the bed, and he returned the favour, and they made love. Shelley seemed to be concentrating as she was enjoying it, but Jack was in absolute ecstasy, so he didn't notice. She knew him and could tell when he was about to ejaculate. As Jack was just about to, Shelley grabbed his bum and his lower back hard, and pulled him in tightly. A thousand thoughts entered and left Jack's mind, but it was too late, and he ejaculated inside her as she reached climax at the same time.

They laid motionless next to each other, not saying anything. Jack was getting his breath back and thinking of what just happened. Shelley clearly planned it and Jack was fine about it but concerned at the same time. It was only a few months or so previously that they weren't talking and had all but ended their relationship. Now they were probably going to have a baby together. The more he thought about it the better, and the more excited he felt.

Shelley felt awkward, as if she had made a mistake not discussing it before making it happen. Her initial thought was how fantastic it felt, but it soon turned to guilt hoping that Jack was alright about it. She looked at him with a wide eyes and pursed lips. 'Are you ok?' she said quietly.

Jack paused for a second then looked into her eyes. 'Fine! So that's settled then, we're going to have a baby?' he said as he pulled her in for a hug. They talked about it for over an hour, laughing when they couldn't agree on names.

Lucy had a plan. The will was likely to be read before probate, and the farm would be sold within months. She had money on her mind. Deciding to stay at the farm for a little longer than expected, she would do chores including doing Theresa's hair free of charge and help with the farm until it was sold.

Theresa knew exactly what Lucy was doing and playing along with it until all was sorted, then make an excuse for not giving Lucy a penny. After all, there was no real connection between them now that Chris wasn't around. The truth is Theresa always knew that Lucy was selfish and out to get whatever she could from people, including Chris, who loved her dearly and gave her everything. Theresa was also playing a game. She would get all the help she could from Lucy then ditch her. After all, she still had contacts with the firm, and they had sworn to Chris that if anything happened to him, she would always be looked after. Lucy however, had upset many people and was entitled to no help at all.

Theresa sat with her solicitor for an hour going through the legalities of the estate and Chris's will. It was becoming clear that he had not left anything to Lucy, and it was looking good. She was heartbroken but there was a good insurance pay-out imminent, and with the sale of the farm, money was not going to be an issue. As she left the solicitors office, she crossed Cathedral Square and passed the hoarded off remains of the hotel which had burned down and into Queens Road. She entered an Italian restaurant and met some friends for lunch. Pat sat opposite her. A well-groomed 54-year-old who had made a fortune from a cider business a few years previous. Now retired and living life to the full, taking regular holidays with her husband in Hawaii, Cuba and Jamaica.

'Is Lucy still staying with you?' she asked.

Theresa gave a look of disappointment 'Yes she is for now, until I sell the farm. I can't wait to see the back of her to be honest.' She said with a deep sigh and taking a sip of wine.

'Did Chris leave her anything in his will?'

'Not a penny. She is going to have the shock of her life when it comes out.' she answered with raised eyebrows. 'When I'm gone there is a percentage of my estate that goes to her but I'm going to change it so my other niece and nephew from my side gets it all. I don't really want Lucy getting anything. She has already had plenty from us. Selfish little bitch. She should be shagging some millionaire and fleecing him. That's the sort of thing she would love to do with no consideration or thought for anyone else.'

As she finished her meal, Lucy, who was sat the other side of a decorative screen left discreetly and left £20 on the bar as she barged out. She was furious. She walked at a pace through to the car park and sat in her Mini, bursting into tears. She was relying on a pay out from Chris to see her through until she had a job. She was going to fleece Theresa in the meantime, but it seemed that Theresa had other plans to ensure that she received nothing.

Lucy sat for an hour in the car thinking of a new plan. Then she reapplied her make up in the rear-view-mirror and drove back to the farm. When she arrived, she tried her best to look like nothing was wrong as she entered the kitchen and faced Theresa. 'Hi, did you enjoy lunch?'

'Yes, thanks darling, it was good to catch up. She is off to Mexico next week, lucky thing.'

'Nice!' I'd love to go there one day.' Lucy said, politely, hardly able to contain the sheer fury burning inside her as she left the kitchen and went upstairs. She had a shower and changed. She logged on to her favourite dating site. She was looking for a man with money, not looks. She was willing to shag anyone with a healthy bank account. She also needed an alibi.

Within five minutes she had a date sorted out. She was meeting a slightly overweight man with greying hair and a trimmed beard. The Bentley Continental was the reason she pursued him. Certainly not looks or physique.

It was 10 am and Jack was sleeping off a hangover. Shelley went to the local supermarket around the corner from the apartment block. She loaded a basket with milk, a water- melon and all the ingredients for a fry up. As she approached the counter, the supermarket owner came into the sales floor from the warehouse. 'Hola Shelley,' he said with a smile.

'Hola Miguel!' she said as she placed her full basket on the counter. She gave him a loose hug and then followed him into the rear office. He closed the door firmly behind them and checked that no one was watching. Shelley produced an envelope from her bag and handed it to him. He checked again through the glazed panel in the office door and started opening the envelope. As he pulled the cheque out, he put on his glasses. As he looked at the amount his face lit up and he placed it back in the envelope. 'Gracias! Tell Theresa and Andrew that all will be fine. I will take care of everything!'

'OK that's great. Thanks Miguel.' Shelley left the office and Miguel followed her back to the check out. 'No need to pay, this is on me,' he said, looking excited.

'Oh, Thanks Miguel!' Shelley said sounding like she meant it, but she expected it. It's the least he could do after the massive favour she had just done him.

'Buenos Dias.'

Chas left the cottage at 6 am and made his way to the farm where the JCB was kept, arriving there 20 minutes later. Unlocking the disused barn and climbed into the cab of the machine, he turned on the ignition to activate the glow plugs and lit the roll up he had held in his mouth for a few minutes. The glow plugs light went out and with a small twist of the key the engine roared into life. He was off to a building site in town and was set to earn a good amount of money for the day as an owner-operator.

As he reached the main road, preparing to hold up the traffic and upset the other road users, he had a knowing smirk. He turned right and headed towards Exeter. Noticing a Ford Mondeo behind, and that the driver seemed to not bother trying to overtake. There was a dual carriageway ahead and Chas thought surely the Mondeo would go for it and take the opportunity to overtake the 35mph excavator. The Mondeo stayed behind, and Chas started feeling concerned. He stopped at a red traffic light and glanced at his rear-view mirror and saw a slightly menacing looking man with a bushy beard and a small woollen hat. Chas rummaged round the cab for a roll up he had prepared earlier and as he found it and put it in his mouth the cab door swung open. As he turned his head, a fist smashed clean into his nose, instantly breaking it. Then hands clasped around his throat and the stranger pulled him in close, head butting him and saying, 'Remember me?'

Chas was in agony. He hadn't been hit like that in years. 'No, I don't know you! What the fuck was that for?'

'Let me remind you, you fucking prick! You tried to bury me alive you cunt! Well, I got out, and I'm alive! Who was the prick in the Subaru? Tell me before I plant another one on you!'

'Callum! He's dead! He was murdered for being a grass!' Chas shouted. 'Let me go!'

Tyrone pulled back his fist and hit him again, this time in the left eye, almost fracturing his eye socket, but not quite. The skin split under Chas's eye and blood started pouring down his cheek.

'Who else was involved?' Tyrone shouted, by this time he was in his element. Intimidating and feeling powerful, just how he liked it. It had been a long time since he felt like this and had been living reclusively in north Devon until the dust settled, with just one single letter written to his mum, telling her that he was fine, but to destroy the letter after reading it.

The incident lasted for two minutes and when Tyrone got what he wanted out of Chas, he punched him in the head repeatedly. Chas was screaming as his head swung back with every punch, trying in vain to stop the punches with his weak arms, compared to Tyrone's. Blood was pouring from numerous parts of his face and his eyes were rolling uncontrollably. He lost the strength in his arms after several hard punches and the screaming stopped. Tyrone kept on hitting him hard in the head until he noticed that he had stopped breathing.

Not taking any chances, he picked out Chas's Zippo lighter from his pocket and emptied the fluid chamber onto his lap. He noticed a cheap lighter on the dashboard of the excavator and set fire to Chas's trousers. He didn't hang around to watch the corpse burn and drove off at speed towards Exeter. Checking his rear-view mirror before losing sight of the excavator and seeing the cab engulfed in flames, he felt excited and full of adrenaline.

Tyrone drove into Exeter town centre and parked in

Corn exchange NCP. He walked onto Cathedral Square and found a cafe where he ordered a cappuccino and sat in the far corner opening a laptop. He plugged a dongle into the side and logged in as Terry Thomas, password K1ngKill. The coffee was delivered to the table by a slightly overweight teenage girl with an attitude which she tried to suppress, but not very hard. Tyrone could see his reflection in the laptop screen. He looked tired and scruffy. He hated looking like this but couldn't afford to be recognised. Particularly from Lucy if she was in town. He typed in 'Brian Chapple'. Various options opened up, mainly social media profiles. He scrolled down and clicked on an online article from local news. An awards ceremony with a member of the Royal family presenting an award to Sergeant Brian Chapple for his heroics during the worst motorway crash in decades on the M5 a year previously. Now he had a face to look out for. He took a picture of the screen on his mobile phone and logged out.

Chapter 20

'It's official.' Shelley said holding the pregnancy test with a nervous but happy look on her face. 'I'm pregnant.'

'Oh my god that's great news Shell!' Jack jumped from his chair and hugged her gently buy lovingly. 'Who should we tell first? My mum or yours?'

'Yours if you like, she could do with some good news.' Shelley said passing him his mobile.

When they had finished telling family and friends, they talked about the house they were buying, the finances and their jobs. All was going to plan, and the house needed updating but not a full refurbishment. A 70's built semi-detached three-bed in Little Stoke, North Bristol.

Four weeks after announcing the pregnancy, the contracts were completed on the house and they moved in, decorating room by room. They were doing everything as cheap as possible, but it didn't show, and they made it look like they were spending a fortune on it. Shelley had an eye for bargains.

Craig climbed into Shelley's car. 'Looking forward to seeing the house Shell,' he said.

'You'll love it. Jack has done a great job on the decorating, the carpets went down yesterday, so it smells really new.'

They arrived and went in, Craig holding a bottle of red

wine for Jack. 'Hi mate, this looks great!' Craig said giving Jack a firm and meaningful handshake.

'Thanks mate, good to see you! how are you?'

'Getting their mate, thanks, started going to the gym recently. I'm limited as to what I can do at the moment, but I'm getting better and stronger week-by-week.' Craig looked pleased with the fact that Jack had asked, and that he was actually on the mend. 'How about you? I hear that you have been promoted?'

'Yes mate. I thought I was being made redundant when they called me in, but it turned out to be a managerial position.'

They held a conversation whilst Shelley, looking pleased that they were getting on, finished the cooking which Jack had started, but seemed to have forgotten about whilst conversing with Craig.

The evening continued, and Jack and Craig were having a laugh and getting on great. Shelley was fully engaged with them, and they all enjoyed themselves.

'Just as well stay the night Craig, hadn't you?' Shelley said.

'Don't worry, I'll get a taxi back.'

'It's fine, I'll drop you off. I'm not drinking anyway, being pregnant and all,' Shelley said.

'Ah ok then, if you don't mind?'

Jack and Craig said their goodbyes and Jack closed the door and opened another can of lager.

As they strapped into the car, Craig's phone rang. 'Hello. Hi Wilksy! What? Oh, shit!' he said rocking in the passenger seat. The phone conversation continued for a couple of minutes. 'Ok mate, thanks for letting me know. I have Shell with me, so I'll tell her. Cheers mate.' Craig ended the call.

'What's going on?' Shelley asked looking concerned.

Craig looked at her with sorry eyes. 'Chas died this morning.'

Shelley slowed down her driving. 'No! how did it happen?'

'Apparently his lighter spilt gas on his lap and he went up in flames in the cab of his digger.'

They were almost silent for the remaining two miles of the journey, the only noise being from Shelley with the odd sniff, and tissue wiping away tears as she drove. Craig stared out of the window and just thought. What if it wasn't an accident? There had been many victims of the mob over the years and maybe a bitter family member had received some info and decided to do some damage.

Tyrone had been walking through fields and dirt tracks for half a mile. He had a head torch on which was offering some light but not enough as he kept twisting his ankles on rough ground. He really wasn't used to being in the country and couldn't wait to be on decent firm ground again. It was 9 pm and the farm-house in the distance looked deserted, apart from a single light in the lounge. Tyrone checked the terrain ahead and turned off his head torch. He approached the drive slowly and cautiously, ensuring that no livestock would be disturbed by his presence. He didn't notice that there was no livestock on the farm, it had all been sold.

Theresa was having a bad night. She had photographs out all over the lounge floor of her and Chris. Holidays, Christmas celebrations, Them with their late daughter. She was drinking wine and was crying hard. Opening the third bottle of chardonnay, she took in a deep breath and changed the CD. Chris loved George Michael's early solo albums, so Theresa put on 'Listen Without Prejudice.' She sat there sipping the wine and sang along quietly, eye liner almost completely covering both cheeks.

Chris's truck was on the drive, along with Lucy's Mini. 'Jackpot,' Tyrone thought. 'I'll take them both out!' he had no empathy and was obsessed with revenge. He was certain it was the mob who tried to kill him for hitting Lucy.

He stayed in the shadows as he approached the house until he could see into the lounge window. He could see Theresa asleep on the sofa, and an empty wine bottle on the coffee table. He knocked on the window to check her response. Nothing. She appeared to be sound asleep and had been drinking. This was good news, but Chris or Lucy could still be around, so he had to be super alert. Walking round the house, he reached the back door. Twisting the knob, he carefully pushed it and it didn't budge. Then he noticed the cloakroom window was left open. It was not a big window, but he was sure that if he tried, he could squeeze through. As he was about to pull himself up to climb through the window, he heard something. He froze. Within a few seconds, the cloakroom door flew open, and Theresa was on her knees, vomiting loudly into the toilet. After ten minutes, she stumbled to her feet and slowly went upstairs to bed.

Tyrone waited 20 minutes and could hear no movement from inside the house. He climbed through the window and slowly opened the door into the hallway. The only light was from the lounge, which Theresa had left on. He made his way upstairs on high alert, and silently. There were two doors in front of him at the top of the stairs and two on the other end of the landing. A fifth door was between the bathroom and a bedroom. A smaller door which housed the airing cupboard and boiler. He turned the knob slowly and opened the cupboard. It was full of blankets and towels, and the boiler was almost buried. He looked around and got to work. Pulling the linen away from the boiler and listening out for people, he knocked his elbow on the wall. A muffled bang, followed by silence, he froze, listening hard. Twenty seconds later it was apparent that no one heard the noise. Exposing the pipes leading to the boiler, he chose a 22mm pipe which was not stone cold, as the water feed was, and not hot. He produced a pipe cutter from his pocket and carefully, and almost silently he placed it round the pipe until it was fully engaged. Pausing for a moment, he listened and heard no sounds apart from Teresa's gentle snore from the bedroom. He thought for a few seconds, if it wasn't the gas pipe, but a water pipe, the plan would be aborted, and he would have to leave quickly.

He started slowly turning the pipe cutter and after five or six twists, he heard a gentle hiss. He stopped turning, feeling for water but nothing, and a few seconds later the smell of gas hit him. He carried on and fully cut the pipe until it fell apart. Putting some of the towels and linen back, but not restricting the flow of gas, he gently pushed the door until it was 2 inches from closed.

Silently he crept downstairs and into the kitchen, leaving the door open. He pulled a lighter out of his pocket and lit the gas hob. Time to leave.

There were keys hung up near the kitchen door which he took with him and silently left by the front door, deadlocking it behind him. He ran to the back door and ensured it was locked, then ran across the field, looking back every ten seconds or so. any second now, he thought. Knowing that the house was filling up from the top down with explosive gas. Climbing over a farm gate, he ran down the lane towards his car and as he opened the driver's door, he heard the explosion, about half a mile away. It was followed by a fire ball which looked like it had removed the entire roof. He drove off at speed, back to Barnstaple, which was 30 miles west, with the music up loud. He felt no remorse, just focussed on the next person to die. Sergeant Brian Chapple! He was well aware that he had to plan this hit meticulously.

'This is more than a coincidence,' Craig said to Shelley. 'Someone's after us. We need to find out who it is and deal with them. Have you called Brian yet?'

'I couldn't get hold of him. Must be on duty,' Shelley said with a concerned look. They were thinking hard and trying to remember who had upset the firm and been dealt with recently. 'Remember that Tyrone guy? The one who had a go at you. He was sorted, wasn't he?'

'Hopefully, but I couldn't be there at the time.' Craig said with a hint of sarcasm.

'I'll try Brian again.' Shelley speed dialled, and Brian picked up after two rings.

'Shell. I'm at the farm- house and it's not a pretty sight. The roof was blown clean off and Theresa was inside. Just as well she didn't know anything about it really. No sign of Lucy though, which is my next line of enquiry. Hang on, she has just arrived in a taxi. I'll call you back love.'

Before Shelley had a chance to speak, the phone call ended.

Lucy was hyper-ventilating as she approached the police cordon. 'What happened?' she asked loudly.

'Gas explosion love. Do you live here?' the police constable asked, as Brian Chapple approached.

'Are you Lucy?' he asked.

'Yeah! Oh my god! Theresa was in there!' she said holding her head.

'I'm afraid she didn't make it. her body was found this morning.'

Lucy burst into tears. It looked like she was crying for Theresa, but she was more upset by her personal belongings being blown up. All her clothes, shoes and make up. She was also thinking of the complications regarding the estate and the money she may lose.

'I have a training course for a few days next week Jack,' Shelley said.

'Oh. OK, where is it?'

'Edinburgh. It's also a conference. I'm going on Tuesday,

and I should be back on Thursday night, hopefully. No mobile phones allowed apparently. Full concentration.'

'What? How am I meant to contact you?'

'I'll call you from the land line. Don't worry love,' Shelley hugged him as she said it.

Tuesday morning and Jack was ready for work but waiting for Shelley to come down. 'I'm going to miss you.'

Shelley came down with a small suitcase which seemed to have plenty of room. 'Me too love. I'll call you tonight and tomorrow night. Don't worry I will be home before you know it.'

Following a long hug, Jack went off to work. He was curious as to why there was a no mobile phone rule, but he trusted Shelley and didn't question it.

Shelley drove to Bristol airport and parked in the prebooked long stay. Two hours later she was in the air over northern France. Looking like a tourist with shades on her head and removing her fleece to reveal summer clothes, in early June. Doing so she didn't attract attention to herself, as all the other passengers appeared to be doing the same, most of them tourists. Not her, she was on business.

She remembered Brian telling her 'If you have any trouble, call me at any time. I have contacts in the area and Miguel will be dealt with. He is expecting you.'

It passed without incident. Shelley counted the money, and it was correct to the last note. She entered a restaurant on the evening and sat and ordered a burger. She really wanted a paella, but seafood was not an option being three-months pregnant. She noticed two Spanish men the other side of the window who she had noticed a couple of times that day. Then she remembered the signal. She looked at one of them and brushed her hair back with her right hand with her thumb, fore-finger and middle finger extended. The guy reacted by tapping the top of his head.

She instantly felt reassured and gave a smile and a nod. The guy did the same, but he was more suggestive as she looked gorgeous.

Shelley was aware that she had one more obstacle. Customs. Getting through with £200,000 cash. Again, with a poker face and looks that could melt hearts, she passed through unchallenged. As she drove back from the airport, she called Jack. 'The most boring training course ever! I'll be home in 20 minutes, but I'm tired love. I'm going straight to bed.'

Lucy went back to Gerald's house. Sobbing her heart out and convincingly looking like it was because of the death of her auntie. 'I have nowhere to stay around here now so I'm going back to Bristol.'

'Do you want to stay here for a couple of nights? Until you have sorted something out?' Gerald said, hoping for another couple of nights of sex.

'Would that be ok? I'll do some chores for you if you like?' she said with raised eyebrows.

'Not necessary. I have people who do that sort of thing for me.'

Lucy was pleased with the response and already knew she had him nailed. She could fake orgasms and pretend to like him for as long as it took.

'All my clothes were lost in the fire. Along with my passport, driving license, shoes, everything!' she said sobbing at the same time.

Gerald held her in his arms and thought for a minute as she cried. 'Come on, we're going shopping.'

She pretended to cry some more as she thought about it, she was certainly convincing Gerald, and she knew it. He was no detective.

Gerald drove into town as Lucy applied her make up. 'I'm watching the rugby while you shop. Here's my card, the pin number is 2670. If you have any problems, call me. The limit is £500. OK?

'What would I do without you Gerry?' she said kissing him on the cheek.

Result! It would only cost her a quick shag. He only lasted a few minutes on a good day. Lucy went straight to the best, most expensive clothes shops in Exeter. She tried on numerous tops, leggings, jeans, shoes and jackets and bought most of them. Underwear and jewellery were next on the list, and she made her way to a famous lingerie store in the Guildhall shopping centre. She had already spent £600 and the bags were getting heavy, but she was enjoying spending Gerald's money, and nothing was going to stop her.

Gerald was on his fifth pint of cider. He had been watching Exeter Chiefs playing The Harlequins and sharing banter with a few mates. He was not used to drinking in the daytime and was feeling it. He received a text from Lucy; 'Can I have the car keys darling? I have some bags to lose and then I can join you xxx.'

Lucy pulled up in a taxi outside the Hole in the Wall sports bar and she ran in to get the car keys from Gerald. He gave her a hug as he loudly said 'Darling' so everyone in the present company would hear, look at him as he hugged his gorgeous girlfriend. She was aware of all the eyes on her and hoped that she looked ok, as she kept her options wide open, hoping that one day soon she would enjoy sex again. Everyone knew the score as Gerald was no looker but had plenty of money and property all over Exeter.

Lucy threw all the bags into the boot of the car and slammed it shut, pressing the lock button twice to set the alarm. As she turned and started walking towards the pedestrian exit, a silver Ford Mondeo caught her eye. She noticed a scruffy looking guy with a bushy beard driving. She tried not to look back as the car went past but couldn't resist. She saw his eyes as he was looking at her through the open driver's side window. Tyrone. She froze. He was supposed to be dead! She ran to the staircase of the multi storey car park and negotiated them with speed, but with caution wearing semi-high heels. She could feel emotions taking hold and was struggling to control them. Fear, anger, shock, all drilling into her stomach as she ran down the stairs. As she reached the bottom of the stairs, she cowered into a piss-stained corner and the emotions overwhelmed her.

Gerald was now seven pints up and struggling. He was enjoying being with some mates and not aware of the time. Lucy had been gone with his car keys for 45 minutes and he hadn't noticed. She eventually appeared, having reapplied her face and looked as cool and in control as ever.

'Lucy! Come and meet the boys. This is James, this is Gabriel, and this is Stephen. Guys, meet my gorgeous girlfriend, Lucy!'

Lucy smiled and nodded one at a time at the men who looked knowingly at her. She already knew Stephen who was in the firm. Gerald put his arm around her loosely and purposely let his hand slide down and stroke her bum, giving it a slight squeeze before raising his arm back up and pulling her tightly into his chest. This made her skin crawl, and she was desperate to pull away, but for many reasons she controlled her anguish and disgust and continued with the game.

As soon as she saw an opportunity, whilst Gerald was in the toilet, she briskly approached Stephen. 'Can I have a word? This is urgent!'

'OK', Stephen said with a confused tone. 'What's up?'

'Tyrone is alive, and I think he burnt down the farmhouse.' Lucy continued and told him the full story worriedly.

As Stephen hurriedly walked away, he reached for his mobile from his back pocket and made a phone call outside. He was on the phone for a couple of minutes and by the time he had ended the call, Lucy and Gerald were gone. Stephen was concerned, but also thinking that Tyrone couldn't have known that he was involved in the attempted assassination. He had another pint of cider and sat quietly as the bar was slowly emptying of the daytime drinkers, and a rock band were arriving and beginning to set up.

Finishing his pint, he stood up and left the bar. He was sure that if he had any more to drink, he would struggle to walk, after eight pints in the afternoon he was more than ready for an early night.

He left the bar and turned right and instantly realised he should have used the toilet before he left the bar. He walked past a cafe bar on the corner and walked into a small private car park where there was a couple of bushes on the side. Swaying slightly, he checked around for people and CCTV cameras, unzipped and started urinating. As he finished and zipped back up Tyrone appeared, but Stephen didn't recognise him, as he was scruffy with a big bushy beard. Stephen started to walk past him, but Tyrone had other ideas. He grabbed Stephen by the throat with his right hand, which was like a shovel and pulled him backwards into the bush which was still wet with piss. Tyrone slammed Stephen's head against the brick wall next to the bush and then raised his right knee and with accuracy, landed it on his balls. Stephen was dazed after his head cracked against the wall which fractured his skull, but then gave out a sharp yell as the knee made contact. Tyrone wanted it to be as painful as possible so slammed his finger into the left eye socket which instantly burst his eye-ball. The sight and feel of fluid bursting out made Tyrone feel nauseous so he made short work of it. pulling the knife from his pocket rammed it into Stephen's stomach three times, hard and fast, twisting the blade the third time. Stephen slumped in his own piss as Tyrone stole his wallet. Stephen died within minutes of the stabbing, his mobile phone ringing in his pocket. By that time, Tyrone was long gone.

Chapter 21

Shelley was breathing heavily and quickly as she was wheeled into the delivery suite. Her water had broken overnight, and Jack had taken her into hospital when the contractions were every three minutes. By the time they arrived Shelley was almost fully dilated and was immediately offered gas and air.

Thirty minutes later the midwife confirmed 'You have a girl.' Jack burst into tears of joy and they both held the beautiful baby. 'India,' Shelley said, 'welcome to the world gorgeous girl.'

Jack was wiping away tears and was totally in love with both girls, feeling like his life was never this complete.

They left hospital three hours later and Jack had time in between to call his Mum and Craig to break the news. They arrived home at 6 pm and went straight to bed, with India in a Moses basket at the foot of the bed. Neither got much sleep as they kept getting up and looking at the baby.

Weeks passed, and the sleep deprivation had started to take its toll on Shelley. She was impatient, and she wasn't thinking straight. India had been ill with gastroenteritis, and it made sleeping even more sporadic. Jack was doing his best and taking control as soon as he arrived home from work and stayed up until mid- night looking after India before handing back to Shelley and getting some much-needed sleep.

Although tired, work was going well. Jack was holding presentations and chairing meetings which made him feel important, and a major part of the company, which he was. He had been given shares in the company and the directors were impressed with his work ethic, drive and ambition. They chose not to big him up too much but every so often showed their gratitude by gifts such as vouchers and other tokens of appreciation.

Jack was attending a regular monthly management meeting and had prepared his report. Sitting in his usual chair in the board room he opened his laptop and started opening emails as he usually did before the meeting started. He was alone in the boardroom at first, then the CEO walked in.

'Morning Jack, How's the baby?' Kurt Summers said, leaning on the back of a chair on the opposite side of the table from Jack. He was an old-school style manager with the left-hand little finger missing from what he said was an industrial accident. In fact, it was the firm, as a warning a few years previously when he tried to rip off a member in a business deal. To save his own life he has been a subs payer ever since. He recently heard that Jack was with Shelley, so he now has a duty to look after him.

'Fine thanks Kurt, teething now so sleep is a distant memory,' Jack said with a smile.

'Oh yeah! I remember that well with my two. It does get easier though, hang in there. Anyway Jack, I have a question for you. Do you have a minute before the meeting for a chat?'

'Of course, Kurt. Is everything alright?'

'Yes mate. More than alright. It's just that Lenny is retiring and he's resigning his position on the board of directors. Me and the other four directors have had a long discussion and we are very impressed with your work, attitude, skill sets and general professionalism. Therefore, we would like to offer you directorship with us. You don't have to take it, as I am fully aware of the commitment, and the fact that it is a big step, but we wouldn't offer you this position as a partner if we didn't have total confidence in you. Take your time and have a chat with Shelley. If you would like legal advice, I have associates in the law profession who can advise you. Totally impartial of course.

'Francis is a barrister working in Bristol Chambers who will be more than willing to advise you, he will give you all the pros and cons of being a company director and you can decide when you're ready. Would you consider this Jack?'

'Of course, I would Kurt. Thanks for the opportunity! I will talk to Shelley, and If you could give me Francis's number, I will contact him tomorrow. Thanks Kurt!' Jack was visibly surprised with the offer, but very excited by it. A company director! He never dreamed he would ever make a director.

Jack made his presentation and sat in a glazed- over state throughout the meeting which lasted two hours but felt like a week. He made his way back to the workshop and worked the remainder of the shift, longing to go home and tell Shelley the news.

He entered the house quietly in case they were asleep, then when he heard Shelley say in a soft voice 'Here's Daddy!' he said 'Hello,' loudly with a big grin on his face.

When he told Shelley, she was overjoyed for him. 'That's brilliant!' she said hugging Jack with one arm, India sat on her other arm. They talked about it for the rest of the evening, in between looking after India, then at bed-time, India went straight to sleep, and they led in bed chatting before falling asleep themselves.

Midnight in Barnstaple, North Devon. A typical Saturday

night, the karaoke had finished, and drunken locals and tourists were leaving the bars. Tyrone needed money. He waited patiently on the corner of Queen Street near a live music bar. There was a dark alley next to the medical centre where men would often go for a piss. He knew that would be the case, so he walked round the block and pretended to have a piss at the far end of the alley.

Sure enough, a drunken man in his early 20s appeared in the alley and unzipped his jeans. Tyrone wandered down the alley towards the guy and as he approached, the guy had finished, and started redressing. Just as he zipped his flies, crack! Tyrone slammed his elbow into the back of his skull. He instantly collapsed to the ground and landed awkwardly. Tyrone sifted through his pockets and made off with his wallet. As he walked casually to his car, he opened the wallet and found £160. 'Result!' he thought to himself.

Saunton Sands was about six miles away and Tyrone drove there from his bedsit. There were surfers milling around the gravel car park, and families getting ice creams and drinks from the beach shop. Tyrone walked down the path and onto the beautiful sandy beach. Not a cloud in the sky, Mid-July and the waves were big, following recent storms. When he reached the compact, slightly wet sand he started jogging. After a few minutes he upped his pace and carried on for 20 minutes until he was out of breath. He wasn't a runner, more of a body builder but it was now necessary to get fit. As he slowed down to a walk, he glanced to his left and noticed a naked woman. He didn't know this end of the beach was a naturist section as there were no signs or other information. She was slightly over- weight, but with everything on show it was a surprise, and he liked it. With all that had been happening, he hadn't thought about sex, but suddenly felt the urge. Then he noticed more naturists in the sand dunes.

He thought to himself, 'Should I or not?' Then again what did he have to lose? He was technically dead. He ran a little longer then wandered back down the beach to where he saw the woman. He walked up to the sand dunes and stripped naked, sat on his clothes and relaxed. A few minutes later a naked man approached. 'Hi' he said, appearing to look Tyrone up and down.

Tyrone chose not to answer, as the guy was clearly gay.

The guy got the message and disappeared into the sand dunes.

Tyrone couldn't resist it and got up and went to look for the woman. He found her and sat about 10 meters away, checking her out. 'Have you got the time please?' he said, getting her attention.

'It's 3.30,' she said, after looking at her phone. She looked over and saw Tyrone, noticing his physique, and cheeky smile. A bit scruffy but he looked good anyway.

They chatted for five minutes, and then Tyrone, clearly enjoying the view, said, 'You look great.'

'Thanks' she said, in a local accent, and a seductive tone. I'm Sharon. What's your name?'

'Terry. I'm originally from Bristol, but I split with my fiancée and moved down here.'

A few minutes more talking and they were in the dunes having sex.

It was over after a few minutes as Tyrone hadn't had any action for months. They laid together and she was stroking his chest and admiring his physique. Tyrone was staring at the sky in ecstasy then, gradually coming to his senses. 'Oh, shit! I need to go! Sorry Sharon, can I have your number? I promise I will call you tomorrow.'

Sharon reached into her bag and gave Tyrone a business card for the florist she worked at. She couldn't hide her disappointment as she watched him pull on his shorts and walk at pace down to the flat sand. Tyrone started jogging towards the car park and couldn't quite believe what had just happened. Grinning to himself.

As he approached the car park, he noticed a police car near his Mondeo. He carefully looked through the windows of the other cars and saw the two police officers sat in the front, looking alert. Tyrone knew they would be looking for him and kept low as he headed for the holiday chalets at the far side of the car park. As he approached the first chalet, he glanced back and assured himself that they hadn't seen him. He was right.

He had left nothing in the car anyway so decided to leave it there. He had used his bum bag to carry his keys, phone and wallet, so it didn't matter too much about the car. He knew that his time was going to run out soon as he had committed murders and the police were on to him.

Walking to the bus stop he thought about the next move. Bristol. The bitch who broke his finger at the bar, and who, coincidentally turned up in court and confronted him. He couldn't remember her name, but he certainly knew people who did. She must have been in on his attempted murder he thought, and therefore she had to be taken out. He sat silently on the bus back to Barnstaple thinking. He now had no transport, hardly any money and was on the run. Not a good situation to be in but he could handle it. He needed to get to Bristol discreetly and not on camera. Railway stations, coach stations and even some buses were monitored these days and therefore the only way back was by car, which he no longer had.

Shelley was taking India to nursery and then on to work. First day nerves and she was not happy leaving her for the first time. As they walked in, they were greeted with an over friendly lady who couldn't have been over 20 years old. Within minutes Shelley felt at ease, this girl was a natural and India took to her immediately. At six months, she was very inquisitive and aware of her surroundings.

Shelley left and as she shut her car door, she was holding back the tears. She took a deep breath and drove to work. Arriving at the office at 8.30 she sat at her desk and waved at the director through the glass screen, and he waved back. Dave lifted his other hand and said 'Hold on a minute, I'll be right back' to the project manager he was in the meeting with. He left the room and headed straight for Shelley. 'Hi Shelley! How are you? Is the baby ok?'

'Fine thanks Dave, good to be back. Has much changed?'

'No, not really, the glad you're back though, Emma couldn't keep up with the workload. Nightmare.'

Within the hour, Shelley was deep into her emails, and realised that the workload was intense. It was as if not much had been done in her absence, and what had been done was wrong. this was going to be a difficult few weeks, only managing a few hours of sleep every night and now a massive workload.

India was asleep when Shelley arrived to pick her up. She quietly said 'Thank you' to Mia the carer and headed home. She arrived at 5pm and India woke up and was clearly pleased to see her mummy.

'Hello my beautiful girl!' Shelley said with a beaming smile, scooping her up into her arms and gently jigging around the lounge. They looked out of the window and saw Jack walking up the path. 'Daddy's home!' Shelley said.

Jack looked pleased with himself and very pleased to be home. It was as if everything was going well. They all shared hugs and kisses and then sat down for dinner. 'Looks like I will be signed up as a partner next week love. I will be given 20% shares instantly and profit-related bonuses. My section of the manufacturing side isn't the most profit -making section but it will still provide me a bonus every six months following the accounts audit. Meantime my basic salary is going up by 20% within a month.

They sat and talked about that, and Shelley's return to work for an hour after India went to bed and they were both excited about their future.

Chapter 22

'I didn't think I would hear from you again Terry!' Sharon said smiling as she wandered around her house talking down the phone.

'Yeah, sorry about leaving you on the beach so abruptly, I had to call my mum. She's been unwell, and I had to check up on her.' Tyrone was about to take a shower and then see if he could meet up with her. What are you up to later? Would you like to meet up for a drink?'

'I'm sorry Terry, I have things to do tonight, how about tomorrow?'

Tyrone thought for a second. Saturdays had had been boring days recently, not leaving the bedsit in case he was spotted. 'Yeah, ok that'll be nice.'

The call ended politely after arranging to meet at a bar in the centre of Barnstaple. Tyrone looked in the bathroom mirror and was sick of the beard and long hair he had been growing as a disguise. By now the police would be looking for him as he looked now. He got dressed and walked up the high street to a budget store. He bought a set of hair clippers and some cheap razor blades and left the store. He was usually far more vigilant about his surroundings but had let his guard down momentarily as he was thinking about having sex with Sharon again.

Looking for a sexual fix, and then getting back on track with the master plan.

He turned left out of the store and froze. There were two community police officers walking towards him. They looked casual and hadn't seen him at that point, as they were looking in shop windows. Tyrone casually walked into the fried chicken take out and ordered a meal, not daring to look behind him. As he turned around with a tray of greasy chicken, chips and a diet cola, he came face to face with one of the officers, the female one. She said 'Sorry' as she side stepped out of his way.

Tyrone held his nerve and replied with 'No worries' in a fake Australian accent then carried on upstairs to eat his impromptu dinner. He sat down and ate the chicken so quickly that he was drawing attention to himself. The officers didn't come upstairs, but Tyrone was worried that he would have to pass them as he left. They may have recognised him and may have already called for back-up. His knees were bouncing with his foot on the rail bending under his weight, and he looked and felt stressed. Slowing down as he dipped his chips into ketchup and having the occasional sip of cola, he went and sat by the window looking down at the entrance. After ten minutes, the officers left and casually walked down the high street. Tyrone was relieved but knew he had to go the same way to get back to the bedsit. He left it another five minutes and then slowly walked down the high street with eyes everywhere. As he entered the bedroom, he let out a big sigh and carried on.

It took an hour to shave off his beard and all his hair. Then he began a close shave of his face and suddenly he felt good about his appearance. He looked younger in his face, and it felt cold and smooth. He couldn't stop touching his face for an hour or so. When he had finished looking in the mirror, getting used to the new image, he had a shower and got ready to go out. He wanted a few beers and needed to get some money from somewhere to take Sharon out.

Leaving the bedsit at 8 pm he headed for a sports bar. As he entered it was predictably busy as Fridays always were. Men fresh from the gym and women dressed for a good time. A band was setting up and there was a party atmosphere building. Tyrone stood in the corner of the bar where he could see most of what was going on and slowly sipped his lager while he observed.

By 11.30 the bar was alive. The band was finishing their set with 'Sex on Fire' and everyone was singing along with their hands in the air. Tyrone sang along too, but he was plotting his next move. He clocked a bloke about the same age as him and noticed he was flashing a fairly large roll of 20s every time he ordered a drink. He was drunk and swaying lightly as he ordered another Fosters. He was having no luck with the women as they all saw he was pissed. A real turn off. Tyrone stood and went to the toilet. As he stood at the urinal the pissed guy entered, heading straight to the cubicle and threw up a couple of litres of liquid which, under pressure also came out of his nostrils. Coughing, spitting and sniffing, he had both hands on the toilet pan and swayed about, with his hips hitting against the cubicle walls. Tyrone took the opportunity. He leant into the cubicle and said, 'Are you alright mate?' as he put his right hand on the guy's back, his left rifling through his pocket, where Tyrone had seen him stuff the money. As the guy started throwing up again, he hadn't even noticed that he had been robbed. Tyrone left casually and walked down the high street, feeling pleased at how easy it all was. As he approached the bus station there were a couple arguing loudly, the girl clutching a bottle of beer and the guy with his t-shirt off and tucked into his belt. He was so pissed he could hardly stand up, and she was not far behind, and getting emotional as she shouted at him, not making much sense. Tyrone slowed down and watched as she tried to slap him across the face, missing and falling into a heap onto the pavement. Tyrone laughed quietly and headed home. When he arrived, he counted the money, and it came to £245. Perfect.

Chapter 23

Another night, another few glasses of the best prosecco on the market, and another fake orgasm. But Lucy was actually starting to like this guy. He was gentle, ridiculously generous, loving and, of course, loaded. It was just the sex was really lame compared to some of the guys she had been with the last few years, Tyrone included.

The truth was that she still thought about Tyrone. Every day something would trigger memories. Whether it was a similar truck would go past, a guy wearing Hugo Boss, a mohawk haircut, or a guy who was particularly muscular. She couldn't forget the fact that he was misogynistic, a bully, selfish and had hit her about. But she loved him.

As Gerald rolled off breathing heavily in ecstasy having had what he considered great sex, Lucy turned to him and put her hand on his chest and kissed him on the cheek gently as his breathing calmed. 'What are you doing today?' she asked softly.

'I'm meeting Stevie for a beer later this afternoon to watch the footy. England are playing. No plans for the morning or tonight, although I may be a bit pissed later.' He said with a slight selfish grin.

'If it's OK with you, I'm meeting some friends in Bristol and probably staying the night.'

'Yea that's fine. I don't own you Lucy, do what you want! Do you need some money? I could get you out some cash if you like?'

'You don't have to do that!' she said, not meaning it.

'Actually, take a card with you. Use it to get cash out, and if you want to pay for a meal carry on. Just don't buy a racehorse or anything.'

That was exactly what she wanted to hear. She got dressed and cooked his favourite breakfast, poached egg on toast with two rashers of bacon and a filter coffee. She had a shower and started packing a small suitcase. Mainly make up and small underwear.

Lucy was trying to hide her excitement thinking of a night out in Bristol as she drove Gerald into Exeter town centre. As she pulled into the bus stop to drop him off, she turned to him, and they kissed and had a brief hug. 'Take care Lucy, see you sometime tomorrow.' He climbed out and headed straight into the shopping centre, and into the sports bar where he was meeting Stephen.

Lucy carried on up towards the M5, music blearing and singing along badly to Ed Sheeran. She called Kerry and arranged the night ahead. They were meeting at a bar on the harbourside which was lively even on a quiet night, so it was sure to be rammed on a Saturday night.

At 7.30, having finished chatting to her Mum and left the car at the hotel, Lucy strolled into the bar full of confidence and feeling good about the way she looked. To any man who didn't know her she looked stunning. She had lost a stone in weight recently and spent almost two hours getting ready. As she approached the bar, almost every man in the bar had noticed her. As she ordered a gin and tonic, she messaged Kerry, but as she was typing, Kerry turned up. 'Hey!' Kerry said loudly as she held her arms out for a hug.

'Hi Kerry!' Lucy said in a near scream 'How are you?'

they were both beaming and genuinely pleased to see each other. Lucy couldn't wait to get started on talking about Gerald and the latest gossip. She got started and continued until Kerry glazed over. As the drinks were in full flow, they were quickly half drunk and giggling at everything.

They moved on to a club around the corner, and Lucy knew the security, which she took advantage of. She kissed him and then they walked in without paying to the disbelief of the other 30- odd people who had been standing outside for half an hour. They ordered cocktails and stood jigging to the dance music which was loud enough to block most conversation.

As the night went on, the club was growing busier, and everyone was at close distance and there was a great deal of physical contact with everyone dancing on a packed dance floor. Lucy and Kerry were pretty drunk at this point, about 1.30, and they were trying to hide it. Kerry went to the toilet and Lucy tried to focus on the fit guy she had her eye on, but she couldn't see him anymore, so she thought he must have gone off with another girl. Kerry returned and looked like she had been sick, with blood-shot eyes and reapplied mascara. Within a few minutes, Lucy screwed up her chin, and legged it into the toilet where she emptied her stomach. Cocktails on an empty stomach was clearly a bad mistake.

They both felt less drunk after they emptied their stomachs of chemicals and they decided to go for a curry. They stumbled down to the city centre and down Hollywood Street, a narrow lane off the centre. An Indian restaurant was open, and they entered, trying not to act too drunk. They were shown to a table, and they ordered a bottle of red wine.

'So, tell me about Gerald then. He sounds great!' Kerry said.

'Well, he isn't bad looking, lovely house, successful,

smart, intelligent, generous, but lousy in bed. I'm desperate for an orgasm or two!'

They both laughed loudly for what seemed like hours, attracting the other diner's attention. Two guys in particular, who had been checking them out since they entered the restaurant. 'Having a good night ladies?' Adam said with a smile.

'Yes, thanks, you?' Kerry said.

'Come and join us if you want to.' Adam asked.

Then it began. Adam was a construction manager from a suburb of north Bristol called Patchway. He was with Justin, a commercial manager he worked with from Filton. They both clearly looked after themselves and weren't hiding the fact that they regularly worked out at the gym. They both had dark hair which was perfectly groomed, and Justin had thin, perfectly trimmed side-burns. Adam was the personality, and he had a permanent smile, which the ladies loved. Kerry couldn't take her eyes off of him as they sat and found the bottom of four bottles of wine and various items from the menu.

'Let's all go back to my hotel. They have a 24-hour bar!' Lucy said with excited eyes.

As they entered the Grand Hotel, on the harbourside, they were greeted by security. Lucy showed her room card and he allowed them all in. As the guys swaggered past the security guard, they looked at him in a smug, down-the-nose manner. They were both taller, and far more muscular than the guard, who didn't respond to their attitude, remaining professional. Little did they know, he was a master of martial arts. Their muscle was simply from pushing weights and just for show.

Tyrone had been lying low for too long. His patience was running very thin. Trips to the local supermarket, runs across the beach and sitting in his bed sit all day were driving him mad. He could not risk joining a rugby club or training in boxing or martial arts as they were all a close community, and his identity would be apparent in no time. He had pictures of Shelley, Sergeant Chapple and Chris on his laptop and was planning his next hit, now that it may have all cooled down. He had lost over two stone in weight and kept his head and face fully shaved so that he didn't look like the Tyrone his former associates would remember.

Donning a pair of cheap spectacles, he picked up from a local pharmacy, he left the bedsit and headed to the bus stop. The look made Tyrone feel weird. He was used to strutting around and everyone being scared of him. It was different now. People got in the way and didn't notice him anymore. He no longer stood out. Somehow it felt OK, knowing that he still had the fighting skills to do the damage if he needed to, but that he blended in. That is what he needed to do for his next move.

Lucy approached the bar first, knowing that Justin and Adam were admiring her figure from behind, and enjoying it. As she reached the bar, she placed her left foot on the low-level marble step, dropped her small hand- bag on the bar and turned her head and upper body round as if she was in a L'Oréal advert and about to say 'Because I'm worth it.' 'What are you guys drinking?' she asked with confidence. They all ordered drinks and sat around a low table. Conversation was shallow and soon the girls were getting drunk again, on double vodkas.

Lucy whispered into Kerry's ear, 'Have you ever had a full-on foursome?'

Kerry burst out laughing but looked interested. 'Adam is quite fit; Justin isn't bad either.' She whispered back, and they both laughed quietly. 'We're going to the toilet. Won't be long, don't go away.'

Tyrone stood waiting for the bus, which would take him

to Barnstaple train station. He was the first to arrive at the stop which was on the A39 towards Lynmouth on the outskirts of town. The bus appeared and as it stopped, he started to board and an elderly man was rushing to board, kind of running towards the front of the bus. He made it as the driver waited for him, whilst Tyrone paid and sat inconspicuously mid-way down, towards the exit door. The elderly man stepped onto the bus and made his way down the aisle and looked at Tyrone for what felt like too long. As he looked, his expression changed from the relief of making it onto the bus, to concern with the site of Tyrone, or so it seemed.

Tyrone noticed this and felt uncomfortable immediately. Inside he was questioning if taking the bus was a good idea, with CCTV and regular users noticing strangers, including persons who may have been in the press, or TV in relation to crime.

The bus seemed to take every wrong turn and stop at every opportunity, with the elderly man glancing at Tyrone every few seconds, from the side which started eating away at him and it was showing on his face. He was tense and glowing with rage, wanting a moment of privacy with the elderly man to take him out. The chance was not going to come, so he knew he had to relax and let it go. The bus pulled up at the station and Tyrone stood up, put his rucksack on his back and left the bus as it stopped. He walked towards the ticket office and noticed two police cars entering the station car park to his left. He lowered his head and headed at speed into the crowded ticket office and purchased a one-way ticket to Bristol Temple Meads, before leaving with haste, glancing around, particularly towards the car park area where the police cars had pulled in. The two officers were talking to the bus driver and the elderly man. Then they head bowed to the bus driver and headed towards the station. By then Tyrone knew they were onto him, so he had jumped over a low fence around the back of the ticket office and headed towards a trading estate to the East of the station. Within a couple of minutes, he was walking around B&Q looking at paint colour charts watching the door using his peripheral vision.

He looked around the DIY store for around ten minutes, hoping that when he left the situation would have calmed and that the police would be searching trains instead of the surrounding areas of the station. He was right on this occasion, so he headed in the opposite direction of the station and thought of how he was going to get to Bristol without getting noticed. Meantime he was trying to understand how this old fucker recognised him, and from what? He was some stupid old bastard who nearly blew it for him. He felt angry and confused, which was not a good combination for him.

The elderly man was in his flat looking out of the kitchen window one night in the centre of Barnstaple when he saw a man urinating in a car park, and as he finished, someone assaulted him, which turned out to be a murder. He never forgot the attackers face, as he is ex-military and was a specialist reconnaissance operative with 2-Para.

The ticket officer told the police that the guy with the ruck sack had purchased a single to Bristol Temple Meads, and the train was just leaving. PC Wilson told the train driver to wait until they had completed a check on all carriages before they left. Two other officers joined the search and the fourth waited at the station entrance in case the suspect tried to slip out during the train search.

Tyrone knew they would be waiting for him in Bristol and so decided to go back to the bed-sit and rethink his plan.

The morning came and Lucy woke to find the hotel room

in a mess. There were empty bottles everywhere and broken glass on the floor. She lay on the bed piecing together the events of the previous night, and more importantly, the last few hours. She had a terrible headache and as the feeling in her body was returning with each minute, it was clear that there was sex involved, and plenty of it for sure. She looked to her left and saw Kerry, still asleep on top of the covers in just a thong. There was a stench in the air of booze and sex, and the sheets on the bed were a reflection of the previous events.

Lucy peeled herself off the bed and slowly walked to the bathroom kicking bottles and avoiding broken glasses on the way. There was no sign of the guys who came back, but she expected that and was somehow grateful, so there was no awkwardness. When she came out of the shower, she wrapped the towel around her and returned to the bedroom where Kerry was sat up in bed with a coffee, looking worse for wear, but smiling at Lucy. 'Hi,' she said in a low-pitched, gravelly voice, still smiling.

'What a night!' Lucy replied and sat next to Lucy giving her a kiss on the cheek. 'That was the best sex I've had in years. You were pretty hot yourself,' she said in a suggestive manner.

'You, too. I've never really thought about other girls, but that was really nice! Best keep it between us, though, eh?'

They both dressed and prepared to leave the hotel room. Lucy noticed that her hand-bag and the inner zip were open. She started rummaging around inside, then her hands started getting faster as she was emptying receipts and old folded up pieces of paper out until the reality hit her. 'My credit card is gone, and all my cash!'

Kerry gasped and reached into her own handbag. It was also open and as she stood there, she emptied the contents onto the table and held her head in her hands. 'So is mine! The fucking thieving bastards!'

Lucy was thinking as she started crying. She could not tell the real story to Gerald, clearly. But the police would have to be called as somehow, she had to pay for the hotel. Then she remembered that the hotel was already paid for and they could leave. She still had her car and some spare cash she hid under the seat so she knew she would be OK for now, but she had Kerry to deal with who was losing control of her emotions. 'We need to call the police, but first, contact the card companies and cancel them before those wankers go on a spending spree on us.'

The police turned up at the hotel and the receptionist pointed in the direction of the bar where Lucy and Kerry were sat. PC White took statements and informed them that these two were at it regularly in Bristol and were likely to be tracked down very soon. The hotel CCTV was of good quality and the footage clearly showed both faces providing good identification.

Then it was just a matter of Gerald. She had told him already that the card had been stolen so he had to cancel it, but he was already piecing it together regarding what kind of night it had been. Lucy said she dropped it in a club, which was far from the true story she told the police, so she knew that sooner or later it would come out. Would it really matter? She was asking herself.

As she was finishing her coffee with Kerry, who by now was much calmer, her mobile rang with MUM on the display. 'Fuck sake, I don't need her laying in the boot.'

'Hi darling, are you still in Bristol? I have a letter for you from Whittaker Solicitors.'

Lucy finished the call. 'I need to go to Mum's. Do you need a lift?'

'Yes, that would be great, thanks.'

Lucy dropped Kerry off in Fishponds and drove the mine or so to her mum's house. Checking her look in the mirror, which was not great, but to be expected, she sprayed mint breath freshener into her mouth and exited the car. Her Mum saw the car pull up and was waiting at the door, greeting Lucy with open arms and a slight smile, as always. 'Coffee darling?'

'Yes, please Mum, how are you?'

'We're bearing up love, you know how it is. Anyway, this came for you, and there are others sent from the flat which I picked up last week.'

Lucy sat in her usual place at the kitchen table and opened the letter from Whittaker solicitors. Most of it was in legal jargon but she could understand that the farm had been sold, and the insurance had been settled to the solicitors.

She also understood that the sole beneficiary to the estate was her. She was suddenly worth just over £1.5 million.

'Everything alright with the solicitors love?'

'Yes, fine Mum, everything is ticking over thanks.' Lucy replied, shaking as she raised the coffee mug to her lips.

Chapter 24

Shelley and Jack were enjoying family time walking down the promenade on Clevedon seafront. India was quietly glancing around at other children and enjoying the view from her buggy which was being expertly driven by Jack. Shelley linked arms with Jack and as she did, looked lovingly at him as they walked towards the loped concrete path leading to a pebble beach. They sat on the concrete with their legs dangling down towards the beach whilst Shelley fed India her favourite Cow & Gate Bolognese and some weak orange squash from a beaker, with Jack watching.

'Hi Shelley,' said a female voice from behind.

Without even looking Shelley replied, 'Hi Rose, how was your ice cream?'

Rose laughed. 'How do you know I had an ice cream? Are you psychic?'

'I saw you earlier near the car park in the queue. We were just getting out of the car and too far to say hello. How's the training going?'

'Fine thanks, I wanted to ask you about a certain kata for my grading. Can we go through it on Tuesday please?'

Shelley replied 'Yes, of course we can. Take care, see you then.'

As Rose left, Shelley turned to Jack. 'She has great

potential that one. She wants to join the army next year and I think she will smash it. When she first turned up at training, she had no confidence at all. Now look at her.' It was clear to Jack that Shelley had pride in what karate was giving people and how watching people develop themselves whilst training under her was so satisfying. She was there for other people, and she loved helping them. It was not about a bit of extra cash, or the status of standing in front of a class and a black belt, or the power and ego of shouting orders. It was about developing people, that was all that mattered.

'I have a project management course coming up in Scotland next week and it's the same briefing as the last one. No mobile phones, due to the government contracts we are tendering for. I will be away from Wednesday until Saturday afternoon. Are you OK with that Jack?'

'OK, that's fine. I'll drop you at the airport and pick you up Saturday.'

'Don't worry the company is doing door to door. They have taxis booked.' Shelley said, hoping that Jack was buying the story. She knew there were similar flight times going to and from Edinburgh and Barcelona.

Wednesday, seven, and Shelley was packed and ready to go. She had a small suitcase and a travel bag with essentials in but appeared to be bursting at the seams. Jack made no comments, as he had made that mistake before and it ended in a blazing argument if he ever questioned Shelley. He decided to go for the peaceful option of not bothering. The taxi pulled up and she gave India and Jack big hugs and kisses and went off to Bristol airport.

The taxi was pre-paid, so she thanked the driver and walked into the terminal building and straight into the Ladies toilets and changed into a summer dress, stuffing her office blouse and trousers into the suitcase. Then she checked the suitcase in at the desk and up the escalators to departures. The body and bag scanners revealed nothing, and she put on her jewellery, watch and belt and headed for the main bar. As she approached the bar, Imogen noticed her and made a point of serving her, asking politely what she would like.

'Hi, I'll have a skinny flat white please.'

Imogen and Shelley both nodded as this was the positive ID and Shelley slowly, discreetly headed for the bar hatch, which was left open as planned. Imogen carried on making the coffee and as she turned, she headed straight for Shelley in the new location and handed a white envelope to her which Shelley carefully placed in her already open travel bag, then slowly zipped it up. The flat white was on the bar and without asking for payment Imogen, 24 and of Italian complexion, carried on serving the next customer, trying not to look preoccupied, but failing. Shelley was picking up on her nerves, and decided the best action was to disappear, which she did, into the crowd and sat as far away from the bar as possible, so she was out of view of the mob rookie.

She made a phone call and simply said 'Hi, I have contacted your supplier, and all is in order for the site visit tomorrow. See you there, Thanks, bye.'

Tyrone decided that it was no longer safe to hang around in Barnstaple so decided to leave the following morning. Fist, he would see if he could go in style, and accelerate things. It was a Thursday night, and he knew exactly where to go. The Champions League quarter finals were on and Manchester United were playing away to Inter Milan. The game was being shown in a sports bar in the centre of town and that's where he knew that Chapple would be there, making no secret of being a United fan.

He arrived inconspicuously at 8:30 pm and ordered a cider. As he drank the first inch from the pint, he lent on his elbow and glanced around the bar, but Brian Chapple was not there. At around 9:05, the door swung open, and a large frame of a man entered, and instead of going straight to the bar, stopped and looked at the screen to check the score line. United were 2-1 up against Inter which made him smile as he headed for the bar.

'Hi Brian, they're playing well tonight. Usual?'

'Yes, thanks John.' Chapple stood and looked at the screen whilst the second half was well underway and felt relaxed as he sipped his pint of lager. He didn't notice as he walked in, a small, fairly lean man in his fifties notice him as he walked in, start to get up from his bench seat, then sat back down again without attracting any attention. Neither did he notice Tyrone, reading a local paper stare over the top of it when he set eyes on him, with a look of anger mixed with excitement, then pull it back up so he could just about see Chapple at the side. But the lean 50- something guy, did notice.

The final whistle blew and there was an influx of mainly men at the bar ordering drinks. Chapple had proactively ordered his last drink a few minutes before full time and was stood enjoying it whilst everyone around him was jostling for the attention of the bar staff. He was passively looking around the bar and as a true professional could never really switch off from policing. He noticed at least seven men who had recently passed through the station, mainly for drunken offenses and he knew that they would barely remember his face, if at all. It was a good thing to be up in the ranks and leave the main confrontational work to the constables and rookies, which meant that he was not a figurehead locally unless he wanted to be.

Tyrone was no longer in the bar, and Chapple turned around, finished his pint, put it on the bar and said loudly 'Thanks John, see you soon.'

John turned his head whilst pouring a pint and said, 'Cheers Brian.' But was too busy to fully acknowledge his old mate.

Chapple left the bar and turned left and down towards the main high street where taxis would be available. Suddenly he realised that he should have used the urinal before leaving the bar, so he found a lane which was dark and discreet enough to relieve himself. He sniggered to himself at the thought of the local police chief getting caught urinating in public, as he started the flow which drained away from his feet. Feeling relaxed, he made himself decent and turned around to be faced with Tyrone three feet away moving towards him at speed with a kitchen knife in his hand, pointing directly at his stomach. In a split second another man appeared and head-butted Tyrone to the side of his head and the fight resumed. Den was an ex-Marine, and rumours were going around that he was in the special forces. The knife was kicked down a gully and Tyrone managed to escape and run down the road.

'Den! Where did you come from?' Brian shouted, in shock of what just happened.

'Hi Brian, I was in the bar and saw him checking you out so I sat quietly knowing it would kick off. You need close personal protection mate!' he said with a smile. They hugged briefly and spoke at length about the incident, the background and their time together in the Marines, many years ago.

'What are we going to do about that prick then?' Den asked.

'Don't worry about him. I'll make some calls and he will be sorted later.' Chapple knew it needed to be a mob activity, not the police, as there was history between them, If Tyrone decided to bleat about the mob trying and failing to kill him then it would lead to serious problems.

Tyrone ran back to the bedsit and packed everything he may need in a backpack and left immediately. He had to leave the area immediately having failed to take out Chapple, and been fought off by his mate, who nearly got the better of him. No doubt in his mind, he had to disappear. He had a terrible headache and the swelling on the side of his head, along with many other bruises were hurting as the adrenaline was fading. He stopped for a moment, looked back at the bedsit which had been home for far too long, momentarily thinking 'should I stay? Should I lay low for a week or so and have another shot at Chapple? NO!' the thought of staying quickly passed and he was planning a trip across country to Bristol.

Chapter 25

Shelley enjoyed the view across the Mediterranean during the taxi journey from the airport into Barcelona centre where her hotel was pre-booked and paid for. She was thinking of India and wandered what she was doing right now, hoping that she was not missing Mummy too much. She was also feeling guilty about lying to Jack. She always did but this time she felt worse, as it was the third time this year that she had done it, and it was going to be for longer. The taxi pulled up at a hotel on a side street just off Las Ramblas and Shelley checked in, having her passport scanned. Her room was bright and airy with a small balcony. Everything she needed for the three nights. After unpacking her case, hanging up her clothes she had a quick freshen-up and headed out down Las Ramblas.

Towards the end of Las Ramblas Shelley took a left turn and headed down a narrow but busy street lined with shops and bars. She walked around 200 meters and then entered a supermarket on the left, glancing around before so. No one appeared to be watching her as she didn't look any-thing other than another British tourist wearing a summer dress with flat comfortable shoes and sunglasses. As she entered, the rear door to the shop closed firmly and the one remaining shop assistant looked at it confused, then looked back at Shelley. 'Hola,' she said politely.

'Hola,' Shelley replied, 'Can I speak to Miguel please?'

The assistant's eyes widened, and her eye-brows raised as she said in good, but broken English 'He's not here at moment. He's away for a while.'

Shelley looked knowingly at the assistant with her head slightly down with a disapproving look across her face. 'What's your name?'

The assistant shrunk in her chair and her face looked worried. 'Emilia.'

'Emilia, I know he's here, but I don't want you to get into trouble. You make sure he knows that Shelley called in to see him and that I'm in town for a while. I suggest you go home and stay there when you finish tonight.'

'OK Shelley,' Emilia replied. At this point she was nearly in tears, and her hands were shaking. She knew what this was about, and Miguel, her father had placed her in danger.

Shelley left the store, and she looked both ways as she headed back towards Las Ramblas, stopping in a bar for a quick cocktail about 50 metres from the store, taking a seat where she could see the store entrance.

Sure enough, after about 20 minutes, Miguel appeared, looking on edge. Looking up and down the street, as he started taking in the sales pitches from outside and closing the shop. Shelley pulled out her mobile phone and speed dialled. 'Hi Darren, how are you?'

'Hi Shelley, all good here love, what's the latest?'

'Well, as predicted, not playing ball. Miguel hid out back and his daughter was visibly shaken by my initial visit. Who have we got locally?'

'Don't worry love, I'll have whoever you need in the morning. I'll call you at 9:30 am and fill you in on the details for the second visit. I'd get some rest love. Tomorrow could be a long day.'

Lucy stayed at Mum's for the night, while Dad was away playing golf in Scotland. She explained to Gerald that Mum could do with the company, and she was feeling slightly shaken after the credit card incident, but Gerald seemed slightly distant, but accepting the bullshit. Lucy was caring less and less as each minute passed and questioning if it would really matter if she never went back to Gerald's house and just left all her belongings there. Not really, but it was Monday, and she had an appointment with the solicitors in Exeter on Tuesday to go through the final points of the inheritance. She was nervous but excited but had to head back for an early appointment. That meant either stay at a hotel in Exeter or go back to Gerald's and face questioning.

She decided to check into Jury's Inn, which is across the square from Whittaker solicitors. Mum paid for it and Lucy promised that the money would be transferred as soon as she had been to the bank in Exeter. It was a flawless journey with no traffic into Exeter and parked in the secure hotel car park. She was aware of having to be careful because Gerald was a popular figure in Exeter, and sightings of her would be around town and back to him within minutes. After checking in and unpacking what was left of her clothes and make up accessories, she left the hotel and crossed the town centre to the Nat West bank. She explained the theft and ordered a new debit card and returned to the hotel. By the time she got to reception, Gerald called. 'Hi Ger, are you OK?'

'Yea I'm fine Lucy. Why are you staying at Jury's?'

Lucy froze. How did he find out so quickly? In a panic, she hung up. Within a few seconds the phone rang again with Gerald across the screen. Lucy cancelled the call and killed the phone. She was not ready to answer to him yet.

The story was not straight and her reasons for dumping him was not fully developed yet. It was now made worse by the pressure of time. He could turn up at the hotel at any time and with his connections could find her room.

She was feeling stressed as she entered the room with a bottle of chardonnay and a glass from the bar. Pouring herself a large glass, she sat on the bed, and paused for thought for a couple of minutes before making the call.

'Hi Ger, sorry about that earlier. I was guessing that you were upset about the card going missing and that you didn't want to see me. I was scared that you were angry at me!' Her voice was crumbling as she spoke.

'Well of course I was upset, but I wasn't angry, I just wanted an explanation from you love. When are you coming home? Why are you at the hotel and not with me? I love you!'

Lucy took a deep breath away from ear shot of the phone. 'I'll be back tomorrow afternoon when you come home from the office.'

'OK love, I'll book a table for us. Love you loads.'

'Love you too, bye.'

Lucy hung up and took a large gulp of wine, knowing what she had to do.

Tyrone was walking towards Porlock. He had wild-camped for two nights and made good progress. The coast path offered shelter in bushes, and he had purchased a cheap pop-up tent and sleeping bag which fitted into his back- pack with ease, along with the other basics he had taken from the bedsit. Beaches provided sea water where he stripped and washed early in the mornings before anyone else turned up and he felt good. He still had a good amount of cash from recent muggings and was eating in local cafes and coffee shops along the way.

Stopping for a rest on a bench overlooking the Bristol

Channel, he reached into his back- pack and found his mobile phone. Dare he switch it on, and risk being tracked? He paused for a moment and then held down the on button for a few seconds until it came to life. It took two minutes to fully activate and when it did, there were 12 notifications. He went through them deleting all, except one. The one that caught his eye was from Lucy. He opened the message which read 'Thinking of you.'

His heart nearly stopped. He suddenly had feelings again and really wanted to see Lucy, hug her, kiss her and apologise for everything. He was breathing heavily and almost crying. He checked the date of the message which was three weeks ago. His battery was at critical, and the phone died.

It was late evening and he needed to set up the tent for the night before it was totally dark, so he headed down to a clearing in a nearby woodland and set up for the night. He did not sleep for most of the night as he was thinking about the text, about Lucy and wondering where she was and what she was doing. More importantly, who with. These thoughts were beginning to eat at him.

'The funds will be in the account of your choice within five working days. Please enter the account details on this form, sign here and here and that will be it.'

Lucy filled in and signed the form with her hand slightly trembling, but with no facial expression. She had £1476 in her bank account at the moment, and within a week she worked out that she would have £1,546,753 cleared funds. She was sure she could lie low from Gerald for one week and then disappear altogether. She politely shook hands with Julian, the solicitor, and left the office, heading straight to the car park. She had already checked out of the hotel and decided that if all was in place not to go back to Gerald's to explain anything, but to simply disappear. She climbed into her Mini and drove out of Exeter in silence. She reached the M5, headed south and then west onto the A30. In a state of shock, she remained almost silent until she reached Newquay, where she sat in a McDonalds car park and stared into space for ten minutes, until she walked in and ordered some lunch. As she slowly ate her chicken sandwich and dipped her fries into the barbecue sauce, she logged on to a hotel booking app on her mobile and looked for accommodation in the area. She found a hotel near Fistral Beach which looked good, so checked in there for a week, half board. At a cost of £680 she was nearly out of funds until the inheritance had cleared so had to be careful. Then remembered she had an overdraft facility of £1000 so didn't have to worry.

Shelley was up and ready at 9 am. She sent Jack a text saying she would call later from a pay phone but not sure what time it would be as the course was a long one which could last until late evening. Jack replied with 'OK, love you, take care xxxx.'

The phone rang at exactly 9.30 'Hi Shelley, a cab is waiting for you outside, black Mercedes. The driver's name is Joao. Let him say his name first. See you later.' The call ended.

Shelley checked her look, grabbed her bag and left the room. She took the lift from her third-floor room and walked across reception out through the open glass doors where, sure enough, a black E-Class Mercedes was there with a smartly dressed, small but white handsome Spanish man stood with the rear door open. 'Hi, I'm Joao.' That was good enough for Shelley, and she nodded and entered the car.

The car journey took 45 minutes into the hills and into a small village. The Mercedes glided over the rough roads and Joao turned right onto a dusty, unkept road with thick evergreen vegetation either side. Eventually they came to an old looking villa type farm building which looked secure and unmanned until Joao sounded the horn, then the front door swung open and a tall, broad-shouldered man appeared with short fair hair. He looked every bit military in civilian clothing with a ripped physique and full self-confidence. He looked like he could run a marathon in a suit and not get out of breath.

He approached the car and opened the rear door for Shelley to climb out. 'Hi Shelley, how are you?'

Shelley gave him a brief hug and replied, 'Fine Dar. Good to see you again. It's been a long time. What's the latest?'

Darren filled her in on the latest whilst they stood outside the house.

'Come inside, you can take it from here.'

Shelley entered the villa and into the hallway, there were three Spanish men with hand- held pistols to their sides sat on chairs. A door led into the room where Miguel was tied to a chair looking like he had already received a few beatings. Shelley didn't show any emotion as she looked at Miguel who was looking desperate and had a piss puddle under the chair.

'What do we have here then Miguel? I thought we were working together. Where's the money?'

Miguel looked at her and said desperately 'I don't have it! My store was robbed, and they took everything!'

Shelley stood up and in a smooth movement punched Miguel clean in the nose, slightly side on, breaking it and sending a stream of blood down his shirt, which already had some dried blood stains.

He let out a low-pitched groan which continued with each short erratic breath.

'Do you know Diego Mendes? The one who owns the casino? Of course, you do. You have been a regular there for the last six-months Miguel. Is that where the money has gone?' Shelley picked her mobile phone out of her bag and produced a photo of the pretty young assistant at the convenience store, Miguel's daughter. She held the picture up to him and asked if he knew her. His eyes instantly welled up with tears and shouted something in Spanish.

'Please, not her! I will do anything, but do not hurt my daughter! I'm begging you! I will get the money just give me time!'

Shelley scrolled down to another photo of the same girl. This time she was stripped naked with her hands and feet tied to the corners of a double bed, and a gag over her mouth. 'She's untouched at the moment. You have 24 hours to get me 200,000 euro's before I let my boys loose.'

Darren untied Miguel and led him outside whilst Shelley watched, looking mainly into Miguel's eyes, in a confident, stern manner. This lack of emotion in times of intensity was why the firm had her do these jobs. Also, she knew the background of this particular case. Now that Theresa was dead, the money was rightfully owned by the firm, as it was intended to be a safekeep for Theresa if she ever needed it. An insurance policy. Miguel was an old hand and had been a trustworthy member of the firm for many years, looking after the business side of things in the Barcelona area from the modest convenience store, which he used as a decoy from a bigger picture. Unfortunately, the refund was now six-months late, and certain people were becoming increasingly impatient, having issued numerous warnings.

Miguel had recently invested heavily in shares which fell dramatically, which resulted in financial difficulties. He resorted to gambling and when the 200k was presented to him, he saw it as an opportunity to put things right. The plan was to reinvest the money and keep enough just in case Theresa needed some back, and make enough to reimburse the full amount, with profit. Unfortunately, the gambling became a habit, and not a good one, as he was regularly losing thousands each week in the nearby casino. He was not aware that the casino owner was known to the firm. Right now, though, he had bigger issues. His beloved daughter was in grave danger and all because of him. He only had 10,000 euros left and had to find 190,000 in 24 hours.

Miguel was cleaned up and driven back to the convenience store where he disappeared in through the back entrance and locked the door behind him. The local firm kept close watch over the premises and his movements, and his mobile phone and land line were tapped. Devices were placed in the first-floor apartment in his absence by a local expert.

Shelley was driven back to the centre of Barcelona where she set up camp in a cafe and logged into her work email account. She told them she would be working from home to save holiday entitlement, but internet access may be sporadic, so she would be off-line at times during the working day. The company were OK with that, being owned by a senior member of the firm, knowing what she was doing, and where.

Whilst sitting, reading and responding to emails, she sent a text to Jack, asking if all was OK at home. Jack replied instantly with 'Yes love! You OK?'

Shelley replied, 'All good here love, boring course regarding cyber security for the government contract but getting through it. Must go, love you XXXX.'

Jack replied, 'Love you too XXXX.'

Shelley was feeling slightly emotional. But she buried her feelings deep, as she had work to do both with the firm, and with the company. She had to stay focussed and not let home life get in the way.

Chapter 26

Wild camping was something that Tyrone had never done before, but he was kind of enjoying it. It was liberating and somehow, he felt safe in the woods near the coast, not entirely sure where he was. He had a small pop-up tent which was just big enough for him to stretch out and fitted easily into his backpack, along with some clothes and toiletries and he made a mattress out of bracken each night, using his backpack for a pillow. Sleep wasn't something he was never very good at, so a few hours broken sleep each night was enough.

He was laying staring at the tent roof at around 3 am thinking of the last year. What went wrong? He was living in a nice flat, fit girlfriend, loads of mates, regular at the gym and rugby club, good job. Now, he was on the run, alone, sleeping rough with an objective to kill more people, having already committed two murders, and seriously injured many others during mugging incidents. He closed his eyes, inhaled and let out a deep sigh. He placed both hands over his face and turned on his front, his body tense and started crying. He had, until now, buried his emotions. Not because he needed to, but because he was not aware that he had any. Suddenly he found himself missing his life. He had everything. What if Lucy had not been unfaithful and the love bite was her friend messing about. He may have made a big mistake. That guy in the pub may have been talking about another girl but described Lucy in detail. That's where it all started. He knew Lucy had links with a gang, and that he was taking risks by even being with her. He hit her and that's when it all went wrong. They tried to kill him.

He lay there for an hour, his tears didn't last more than a few minutes and he led with his eyes closed, faced down with his hands over his face.

His thoughts turned to the accident in the truck. He started remembering the chase with the Mitsubishi and then he vaguely remembers hitting the windscreen of the truck, and waking up in darkness, blood everywhere with hardly any air. Using the broken bits of the truck to dig his way out and laying in a field for an hour not knowing where he was, who he was or what had happened for hours, in the middle of the night.

His anger started returning. He was Tyrone O'Mally. Everyone was scared of him. Hard as fuck, on and off the rugby pitch. Every one of them are going to pay for this, with their lives. Chapple was lucky but he will get it soon, whoever was on his side that night had better watch his back as well.

At 4.15am Tyrone was packing the tent away with a new-found determination. He had to get to Bristol to get to that Bristol woman who broke his fingers in the club, and her brother who he hadn't quite dealt with. Then back to Devon when the dust had settled. No time to lose.

Lucy was in the spa relaxing in the whirlpool. She was planning her next move and was considering where to live when the money cleared in her account. She thought about all the places she had been and where she had always wanted to go. Mainly Europe, as it would be easier. Mallorca would be good, Ibiza, Greece, Turkey maybe? She could visit them all and pick the best one and set up home there.

She returned to her room, opened the French doors leading to the balcony and took in the perfect view of Fistral Beach, with surfers enjoying the late evening when the regular beach users had left them to it. It was 7.30 and she was starting to feel hungry, so pulled on a mini dress and fixed her hair and make-up quickly before heading for her usual place in the restaurant.

She ordered a large glass of pinot grigio and logged into mobile banking. The waiter set the large glass of almost freezing wine on the table, and Lucy nodded and smiled at the Eastern European girl as she returned the smile and walked off. The mobile banking app revealed her current account a few seconds later revealing that the inheritance had cleared. Lucy gasped and put her hand over her mouth, looking left and right but no-one noticed her. She logged off and locked her phone screen, still covering her mouth, staring into the distance. It took a good five minutes for it to sink in, and the Eastern European waitress came over and asked if she was alright, slightly leaning forward with a look of empathy on her face.

Her question snapped Lucy out of her trance. 'Oh, yes I'm fine thanks, can I have the menu please?' she replied, with a smile.

She ordered rib-eye steak, her favourite and called a taxi into the town centre. Time to celebrate. The town centre was getting busy with stag and hen parties doing the rounds, and plenty of other groups of people out. The first few drinks went down in the first ten minutes and then onto the next bar. Even livelier, with a band setting up their equipment for a gig. She took a table near the stage and sat eyeing up all the men walking in. If only they knew, but she was keeping her secret to herself. She should not need to tell anyone she was loaded as she had the looks anyway.

As she sat drinking, she was deep in thought. Barcelona for a while, do some shopping, enjoy the climate, then come back and set up home. She was sure everything would be settled by then, including Tyrone. She started chatting to a dark-haired lady who came and sat next to her, and without giving away all the information about her new found fortune, told her about her plan to move to Spain for a while, enjoy some sunshine and have a think about what to do with her life. The lady seemed warm and friendly, if a bit old for Lucy, as she was probably going home, to bed around ten, just as the party starts. She was right. Hayley said her goodbyes and left the bar, pulling out her mobile phone as she walked out to call a taxi, Lucy assumed.

Tyrone was marching up the A-39 and was nearing Minehead. As he approached a lay-by on the left, a fairly new looking Harley-Davidson was indicating left, and pulled in to the lay by. The rider dismounted and pulled off his full-face black helmet revealing a 50-something man with a greying goatee. He was fairly lean but had a slight beer gut showing through his protective clothing. He was roughly the same hight as Tyrone, which sparked the idea.

'Nice bike mate.'

'Thanks.' The rider replied, as he lit a cigarette, having hooked the helmet strap over the handlebar of the Harley.

Tyrone didn't waste any time. He looked left and right, no one around. Punched the rider clean in the face with his right fist, knocking him clean off his feet and into the bushes behind. Tyrone quickly followed up and pushed him hard further into the bushes and stamped on his head. The rider at this point was out of it, his arms and legs lip and motionless. Tyrone sifted through the victim's pockets and took the wallet, bike key and mobile phone. He took the victim's right hand and used his index finger to unlock the phone as fingerprint recognition and was relieved when it worked. When he had what he wanted, he rolled the victim into the ditch and dialled Lucy's number from the new mobile.

It was 10.45 and Lucy was searching for flights from Newquay airport to Barcelona and the mobile rang. She didn't recognise the number so was not sure whether to answer it or not. She did, and curiously said, 'Hello.'

Silence. Lucy's voice had Tyrone stunned for a few seconds.

'Hello!' Lucy said impatiently, and then she could hear breathing. It was Tyrone! She thought her heart had stopped, and she dropped the phone onto the dressing table, and almost broke her laptop.

'Lucy, it's me.'

Lucy composed herself and took a deep breath. 'What do you want? Where are you?'

'I'm sorry about everything. I love you. I want to see you again.'

'I love you too. I can't see you, I'm going to live in Spain. You're wanted by the police. Where are you? Why don't you turn yourself in?'

'I've done too much. I'll be given life.'

'Come with me to Spain. I'm in Newquay and I'm flying out on Thursday to Barcelona. I can arrange for you to get there somehow. Come to Newquay and meet me! I need to see you!' Lucy was crying hard. Suddenly nothing mattered but seeing Tyrone again and escaping to Spain for a new life.

Tyrone adjusted the crash helmet and started the Harley. He had only ridden scramblers and smaller bikes before, but how hard could it be? He soon got the hang of it and it was just a case of not pulling the throttle too hard. He headed back down the A39 into Devon, through Barnstaple, Bideford and towards Bude into Cornwall, stopping once to refuel and to ditch the stolen mobile. He arrived at Watergate Bay at 3pm, where he ripped the number plate off the back of the Harley and walked the rest of the way into Newquay and to Towan Beach, where he had arranged to meet Lucy, under the suspension bridge.

Tyrone arrived and looked around for her. The tide was out which made the beach stretch way out and the island to which the bridge provided access was surrounded by sand, until the tide came back in. He looked back towards the surf school and there in the distance he saw Lucy walking towards him holding her shoes in her left hand with a small hand-bag over her shoulder. He was in a summer dress and looked amazing. He looked as expected. His hair was mid-length and messy, he had a beard, in scruffy clothes and had not had a decent wash in days. His teeth were yellow, and he had lost a significant amount of weight. He had a cut on his right fist which had dried up blood over his hand from the biker and his walking boots were badly worn out.

Lucy slowed down as she approached him and was taken aback when she saw the state that he was in. It didn't stop her dropping her shoes and rushing in and hugging him tightly for a full two minutes, both of them in tears.

She took him back to the hotel and left him in the room while she went back into town and bought new clothes for him. She arranged a hair appointment, but he refused to go so she tidied it up for him Later that night, after sex, they went to the marina and had a walk around. Tyrone was on edge and did not know what Lucy had planned for the future, or for the night, but he was concerned that she was going to turn him in.

By then there was a high tide and there was a yacht moored on the dockside. It was at least 40 feet long and was being prepared for a long trip. 'Where are you going?' Lucy asked politely.

'We're going around the Med tomorrow morning,' the woman answered excitedly.

Lucy saw the opportunity and immediately started a long conversation with the woman and her husband. 'My friend wants to go to Barcelona. Would he be able to come along? I will pay for him, name the price.'

The couple looked at each other and the husband looked at Lucy and Tyrone and asked 'Can you give us a minute please?' and they disappeared into the cabin.

Tyrone looked at Lucy 'What are you doing? You can't afford this?'

'Don't worry about a thing. I've got it sorted.' Lucy replied.

The couple reappeared and the woman looked at Lucy and Tyrone. 'Well, we have had a chat, and we can take your friend if he helps out throughout the trip and you pay us £500.'

Lucy looked at Tyrone 'You will help out, won't you?'

'Of course I will, but.'

Before he could finish, Lucy looked back at the couple and said, 'I'll give you £1000, but here's the deal.'

Chapter 27

Shelley was laying on the lounge carpet playing with India. Wearing loose cotton trousers and a fleece with her hair tied back feeling relaxed and content with being home. It had been quite a trip visiting Spain secretly and doing what she did best for the firm. Keeping it a secret from Jack was the tricky bit. She thought he must suspect something as she often disappears to these secret conferences and never talks too much about Scotland. She had actually only been to Scotland twice in her life.

Jack came home from work and as he closed the front door behind him, said 'Hello!' In a gentle but loud voice.

'Daddy's home!' Shelley said with a look of glee as she raised herself off the floor and as Jack entered the lounge, she wrapped herself around him. 'I love you! I've missed you so much.'

Jack hugged her too, and kissed her, but she noticed that there was a lack of warmth. 'Are you OK love?'

'Yes, fine love, I'm just tired. It's been hectic at work.'

Shelley's phone vibrated on the carpet and India picked it up and went to chew the corner. 'No love, I'll have that.' As she gently replaced the phone with a squeaky toy. She looked at the screen and opened the text message and felt Jack behind her. She closed the screen and turned to Jack to hug him again.

'What was the message?' He asked, half smiling.

'Just work love, it can wait.'

'Come on, what was it? Don't be shy, we don't have secrets, do we?'

Shelley tried to hide her nerves as she opened the message. 'Miguel paid up. No further action required'. 'There you go love, just work. A client hadn't paid so we don't have to get the solicitors involved.'

Jack looked serious, but he had to believe her. For now. Shelley discretely breathed a sigh of relief for dissolving the situation, but she knew it was just a matter of time. She knew she would have to tell him the truth one day. What if she got hurt during a job? That would be unexplainable.

Tyrone prised himself from Lucy looking deep into her eyes and rolled onto his back lying next to her. Lucy rolled onto her side with her head on his upper arm and her hand on his chest. They were silent for ten minutes knowing that they had to get up and prepare shortly as they had arranged to meet at the marina at ten. It was 7:30.

Lucy arrived back from shopping at 9:30 and Tyrone was dressed and packing the new clothes which Lucy had picked up the day before. All designer gear including a North Face sailing jacket which must have cost hundreds. He was still curious about all this money she was willing to spend, but when they were in Barcelona, he would have plenty of time to ask.

They arrived five minutes early, but Ann and Mike were all set to go, sat on the stern prepared to greet their new friend. Tyrone put on his friendliest face and smiled as he approached the yacht wheeling his suitcase, with his brand-new backpack bursting with food and toiletries. Lucy grasping his right hand as they approached.

'This is it then, enjoy the trip and make sure you call me when you get there. If you can't get through, I'll be at this location every day at 6 pm.' Lucy gave Tyrone a piece of paper with a name and address of a bar on Las Ramblas. He hugged him tightly and kissed him on the lips before watching him hand his luggage to Mike on the deck, which was almost level with the dock during high tide, then climber on board and shook hands with both his shipmates, still half smiling. At this point Ann could sense immediately that separation anxiety was already hitting Tyrone and Lucy as her eye-brows were sloped from inside to out and she was smiling slightly downwards. Tyrone was also sighing loudly with each breath and glancing at Lucy blinking and waving. He was trying his hardest but failing to hide his emotions. This was unlike him, as he never could display emotion even in times when others would seriously struggle.

Mike untied the yacht, and they were away, negotiating through the marina and within a few minutes they were a few hundred meters into the Bristol channel. Mike and Tyrone were getting to know each other whilst Mike was at the wheel. 'So, you were a machine operator then?' Mike asked.

'Yes, I started as a labourer, and someone asked me to jump on and give it a go when I was about 18 and I enjoyed it so much I took all the courses. Never looked back. Easy work really. How about you? What's your background?'

'I was in the Royal Marines for 20-years. Retired last year with a pension. I had a great time seeing the world, but it took its toll on me a bit. Particularly Afghanistan.'

Tyrone felt slightly inadequate knowing that Mike had served in an elite force for 20-years. They were similar in size, but Mike was still extremely fit looking and had an edge to him which Tyrone liked but was slightly intimidated by. A direct and fairly loud talker who without fail made eye contact, but friendly and welcoming at the same time. Knowing that he had to behave himself on this trip which he was not used to made him uneasy.

Ann came onto the deck with a tray full of sandwiches and three bottles of lager. 'How's it going?'

Mike replied, 'Fine, we'll have some lunch and then kill the engine and set the rigs up. We should be away from England before sunset.'

Ann handed out the bottles and turned to Tyrone. 'Glad Mike knows what he's doing, this is all new to me Tyrone, how about you? Have you ever done any sailing?'

'Just a bit with my uncle years ago. We went around the Isle of Wight. He had a small yacht he kept at Cowes. I think he still has it, but I haven't seen him in years. I really enjoyed it but can't remember much about how to sail unfortunately. I am a quick learner though,' Tyrone replied sheepishly, hiding the fact it was a pack of lies. His uncle hated him.

'Don't worry mate, By the time we get to the Med, you'll be a qualified sailor,' Mike said as he offered his bottle up for a cheers.

The sea was unusually calm as they passed the Scilly Isles, and the sun was disappearing slowly on the perfect horizon. It was the perfect summer evening, and they could only hear the sails and the water lapping against the bow. Tyrone knew there was no turning back now, but he was also feeling relieved that he was not on the run. He felt safe in that the police could no longer find him, but unsure of the sailing trip he was on. He stood on the bow alone for around 30 minutes thinking and staring into space before Ann appeared next to him. 'Mike asked if you could take the wheel for a couple of hours. He will show you what to do, then he's going to get his head down for a bit.'

'Yes, of course I will.'

Mike showed him what to look out for and confirmed

that if there were any issues just to shout for him. Tyrone was then steering a 40-foot yacht in the Atlantic in the dark. 'Shit!' he thought.

Around midnight, Mike re-appeared with just shorts on, and Tyrone was relieved, but felt that he enjoyed the experience. Mike checked the sat-nav and looked up at Tyrone with a smile. 'Bang on course mate. Great work.'

'Thanks mate,' Tyrone replied, noticing a tattoo on Mike's upper right arm, and there was no mistake what it was. He was ex- special forces. The tattoo was the symbol of the SBS! Tyrone had instant respect for Mike, as he noticed scars all over his body but looked away and tried not to stare. 'Better behave myself,' he thought.

Tyrone went to bed and noticed Ann was still up reading. She had a small light on as she sat up in bed with her glasses on and looked over them giving Tyrone a nod and smile as he climbed into his bed at the other end of the yacht. 'Good night Ann,' he said politely.

'Sleep well,' she gently replied, turning a page of her book.

Tyrone slept like never before. He seemed to be rocked to sleep by the motion of the yacht and fell into a deep sleep which lasted until 6.30 am. He got straight up, seeing that Mike was asleep in the bed opposite and headed for the deck where Ann was at the wheel. 'Good morning Ann,' he said looking around at the sea.

'Hi Tyrone, sleep well?' she asked, sipping coffee from a plastic cup with a lid.

'I haven't slept that well in a long time,' he replied.

'Great! Help yourself to coffee and breakfast, then you can take over for a bit if you want?'

Tyrone made himself toast and coffee and sat next to Ann who was still behind the wheel. There was something warm about her which was drawing him to her. She was gorgeous with shoulder length brown hair, which was lighter at the ends, due to the sun. She was thin, but not skinny and wore which he would describe as 'clean hippy' clothing. She was probably mid- 40s with her intelligence and maturity but would get away with saying she was in her 30s with her looks. Tyrone was totally back in love with Lucy so there was no way he would try anything. Also knowing that her ex-SBS husband was a few feet away. With that in mind, Ann also felt safe.

'How long have you been with Lucy then?' she asked.

'Well, we have been together for about six-years, but we recently split up. We just got back together and decided to start over in Barcelona. The trouble is I don't like flying,' he said, eyebrows raised.

Ann saw the lie before it came out, but let it go. She knew she had time to get the truth out of him. She would try today though. That was the plan.

Flight number BA2152 to Barcelona, please make your way to Gate Number 17, as your flight is now boarding.

Lucy was on her third glass of wine and feeling it. She was high on life, knowing that there was a clean break and a new beginning in a beautiful country waiting for her. She was glancing around at the tourists in Bristol airport with a satisfies feeling that they would be returning to their 9-5 jobs a week or so later and that she had a one- way ticket.

She picked herself up and headed for gate 17 and passed by the queue as she was priority boarding and first class. She said nothing as her ticket and passport was checked, and hardly made eye contact with the officials, in an almost arrogant manner, and then glided across the tarmac, up the steps onto the Airbus A320.

As the plane reached altitude the hostess approached Lucy. 'Can I get you anything madam?'

'I'd like some Pringles and a Prosecco please.' Lucy said, making eye contact.

The hostess gently nodded and turned away with a professional look. Lucy looked out of the window seeing the west of England and the Bristol Channel in the distance as the flight moved South towards the English Channel. She was feeling drowsy at this point as she had been drinking since 9am, and it was nearly 1 pm and another drink was on the way, courtesy of first- class service. Glancing around at the other passengers in the vicinity, there were only six as the first- class part was fairly small, but she didn't know any better as she had always travelled economy before today. There was a 60- something wiry man sat reading what looked like legal documents, a woman in her 40s, well dressed but flat out snoring with saliva falling from her open mouth and a 20- something man who appeared to be a football player with all the trimmings from a super-fit body to all the designer gear and expensive jewellery. She took the mirror out of her bag, checked herself out and reapplied her make-up momentarily. Not that she was interested, but seeing this guy just prompted her to ensure she looked OK. Usually, she would have been there trying to attract his attention but with Tyrone back on the scene she was keen to rebuild her relationship and new life with him.

'Tell me about Lucy, Tyrone.' Ann asked, over the cabin table.

'We were together for six-years, then we split for a year or so. We decided to get back together having met up again and start a new life in Spain. She's the love of my life. I was lost when we were apart,' Tyrone said trying unconvincingly to be sincere. Although he actually meant it.

Ann looked into his eyes sympathetically for what seemed like five-minutes to Tyrone. He started feeling uneasy. As he looked as if he was about to leave the table, Ann asked, 'Why did you separate?'

Tyrone was visibly unhappy with the question but felt

compelled to answer. Trying hard to think of an answer which was not going to give away too much. 'We had a big argument after she stayed out all night and I accused her of sleeping with someone else. I will never know if she did, or not but she left that day and went to live with family in Devon.'

Ann was motionless and looked sympathetically at Tyrone over the table, as Mike passed by the porthole window and back to the stern wheel whistling to himself, knowing what Ann was doing. 'Did you know Lucy when you were a child?' she asked, not changing her facial expression.

'No, I met her in a rugby club through a friend. He was dating a girl and Lucy was her best friend at the time. I played a cup game in a place called Chipping Sodbury and we all met in a bar near the local rugby club. We started chatting and got on well. She likes the rough guys. You know the type.' He said smiling, then remembering that Ann was married to an ex-SBS operator. His face sank momentarily. 'How about you? Do you work when you are not travelling?' he asked, trying to divert the conversation.

'I am a CEO of a national charity. Have you heard of Resting Hearts?' Ann asked.

'Yes, aren't they a big organisation helping ex-military with PTSD?'

'That's part of what we do. I'm the lead counsellor, trainer and CEO. I'm on a sabbatical for the summer.'

Tyrone was silent, eye-brows raised for a moment. He was on a yacht with an ex- elite soldier and a counsellor sailing to Barcelona. How did that happen? 'Wow! You two are incredible! I'm just a digger driver from Bristol. I feel like a bit of a loser.'

'Don't be silly! It's not about that. You're building a new life in Barcelona, what an adventure! You should be proud!'

'How about family at home? Who are you leaving behind?' Ann asked, with a plan.

'Mum was fine about it,' Tyrone said, with every inch of his persona screaming the lie. 'She's looking forward to visiting now and again and getting cheap holidays.' He said smiling.

Ann looked at him, expressionless. She held the look for 20- plus seconds and Tyrone was getting agitated. 'Was it just you and Mum at home?'

Tyrone breathed in deeply and looked into space, between Ann and the far end of the cabin. He exhaled and took in another breath before talking again. 'Dad died when I was eight- years old, so yes, just us two.'

'What can you remember about your dad?' Ann asked, feeling like she was finally getting somewhere.

Tyrone was reluctant to talk about it, as it hurt when he remembered what happened. His mum tried her hardest to make him erase it from his memory. 'He was a brick layer, and most days would go to the pub after work, coming home at around 8:30 – 9:30, most of the time, drunk. Mum used to jump out of her chair when she heard the door open and serve his dinner up and make him a cup of tea. She seemed scared of him.

Most of the time, he would just eat his dinner, watch telly and that was it. But sometimes he would get angry about stuff. I didn't know what was going on because they were talking about adult things. I'd just be playing with my toys on the floor.

'Sometimes he used to slap Mum across the face, sometimes punch her hard in the stomach. She would curl up on the floor and struggle to walk when she took me to bed, but she always did. She made a point of it.' Tyrone was welling up and his chin was raising, remembering his Mum being abused.'

Ann sat back with a sympathetic look and listened intently.

'There was this one time when Dad came home earlier

than usual but had been drinking more. They had been raised off from work so spent the day in the pub. He was really drunk. I was a bit scared, but it I thought at the time that it always ended, and we would always go to bed and forget about it. They started shouting at each other as I played with my toys on the carpet and out of nowhere, Mum landed next to me, unconscious. I still don't know the full story and never will. She spent two nights in hospital with a fractured skull and concussion.'

'How did you feel when you saw that happen?' Ann asked.

Tyrone had never been asked that before. In fact, no one had ever asked him how he felt about anything, or he never let them. He looked gaunt and unsure how to answer the question. Not that he didn't want to answer, he simply did not know. He was silent for a couple of minutes reliving the moment, thinking about it. 'I thought she was dead,' he said quietly. 'I poked her in the arm and said "Mummy", but she didn't say anything, so I thought she was gone. I started crying and dad picked me up, looked me in the eyes and said, 'I'm taking you to bed, and you're staying there.' He basically threw me onto my bed and slammed the bedroom door. The next thing I knew was the following morning when he woke me up and took me to hospital to see her. On the way he said she had fallen over and hit her head. He kept saying it to me all the way to hospital.'

'Did anything like this happen again?' Ann asked.

'Yes, most weeks they would kick off. Same old crap, Dad getting drunk and Mum getting mouthy. He broke her arm once, she often had black eyes, you name it.' Tyrone looked angry as he was telling Ann about it. Like he wanted revenge.

'You said your dad died when you were eight. How did that happen. Do you know?'

Tyrone shook his head slowly. 'I still don't know how he died. I wasn't allowed to go to the funeral either. Not that I wanted to after all he did to Mum over the years. He was just not there anymore, and Mum seemed much less stressed. Although she worked three days per week and I was picked up from school and looked after by one of her friends, it was just us two.'

'How was that?'

Tyrone was slow to answer. He took a long drag of coffee and closed his eyes. 'I was bored. I loved Mum and wanted to protect her from anyone who came to the door, or came in for a cup of tea, or just about anyone. Not that she needed it by then, she was hard as nails, and the proper Irish mouth on her.'

'Did you have may friends?'

'Yes, but not many. I was seen as the quiet one. I was bigger than most of the other kids and had a reputation for being a bit of a hand full. Most other kids my age kept away from me, so I used to have mates who were a year or two older. Mum used to have friends whose children used to come around to ours sometimes when I was young. Some were OK, I guess. They never lasted long though, never came back but I didn't get it at the time.' Tyrone held his hands over his face, holding back tears.

'What didn't you get?'

Tyrone sniffed through his closed hands. Wiped his face and his eyes repeatedly with his palms, leaving his eyes bloodshot and his upper cheeks red. 'One of Mum's friends had a girl the same age as me. Her name was Kelly. I could not keep my eyes off her at the time. I was eight and she was six. It was not long after my dad had disappeared, and I was not sure what was going on. We would play on the floor in my bedroom while our Mums would chat downstairs and I would just watch her. It was the first time I ever really liked someone.' Tyrone stopped talking and stared into nothing.

Ann looked at him, observing his expression, waiting for him to continue. A tear started forming in his eye, but he quickly wiped it away.

'She used to play with the toys, but not pay me any attention. I wanted her to play with me. Talk to me. Look at me. But she wanted to play with my transformers and Pokémon toys instead. So, I pushed her, but she just shrugged me off, thinking that I did it by accident.' Tears started appearing in Tyrone's eyes, and he was struggling to stop them. 'Then I grabbed her arm. Not hard, but enough to get a reaction. She looked at me and said "OUCH!" It felt good, because I had her attention. But she carried on playing with the toys, ignoring me again for what felt like hours. I was just looking at her. I really liked her.' Tyrone looked at Ann with desperate eyes, Ann looking back expressionless.

'It was then,' Tyrone held his face silently for a few seconds. 'I slapped her.' He continued to hold his face with his elbows on the cabin table. His hands damp with tears.

'I though, if I hurt her, maybe she would pay attention to me. She ran downstairs crying, and we ever saw them again. Soon after apparently, they moved to Devon and ran a farm. We found out that she died two years later from meningitis. And I didn't find out until a couple of years ago that she was actually Lucy's cousin.'

Ann handed Tyrone some tissues and he wiped his face repeatedly until they were saturated with tears. Then he took some more tissues and did the same. He was confused, as no one had opened him up before, like he was just a badly behaved boy and that was it. Suddenly, there were reasons why he was a dick head. He always knew he was acting up, and that it was upsetting for everyone around him, particularly his Mum, but he didn't know why. Neither did he know how to change.

Chapter 28

Shelley was in the meeting room on her laptop reading through her PowerPoint ahead of the upcoming board meeting. She was fully focussed on her work with the construction company whilst in the office and had a strength removing all other aspects of her life whenever she was in a separate application.

In walked Paul. A senior project manager who loved himself and joined the company six-months previously, actively licking butt. Wearing a tweed suit style jacket and black chino's which were slightly too tight, dark grey shirt with the top two buttons open and curtained, brown hair. He threw down a coaster onto the table opposite Shelley like throwing a frisbee and landed his coffee mug on it before loudly kicking a chair back and sitting down with a loud sigh, looking straight at Shelley, mainly at her breasts.

Shelley was aware of him before he entered the room but coldly ignored him, concentrating on her work, or at least pretending to.

'Alright Shel?' he said with a smug look on his face as if they were close friends, or he owned her, head slightly tilted back.

Shelley took her time answering. Then without looking up and typing on her laptop she replied. 'Fine thanks Paul,

How's Basingstoke going? I hear you have had client issues?' not taking her eyes off the screen or changing her facial expression.

His face slightly dropped, and Shelley's comment had the desired effect, damping down his ego.

'That's all sorted now, it was a misunderstanding regarding a planning application for block B. What the hell has that got to do with you anyway? I'm a senior PM, and you're a glorified secretary. Be careful talking to me like that darling, I'll have you fired!' he said leaning back, looking slightly annoyed and then taking a large gulp of coffee before firmly placing his mug back on the coaster louder than necessary on purpose.

Shelley did not respond verbally or physically. Her expression did not change or her facial expression. He would be great at acting because inside she was burning up. This guy in front of her was failing at his job but so blind-sided by butt licking the directors that he could not see what was actually happening on his own projects.

'Did you hear me?' he asked, in a raised voice.

Shelley knew that her next response would be the big one. She waited a few seconds and said calmly, 'I heard you.' She tilted her laptop screen forward, so she had a full view of the egomaniac sat opposite. 'So, if you have any issues, contact HR,' she said, with a poker face. 'By the way I manage the HR department. I must say, this chat has highlighted a potential observation issue on your side. Anyway, if I were a glorified secretary, would you still talk to me like that? As this could be a HR issue?'

Paul looked away and shook his head slowly, lips pursed and right leg shaking gently. 'Unbelievable. I can't believe you're getting away with this. In my last job. I would have fired you on the spot!' he said just loud enough, but not so that it could be heard outside the room. 'What is it about you that's so special to this lot then? Or is it obvious?' he said, eyebrows raised, making no secret about staring at her breasts. 'You obviously look after yourself, what do you do for fitness? Cycling? Swimming?' he started to smile.

'Keep talking Paul, this is starting to get interesting,' Shelley replied, looking straight into his eyes with a poker face.

'Well, you're clearly the best- looking bird in the office, so what's your secret? Implants? Botox?'

'What do you mean Paul?' Shelley asked, gently, knowing she probably already had enough to get him fired for sexual harassment.

'I'm just paying complements darling.' He said with a smug grin. 'What are you doing after work? Dinner is on me.' At this point he thought he had it nailed.

Shelley paused for a few seconds, gathering her thoughts. 'I appreciate your complements, albeit slightly sexist, misogynistic and damn right inappropriate, but I am engaged with a young baby. When you ask what I do to keep fit, you really do not want to know. And anyway, I really would not be interested in you even if I was single and desperate. By the way, did you see the notice on the door stating that all conversations in this room are recorded for training and security purposes? Well, the questions relating to implants and Botox were far beyond the boundaries of friendly office banter and could quite easily get you fired in the next five-minutes. So, if you will excuse me for being rude, I have a presentation to complete for the board of directors who will all be in this room in approximately three-minutes. My advice to you, is to sort out your pathetic ego, your failing Basingstoke project, your failing Hounslow project and be very careful how you speak to everyone in this company, in particular, the ladies.'

Paul looked at the door with a concerned expression. He

knew he had made a mistake and was anxious thinking Shelley was going to get him fired. He was looking around the room for CCTV and recording equipment hoping she was bluffing.

Shelley looked at him and then at the desk pod, which had a green flashing light indicating 'record.' Paul raised himself from the swivel chair, grasped his coffee mug and left the room. Doing so, the glazed fire door struck the rubber wall mounted door stop loudly and the over-head closer slowly eased the door to the latch with a gentle click. Shelley took in a long breath and exhaled deeply. Paul was a smoothie and needed taking down a few notches, but she had this harassment in the bag and could turn to it at any time now. He probably should be given a chance to change his ways. He may turn out to be a good project manager, she thought. She looked at the wall mounted clock to her right and decided that she just had time. Leaving the meeting room and to the server room of which there was a restricted access code of which she knew, she entered and closed the door behind her. Alone, as planned, she sat in front of the monitor which had a view of the meeting room up and went onto the options bar. Opening the audio recordings tab, she stopped the recording of the meeting room and took the timeline of the previous 20 minutes. Saved it as a file and emailed it to her personal google mail account. She then resumed the meeting room recordings and left the server room unnoticed.

She sat down just in time, as the directors started arriving. Andrew was a tall, smartly dressed guy with short brown hair. He was the managing director, and everyone feared getting on the wrong side of him, for good reason. He had a history of tearing people to pieces verbally in meetings if they were not performing to his standards also, but secretly he was leader of the mob. He was followed into the meeting room by all the other board members who were calm, but business like as they sat around the table finishing off small talk before business.

Andrew looked at Shelley. 'How are you, Shelley? How's Jack and India?' with a genuine smile.

'They're fine thanks Andrew. A full night's sleep would be nice,' she said smiling back.

The meeting lasted two hours and Shelley finished her presentation with the latest statistics and asked if there were any questions. Going around the table, no one had any further input and the meeting ended. As the directors started back onto small talk and the weather, Andrew looked at Shelley over the table and said quietly, almost whispering, 'Can we have a chat after please?' with his eye-brows raised.

'Of course.' Shelley replied, knowing it was not going to be construction-related.

The rest of the directors filed out of the room chatting and Andrew stayed behind as Shelley unplugged power and HDMI cables into her bag, followed by her laptop. She looked up as Andrew was closing the door.

'There's news from Barcelona Shelley. Apparently, your friend Tyrone is on his way there to start a new life, not on the wanted list. Lucy is already there looking at property. She was the legal benefactor from Chris and Theresa's estate and now back looking after Tyrone. He's sailing there privately to avoid border control and due to arrive this week some time.

'He needs to disappear permanently Shelley, and I thought you might want the job after what happened with your brother.'

Shelley was staring at Andrew, all sorts of thoughts running through her head. This bastard was supposed to have been taken out a long time ago. It also explained significant losses in the firm since the initial attempt on his assassination. She started breathing heavier than usual, the adrenaline hitting her. 'No question Andrew. I'll do it. Just pay my expenses and we can put a plan together with the locals.'

'It is unconfirmed, but we strongly believe he is behind all the losses over the last 18-months. This needs to hurt, Shelley, but we can't have you putting yourself in danger. You have a family now, and you are too important to the firm, and this business. I need you to assure me that you are up for this and that you will be alright.'

Shelley stood up from her swivel chair. 'I will do most of the work remotely and take a flight over when the good news is delivered to him. I'll be fine Andrew. We have good assets there who we work with regularly. I'm going to make him uncomfortable first and then personally deliver the news. That's the intention.'

'OK, that sounds fine. If you have any issues, call me or Brian. I'll let you take this one on in its entirety and report back with regular updates. Just be careful, this guy is actually quite dangerous.'

'I know, I have had the pleasure, Andrew. I broke his finger in a bar last year and I'm surprised he hasn't come after me since.'

Andrew laughed and left the boardroom heading straight to the server room to delete the dialogue from their conversation. As he approached the door, Paul was leaving, and looked slightly wide-eyed as Andrew approached. The server room door was slowly closing behind him,

'Hi Paul, what were you doing in there?'

'Ah just a restart Andrew, I couldn't connect to the printer for some reason,' he said slightly nervously.

Andrew entered the room and went straight to the monitor. Tapping the same password as Shelley did earlier, he scrolled back through the dialogue, but it had been removed.

He thought it was strange but didn't dwell too much on it. As he left, Shelley was entering, 'I was just going to remove that conversation, Andrew. Have you already done it?'

'It was already gone. It may have been a glitch in the system so don't worry, Paul was leaving as I entered, and he has had some IT issues today apparently.'

Shelley froze. 'Andrew, we need to be careful here. Can I talk to you?' She told him everything.

'I can take this firm down now; I have everything I need. They're corrupt gangsters and I could get some serious money out of this!' Paul said on his hands free whilst driving back home to Swindon.

'Be careful mate, it sounds like the are big players. You could be banging on a very big door there.' George replied. George was an old workmate who stayed in touch for the last 20-years and Paul believed he was his best friend. George thought differently but still liked him for some reason. He didn't know why, as Paul was a married man but had numerous affairs of which he badly kept secret. He wasn't bothered if his wife found out, as he was the bread-winner and he could do what he wanted. George disagreed with him but liked him for some reason.

'Nah, don't worry mate, I can look after myself against some small- town gangster wannabes,'Paul said arrogantly. As he finished the call, the agency called him.

'Hi Paul, its Phil, from People Resourcing. The company have a number of outstanding invoices, so we are pulling resources from your site tomorrow in Basingstoke. Sorry mate.'

'What? I'm not getting any site managers tomorrow. That's ridiculous! Send them in and I'll sort it out mate.'

'I can't send any resources until the invoices are settled mate. Company policy. Sorry Paul,' Phil said, pretending to be sincere.

Paul ended the call and dialled the accounts department in the office. 'This is Paul Burton. I have had a message from People Resourcing saying that they have not been paid. They have pulled all resources from my project so I would appreciate it if this could be sorted out tomorrow at the very latest. Please call me back urgently.'

No answer or call back. After the fifth call, at 5 pm, Paul finally got through to Chloe.

'Yes, there is a dispute on their invoices Paul, so Andrew is not authorising payments until it is cleared up,' Chloe said nervously.

'Let me know when its sorted please Chloe. I will have to run the project myself until then.'

Paul was approaching home and thinking about how to wriggle out of being site based where everyone knew where he was. He would have to cancel golf in the morning at South Marston and go to Basingstoke to cover the site until the idiots in accounts have sorted the issue out. He arrived home too early, and his wife was still there which he didn't want. She was due to go to tennis club at 4pm but it was 4:10 and she was still there.

'Hi love' he said as he entered the 2- bed semi in the middle of Swindon.

'Hi, I'm not going tonight because I have pulled my calf. Shall we eat out?'

'Yes, OK, but I need to be in Basingstoke early in the morning so not a late one love.'

Six-thirty in the morning and the traffic was virtually non-existent driving from Newbury to Basingstoke apart from the odd lorry Paul was driving too fast in his BMW 3 Series and enjoying it. It was a distraction from the latest developments with the agency and the face that he had two site managers which were not likely to be back on site for the coming week, probably longer. He arrived on site at 7.15, earlier than anyone else to give him time to bring himself up to date with the previous week and prepare to run the project hands-on for the foreseeable.

As he sat in the site office which was stacked above the canteen in a portable unit, he sorted through his emails and decided which ones to reply to whilst looking out of the window. A couple of contractors' vans pulled into the car park and the workers were stretching and yawning as they left the cabs and started putting on their safety boots and high visibility jackets.

More vans and cars turned up and the canteen was becoming loud with activity, and Paul noticed a black Land Rover Discovery Sport park up. As he completed a phone call to a supplier he watched as Shelley climbed out of the passenger door and Andrew from the driver's door. He had a tremor of anxiety momentarily running through his chest and then carried on working.

Whilst typing an email, Paul watched in his peripheral vision as Shelley and Andrew changed into their safety boots at the rear of the Discovery, appearing to be in calm conversation. Paul was still confused what it was about this young, attractive woman that was so important to the managing director? Maybe they were having an affair? Anyway, they were entering his site, so it was his rules. He raised his head and straightened his back with his shoulders back as he heard them coming up the temporary metal stairs. Andrew was first to enter the office. 'Hi Andrew, this is unexpected. To what do I owe this pleasure?' as he said it, he deliberately put his back to the door to make it difficult for Shelley to enter.

'We're going to base ourselves here for the day, me and Shelley,' Andrew replied, gently pushing Paul's shoulder to make way for Shelley.

'Hi Shel,' Paul said passively with a lower tone, 'Do us a

favour, put the kettle on. I'll have a coffee with one sugar. Tea or coffee Andrew?'

Shelley looked at Paul with a slight grin.

'You can make the coffee Paul, I'll have white with no sugar, Shelley will have one sugar. Thanks.' Andrew stared at him sternly as he said it, and then turned away, putting his laptop bag on one of the spare desks, Shelley sitting at the other spare desk opposite Andrew. Both raising their eyebrows as Paul loudly filled the kettle and slammed it back onto its base before flicking the on switch. As the kettle boiled, footsteps could be heard on the metal stairs and then the office door swung open and a rugged, six- foot tree guy in a high visibility vest over a t-shirt blocked the sunlight, and quietly, but deeply asked for a site induction.

Paul served the coffee to Andrew and Shelley and said, 'Yes, come into the back office and I'll induct you. Who do you work for?'

'The groundworkers mate,' Tony said, glancing at Shelley and Andrew as he followed Paul into the other section of the portable office. 'I'm here to help with concreting the pile caps later this afternoon.'

Paul ignored him and started giving the site health and safety induction, giving Tony the form to fill out. Shelley and Andrew remained quiet as they logged onto their laptops.

The day went slowly, and Paul was rushing around, trying hard to impress Andrew with his management skills and assuring him that he was in control of the project. Andrew just sat at his laptop, not paying attention and leaving the office to make the occasional phone call in private. Shelley was doing the same, expressionless as Paul seemed to get too close to her when he passed her desk, trying to see what was on her screen as he went. Just emails were on show and

Shelley was conscious of his irritation, as it appeared that she was not doing much, and he was flat out.

Andrew returned to the site office and started putting on his high visibility vest over his suit jacket. 'Paul, can you show us around please?'

Shelley stood up slowly, locking her laptop screen and reached for her high vis and hard hat from her bag. Whilst she did, Paul was watching from behind, in admiration of her gorgeous bum.

They walked across to the site and into the building. Most of the workers were on lunch, which Andrew planned, and Paul was narrating the progress as they went. 'This is the lift shaft which was built using 7-newton 140-millimetre concrete blocks. The base is being concreted tomorrow to bring it up to level. That's the reinforcing being fitted at the moment.' They peered over the edge of a lift opening which had scaffold tubes as edge protection. The drop from the ground floor was around two- metres into the pit where a steel cage was being fitted.

'Should this have been done before the blockwork went up Paul?' Andrew asked. 'Now you are going to struggle getting the concrete in.' His voice slightly raised.

'Jeff was supposed to have done it but for some reason it didn't happen at the time,' Paul replied defensively.

'Jeff was an agency manager mate. You need to be on top of this sort of thing in future. Never assume it's done unless you see it for yourself.'

Paul knew he was right and the lie he told was not going to stick. He forgot himself that this work needed to be done at the time but tried to blame someone else, which he often did. They continued up through the building using a scaffold staircase to the fourth floor. The main structure was up and there were window openings providing a view over the rear part of the site where the ground workers were preparing for concrete. As they watched a concrete wagon reversed into position and released a full load into a pit, covering a steel cage, but the trench was only half full. The groundworkers started up small generators and started poking the concrete with vibrating rods which crudely levelled it, expelling air from the mix as it settled.

As they started walking back to the staircase, Shelley walked over to the lift shaft which at fourth-floor level had a fence across which was screwed into the masonry firmly. As she approached, Andrew appeared next to her, and they pretended to observe something in the shaft. Paul curiously walked over, not wanting to lose sight of the two visitors, and stood slightly back, and between them. 'Is there a problem?'

'We do have a slight issue Paul, yes.' Andrew said, looking straight at him. 'And I think you know what it is, don't you?'

Paul looked stunned. As he glanced between Andrew and Shelley, he heard footsteps, and the light from the stairwell darkened as the man mountain that was the new site arrival appeared. 'What are you doing here? We're having a private conversation if you don't mind. You should be helping with the concrete!' he said angrily.

As he stared at John, Shelley's elbow connected hard into the back of his neck accurately beneath the skull, knocking him forward, stunned but not unconscious. As he landed, Tony produced a battery drill from his coat and proceeded to undo the wire fencing from the lift shaft. As he did, Shelley held Paul in a double goose neck with his wrists twisted. Paul was groaning and didn't know what was going on. Andrew emptied Paul's pockets of tissue, a mobile phone and his wallet before Tony came over and picked Paul up by the rear collar and belt, as if he was a bag of sugar. He carried him to the lift shaft and dropped him head-first without hesitation, then replaced the fence. They all headed down to the ground floor at a rate, and Shelley went straight to the canteen where she held a lengthy safety briefing for all the site attendees.

Andrew supervised as Tony poured a tonne of concrete into the base of the lift shaft and then another one until it reached the level line markers. The concrete easily covered the body with an extra cubic meter of concrete on top. Andrew handed him the phone and wallet, shook his hand and said, 'Well done mate. You know what to do with the car, don't you?'

'Yes mate, leave it to me.' Tony said with a menacing smile. He went straight to the changing room and put on a complete change of clothing, bagging up his soiled site wear and placing it under Shelley's temporary desk before taking the BMW off site. He drove out of Basingstoke and headed towards Southampton, then West towards Bournemouth.

Shelley completed her safety briefing regarding working at height and when she witnessed all attendees sign the register went back up to the site office. Andrew was already sat at his laptop tracking the BMW on the map, ensuring there were no issues.

Tony drove at the speed limit to ensure he was not attracting the attention of the police, or any other motorists as he headed for the coast. He arrived on Bournemouth sea front as night fell and placed the mobile phone and wallet in the glove compartment on top of the CDs. Reaching into his bag, he produced cleaning gear and wherever he had touched the car, wiped the surface after spraying with cleaning fluid. He then placed the sealed envelope on the passenger seat with the faked suicide note inside, locked the car and walked off down the sea front towards the station. He left it a couple of minutes before throwing the car key as far as he could into the sea.

Chapter 29

It was day four of the 16- day sail to Barcelona. Tyrone was loving it. He was spending more time at the wheel now that he was getting used to it and recognising issues when they occur, but more importantly, knowing what to do about it. Mike was able to relax and enjoy the view across the sea and relax with Ann. They were lying in bed mid-afternoon having had sex, whilst Tyrone was at the wheel.

'How's it going with Tyrone?' Mike asked.

'He had a bit of a bad start in life which made him angry. I'm still working on him, but he'll be a different person when he sees Lucy again. The main thing is, he trusts us.' Ann said, in a relaxed voice.

'He's picking up sailing really well. Listening, learning and doing what he's told. I actually quite like him. He reminds me of some of the lads from the marines. Bit of a handful, full of issues but willing to learn and put in the work.'

Lucy was looking at properties in Barcelona. It was her second day in the hotel but not wasting any time. If she stayed in that suite too long, she would get too used to it and not buy anything. It would not take long for the money to start to disappear.

She had viewed two villas that morning, but both failed

to meet her expectations and seemed over-priced. She decided that was enough for the day and found a cafe bar where she ordered a snack and a glass of chardonnay. The weather was hot, but not overwhelming, around 27 degrees with a light breeze. Perfect for a relax watching the world go by, dreaming about the future. She was already in love with Barcelona and was never planning to return to the UK. Life was good, and when Tyrone arrives in a couple of weeks, it would be even better.

After a couple of glasses of wine, Lucy paid the bill and strolled along the sea front, watching the volleyball. It seemed that the only people allowed to play volleyball were beautiful topless women and super fit men. She strolled further and there were fitness frames where people were exercising joggers wearing ear- phones and Segways gliding past silently. She stopped and looked out to sea for a moment, thinking about Tyrone. Was he getting on with Ann and Mike? We didn't even know them, and it was a gamble sending him off with strangers. She knew Tyrone could handle himself and that Mike guy would not stand a chance. She assured herself that everything would be alright, and she would have him back soon.

She took a deep breath and started walking again, this time back the way she came, in the direction of the hotel which was about 400 yards away. She walked slowly taking it all in, almost day-dreaming and then suddenly she was hit in the back hard which knocked her to the ground, nearly scraping her face on the paving. She let out a distressed screech and rolled over onto her back, immediately sitting up to assess the damage to her elbows and knees. She looked around in shock and saw people coming over to help, speaking Spanish. There was no sign of the person who hit her except one guy, an elderly local waving a walking stick and shouting in Spanish at someone disappearing into the distance. Both of Lucy's elbows were skinned and were dripping with blood. One of her knees was also bleeding and both were bruised and already beginning to swell up. A lady came through the crowd with tissues and started patting the wounds. 'Are you OK?' she asked, Lucy was shaking but not emotional at this point.

'I'll be OK, thanks. Are you English?' she asked.

'I'm from Birmingham love. Here for the weekend with my husband. How about you?' Julie asked.

'I've just moved here. I'm looking for a permanent home at the moment, staying at the Icaria Hotel until I find something for me and my Fiancée.' Lucy replied, feeling sorry for herself, but also bragging about her wealth.

They spoke for a couple of minutes and Lucy thanked Julie and Ken for helping her, and invited them both for dinner, on her that evening. They arranged to meet at 8 pm in a bar, then on to a seafood restaurant in town, where Lucy went on her first night.

Lucy went back to the hotel, had a shower and put on a long-sleeved blouse and long skirt so to cover the damage. Looking slightly worse for wear after the events earlier, she knew it would take a while to do her make up. As she started, her mobile phone rang, no identification. 'Hello?' she answered.

'Is that Lucy?' the female caller asked in a Northern English accent.

'Yes, speaking, Who's this please?'

'Hi, this is Bridget Ford from Avon and Somerset Constabulary here, sorry to disturb you, do you have a few minutes?'

Lucy felt her stomach turn, like it was tied in a knot. 'Yes, OK. What's it about?'

'We are following leads regarding your ex-fiancée who is wanted for grievous bodily harm on a police officer. We have reason to believe that you may have been in contact with him recently in Newquay. Is that correct?' Bridget asked.

'No, sorry. I haven't seen him since we split up about two years ago.'

There was a pause for a few seconds. 'I was hoping you could come to the station to have a chat. New Bridewell, in central Bristol. I'm guessing by the foreign ring tone that you're on holiday. When you return, please contact me personally. When are you coming home?'

Lucy thought hard for a second 'I should be able to come in next week. I'm back in England Wednesday so let's say Thursday?'

'Ok, that will be good.' She gave Lucy her mobile number and hung up.

Shelley hung up and went back in the lounge where India was playing on the carpet. 'Hey- up duck, she fell for that one. That should put the shits up her.'

Shelley put on her karate gi, tied on her faded black belt and waited for Jack to come home, feeding India at the table. She was looking deep into India's eyes feeling like the world had stopped. India was her world, and nothing else mattered. She suddenly felt anxious about India's future and if she could protect her from this nasty world. But also protect her from the truth of what she herself was involved in. She started doubting herself. How could she be a loving mother, a soul-mate to India if she was also a major player in a nationwide gang?' She may have to get out sooner that she thought. Always planning to scale down her active role in the next year or so, but, at that moment, looking at her baby daughter, she suddenly wanted out. She also knew that there was unfinished business with Tyrone which needed to be completed. Lucy needed to pay her share from the inheritance and maybe she should also disappear. Miguel had already made contact with Lucy, quite literally, as a 'bit of bad luck', but soon the job would need to be finished. Very soon.

Jack arrived home and walked straight in to greet Shelley and India, who was plastered in baby food, but managed a big smile. 'Hello by beautiful girls!' he said with a big smile, giving Shelley a big kiss on the lips. 'How was your day on site love?' absolutely clueless as to what actually happened.

'Fine thanks love, interesting to see it all happening. I usually just sort it all out remotely, but it was good to spend some time out on site to actually see things like concrete being installed. I enjoyed watching that bit,' she said with a look on her face which Jack could not work out.

Jack picked up the calendar from the kitchen wall and took it into the dining room where Shelley was cleaning up India with wet wipes. 'I'm off to London in two- weeks on a training course for health and safety. It's a condensed Level 3 engineering focussed course which is going to be quite intense apparently.'

'OK Shelley replied, already planning the opportunity. What are the dates?'

'21st to the 25th of September.' Jack replied.

'Oh. OK, that apartment in Barcelona is available that week. I was going to surprise you. That's a shame, I can get cheap flights for all three of us then as well, as schools are back. Don't worry. There will be other times,' she said, looking disappointed.

A few seconds passed, and Jack said, 'Why don't you take India? We can all go together another time. Take the week off and have a break. You deserve it.'

Exactly what Shelley wanted to hear. She paused and said, 'It wouldn't be right without you love. No, I don't think so.'

'Go on, have a rest love. A change of scenery will do you the world of good.'

Shelley was already planning it silently as she left for karate. She would use local resources to look after India while she got to work on her final task. As she pulled up at the leisure centre, she made a phone call from the car. 'Hi Andrew, I have a date for Barcelona, and I need resources and return flights for myself and my daughter. I also need a child-minder whilst working.'

'OK, nice work Shelley, just list down your requirements and I will make sure it happens.' The call ended.

The Karate session felt better than usual, and Shelley taught a good class. She suddenly felt energised once again. She felt like now that there was an opening, she could do the job discreetly and Jack would not have any idea what was going on. She was now looking forward to it.

Lucy worked her way through the crowds as she made her way to the bar where she arranged to meet her new-found friends. She was trying hard not to think about the phone call from the Bristol police earlier, but she could not blank it out. Could they collude with the Spanish and send her back for questioning? And if Tyrone was arrested and sent back, she could also be deported.

She entered the bar with a smile and Julie and Ken, both greeted her with hand-shakes. Ken was a 50-year-old guy who wore a white tucked in shirt and beige chinos, with a dark brown leather belt. He had dark brown wavy hair, which was greying at the sides and a slight gut, but not greatly over-weight. Julie was a skinny woman of the same age with flowing brown shoulder-length hair and a long dress. She also had some grey hair beginning to show but still attractive for her age.

'Are you OK after the accident Lucy?' Ken asked with a genuine look of friendly concern.

'A bit sore but I'm fine thank you Ken,' Lucy replied with a polite smile. 'What can I get you? I'll order a couple of bottles of wine to start with, then we will look at the menus.'

'We don't expect you to pay for everything Lucy, we'll pay our share, we insist,' Julie said.

'I just really appreciate you helping me earlier. It's the least I can do.' Lucy replied, thinking Julie was probably right.

As the evening continued, they all loosened up and Ken turned out to be a successful business entrepreneur, and Julie his ex-PA who became particularly close, eventually marrying him. They were both great company and enjoyed the evening of loose talk, Lucy, although struggling after two bottles of wine, kept the truth to herself.

They said their goodbyes and hugged before leaving in opposite directions. Julie and Ken heading back to their hotel, and Lucy into town. She was up for a good night.

Barcelona was a hive of activity, and she was high on life. Walking up The Rambles, she felt relaxed and slightly drunk, looking for a bar to end the night in style. She walked into a small street to the right and found a lively bar with an Irish theme. Perfect. The music was loud, and the atmosphere was good. She immediately caught the eye of a group of English guys and she smiled to herself as she walked past, straight to the bar. As she stood waiting to be served, one of the English drunks staggered over and leaned on the bar next to her. He was swaying and grinning, clearly smashed but not realising that he was acting like it. Wearing long shorts and a black muscle vest with his shaved chest on show he stammered as he asked, 'Can I get you a drink love?' in a London accent.

'No thanks, I'll get my own. You should get some sleep,' Lucy said, staring at him.

He staggered back to his four mates, and they all laughed at him for being rejected, before they all left the bar. Lucy ordered a Bacardi and Diet Coke and sat on the bar stall. She noticed a tall, quiet guy sat alone at the end of the bar.

Ridiculously good looking with short fair hair, with a quiff at the front. He ordered a drink in Spanish and the bartender prepared a double vodka and lemonade for him with ice. She was intrigued by him as he seemed to not pay attention to anything, like he was in his own little world.

Lucy returned from the toilet and sat on a stall slightly closer to the guy. He acknowledged her presence by glancing at her and giving a subtle nod with a slight pursed-lipped smile before returning to his inner zone. Lucy was determined to get his attention and start a conversation. 'Do you speak English?' she asked.

He took his time and then slowly turned to Lucy and said in a broken accent, 'Yes, a little.'

'I'm Lucy' she said, extending her right hand.

'My name is Karl,' he said, shaking her hand gently. 'I am Swedish, here for the week on vacation from the army.'

Lucy felt a rush of excitement run through her body as he spoke. He was clearly super fit and ridiculously good looking. 'Can I get you a drink?' she said as she ordered herself another Bacardi and coke.

'OK, thank you,' Karl said.

They started talking and Lucy took a couple of sips of her drink. After ten-minutes, she felt totally out of it, like she had necked a bottle of whisky. Karl held her up as he bundled her into a taxi and sat next to her. As he did, he went through her hand-bag and found the hotel room card. He told the driver the hotel name and as they pulled in, he used her debit card to pay contactless. Karl helped her up the steps and asked the receptionist which room Lucy Gardener was staying in, and that he was helping her to the room.

He took her to the room and ensured the door was firmly closed. Not wasting any time, he slung her on the bed face down and reached up her long dress, removing her thong revealing her naked bum. He started undoing his belt as there was a loud knock on the door. He quickly pulled the dress down over Lucy's bum and buckled his belt, suppressing his erection as he opened the door. The receptionist and a security guard stood at the door asking in Spanish if Lucy was safe.

'She will be fine. I am going to look after her.' He said, attempting to close the door. The security guard shouted something in Spanish as he placed his foot against the bottom of the door and Lucy let out a drunken moan as she turned over on the bed. Karl brushed past him and left the room abruptly. 'You look after her then!' he shouted, as he headed down the corridor.

The security guard checked on Lucy as the receptionist stood at the door before they both left, closing the door gently.

Tyrone was setting up the main-sail under the watchful eye of Mike. He was loving the sailing and didn't want it to end, really enjoying Mike's teachings and his and Anne's company more than he ever imagined. Even taking over the night sailing duties.

'That's perfect mate. I'll leave you at the wheel and get some rest.' Mike shouted over the steady force 3 wind, which was taking them past the Portuguese coast at speed.

'OK Mate, no worries,' Tyrone answered as he headed for the stern, taking the wheel from Mike. As he stood leaning against the upturned seat, he gazed around himself. The main sail was full, the bow was cutting through the ocean which had a gentle swell. To his left, the coast of Portugal with the flickering lights about two miles away. He took a deep breath and fully appreciated everything. There was something about sailing at night that he really enjoyed.

Mike had been in the cabin for over five-minutes and Tyrone could faintly hear him and Ann having sex. Tyrone let out a sigh, as he could do with some action, but would not dare try anything with Ann. Mike would probably kill him and lose him overboard. There would not have to be an explanation as according to Spanish authorities, he did not exist. Best forget it and enjoy the sailing.

Chapter 30

Shelley arrived at the apartment and settled India down on the bed for an afternoon sleep, whilst she quietly unpacked. It was 28 degrees and there was a slight breeze from the sea. Shelley hung up the last of the clothes and took a shower before India woke up. She picked her up into her loving arms and sat on the balcony showing her the view before feeding her. As India finished her meal, Shelley's phone displayed a text message.

'Shelley, I have a Nanny coming over in the morning. Her name is Isabel, a local asset.'

Shelley's heart sank, and she held India close in, kissing her on the head, rocking gently from side to side.

Lucy woke up at 7:30 with a terrible hangover, trying to remember the night before but failing to get past the meal with her new friends, and then on to the Irish bar. She made a coffee and sat on the balcony trying her hardest not to throw up and line her stomach before going down for breakfast and facing everyone.

As she stood in the shower, she started vaguely remembering the guy she was chatting to at the bar. A good -looking Swedish soldier. She knew she had not had sex, as she would feel it, but when she woke, she was semi- naked and on top of the bed. It didn't feel good not knowing how she got there, or if anything else happened. She simply could not remember.

At 9:30 she took the lift to the ground floor, checking her appearance in the faded mirror above the line of buttons. She still had puffed eyes despite of all her efforts, and still felt dreadful. Hopefully a breakfast would help. The lift doors slid open to a bustling reception area with people checking in and out, suitcases everywhere and a security guard noticing her as she crossed and down the steps to the dining hall. He followed her and as she picked up a tray, patted her on the shoulder.

'Good morning, Miss Gardener. Are you OK?' he asked, not knowing how she would react.

'Hi, no I feel dreadful actually. Can I ask you something? Did you see me last night? It's just that I don't remember anything. I didn't drink that much but I was so out of it I can't even remember getting back.'

'I thought that was the case. You were literally carried in by some guy, and he was putting you to bed. I saw you both enter the hotel, and I was suspicious, so I came up to check on you. I think he was going to have sex with you while you were out of it, so I banged on the door. When I left you, I ensured you were laying on your side, so you were safe.'

Lucy had her hand on her mouth, holding back the tears as Alexandro spoke. He was in his forties, stern but friendly looking and wiry under his light blue security shirt.

'Thank you, Alexandro! Thank you so much!'

'That's fine Miss Gardener. Do you want me to inform the police?'

'No, don't worry. My fiancée will be here in a couple of days. He will sort him out,' she whispered.

Lucy had a light breakfast and four glasses of fruit juice and disappeared back to her room, where she stayed for most of the day, drifting in and out of sleep watching TV.

Shelley slept with India next to her, although she hardly closed her eyes. She spent most of the night watching India sleep, gently kissing her every so often. She had most certainly made up her mind that this was her last job for the firm and was going to take a back seat. More of an admin role, as she had told Jack she was already doing.

The morning came too soon it seemed, and at 7 am India was wide awake, talking gibberish in the cutest manner whilst Shelley was getting ready for the day ahead. She was pulling stretch jeans and trainers, and a loose t-shirt over a tight sports bra. Today was going to be busy, and she had to meet the locals for an update before planning the operation.

There was a gentle knock on the wooden door and Shelley said 'Hola,' from the hall.

A female voice came from behind the door 'Queen and Country.'

Shelley, concealing a sharp, small kitchen knife opened the door just enough to see that Isabel was alone. 'Hi Isabel, come in.'

Isabel entered and saw India laying on her belly on the floor playing with some toys. She gently knelt beside her and began to bond. Shelley's mind was put at ease. She briefed her on feeding and sleeping patterns and they took a walk, all three of them to the park. Isabel chose to push the buggy so that India would get used to seeing her.

Lucy was up early and heading to a viewing. The villa looked perfect on the brochure, just out of town and a private pool. Needing slight redecoration but that was exactly what she wanted. She walked down to catch the bus and noticed Shelley across the road, Picking India out of the buggy for a hug. 'What the hell is she doing here?' she thought, as Shelley handed India to another woman and walked off. Lucy observed from a distance and Shelley walked at a rate down the road towards the marina appearing to wipe a tear from her eye as she went. Meantime, the woman gently placed India back into the buggy and took a side street. Lucy followed from a distance, not knowing why she felt curious, but following her instincts.

Isabel pulled the keys out of her hand-bag and opened the door to the apartment block communal door. As she held the door with one arm, she pushed the buggy up the low step into the apartment block. As the door was closing a dark-haired, well-dressed woman entered the communal door and said 'Hola,' politely. Isabel pressed the lift button and waited with the woman waiting patiently behind her. The lift doors opened, and she pushed the buggy in, pressing the number 5. Lucy reached across and pressed number 6.

The lift doors opened at the 5th floor and Isabel backed the buggy out, smiling politely at Lucy who returned the gesture. The lift doors started to close, and Lucy waved her foot discreetly so that the doors reopened, so she could observe. Isabel did not notice as she pushed the key into the lock of room 517. Lucy hardly noticed as the lift doors opened at floor 6. She was stunned with confusion. She eventually pressed the GF button and left the building, walking slowly to the property agent preoccupied with scenario's, thinking that she and Tyrone were in trouble before he had even arrived.

Shelley had arrived at the restaurant on the marina at 9:50, as the meeting was planned for 10. She ordered a coffee and the waiter served it up and nodded politely as he left. She sat admiring the cruisers crammed in with little room between, and pontoons gently swaying as cleaning and maintenance staff carried out their duties. As she watched, a tall fair-haired figure was walking up the marina wearing a white cotton shirt and light brown chino's, expensive sunglasses and comfortable walking shoes.

'Hi Darren, how are you?' Shelley said, as she stood and gave him a gentle hug. 'How did you get on the other night?'

Darren let out a slight laugh. 'Not my type, Shell. But I have mastered the Swedish accent.'

They both laughed and headed into the back of the restaurant where Miguel was waiting. As they entered the private room, Miguel looked startled, even though he was expecting them both. The memories of their last engagement still affected him. 'Hi Shelley, Darren,' he said in a low, almost fearful voice.

'Hi Miguel, relax, no hard feelings. Let's all work together from now on, shall we?' Shelley said offering a hand-shake. 'I hear you have contacted Lucy. Hopefully did a bit of damage?'

'Yes, she went down hard, but no hospital treatment.' Miguel said shaking Shelley's hand with his eyebrows so high that his forehead resembled a ploughed field.

'Perfect, well done. Now, Tyrone O'Mally is on his way to Barcelona on a private yacht. He will be arriving in about three-days, and here is the plan,' Shelley said, producing a photo of Tyrone.

Gibraltar to the left, Morocco to the right. They were entering the Mediterranean. The temperature had become noticeably warmer, and Mike was stood at the wheel in his boxers. The mid-afternoon sun topping up his already bronze tan. Tyrone was sat in the cabin enjoying a coffee with Ann. They were chatting.

'Where are you heading after Barcelona?' Tyrone asked.

'We're planning to go across to Sardinia. Mike has friends there,' Ann answered with an air of excitement. She raised herself from the seat and reached down into the fridge and handed two beers to Tyrone, taking a third for herself.

Tyrone climbed the steps and handed Mike his beer and then they both joined him on deck. Tyrone was feeling slightly emotional as he knew it would be one of the last days at sea, and with Mike and Ann. He was enjoying their company far too much, and it showed. The feeling was mutual, as they really liked Tyrone too. His work ethic was really good and, although fairly quiet, really friendly. 'I'm going to miss this. I hope I'm going to like it in Barcelona. Lucy and I have had issues lately and I just hope we can get on in this new place,' he said, looking straight ahead.

'You'll be alright mate. Barcelona is a great place. One of my favourites. Apart from the jungles of Borneo. I need to go back after this trip for a few months to get some training in,' Mike said.

'Training in the jungle? What for?' Tyrone asked.

'I train the military there. I just love the environment. Proper survival.'

'Are you still in the military?' Tyrone asked.

'Yes, but part time now. I'm in 23 squadron SAS. I was in SBS for ten years and retired from full time service after Afghanistan. Now I am directing staff.'

Tyrone already knew but was still impressed. This is the first time Mike had spoken about the Special Forces and he stopped before giving too much away. Tyrone wanted to hear more, but Mike changed the subject each time it came up, looking at him as if to tell him not to ask. Tyrone got the message instantly and stopped the questioning. If it were anyone else, he would have driven them mad with his questions until he got what he wanted, but he respected Mike. The first man he had actually felt any respect for, probably ever.

Chapter 31

Entering the dock in Barcelona, Mike was in full concentration. Tyrone was in the cabin packing the last of his clothes into his back-pack and keeping his head down so the port authorities would not see him. Mike and Ann knew he did not have a passport, so they had agreed a discreet exit from the yacht. Mike manoeuvred the yacht into position before reversing into the designated space where it would be moored for the day whilst they picked up supplies and said their goodbyes to Tyrone.

'Hola,' Mike shouted, as the official approached the vessel. They held a conversation in Spanish and after the official checked Mike and Ann's passports, and taking a wad of cash, he strolled back to the port office, looking pleased with himself.

Mike told Ann to stay put and walked off the pontoon and headed towards town. He returned an hour later in a Chrysler Voyager which had blacked out windows at the rear, reversing it up to the mooring. Ann started loading bags into the back and then signalled to Tyrone, who, with his back-pack darted into the vehicle before Ann quickly closed the hatch door behind him, not checking if he was in safely or not. As she closed the hatch, she locked the cabin on the vessel and climbed into the passenger seat at the right of the voyager. Within a few seconds they were clear of the port and in the town. Ann was dropped off at a launderette and they checked their mobile phones were working before Mike drove off with Tyrone in the back, his back-pack on the seat next to him. A text message alert came up on Mike's phone, and he answered it whilst driving up through the town, towards the hills.

'Where are you taking me mate?' Tyrone asked, with a smile.

'I don't think it's safe to drop you in the centre of town at the moment mate. We'll go for a drive first. I've always wanted to see the mountains of Catalonia. Let's go up there for an hour or so, in case the authorities spotted us leaving the port,' Mike answered.

Tyrone thought it was a good idea but was also keen to see Lucy again. 'OK, sounds good,' he said, slightly disappointed.

They headed up the BV 1468 out of Barcelona and started climbing the hills, the Voyager not having any issues with the terrain or the steep inclines. Around 30-minutes after leaving the port, Mike pulled into a layby, which had a view of the city. It was deserted, apart from an old looking man sat on a rock at the side of the road, glancing at the car as it turned into the dusty track off the main road.

'I need a piss mate.' Mike said, looking in the rear-view mirror at Tyrone.

'I do too, actually.' Tyrone answered, feeling relieved to leave the car and stretch his legs.

They climbed out of the car and Tyrone walked to the left where the bushes were dense. He relieved himself and fastened his button flies before turning back towards the car. As he started to walk back there was an almighty 'bang' and then excruciating pain, like he had never felt before. He looked down and his left knee had been obliterated beyond recognition. He began to scream in agony as he fell to the floor. A skinny Spanish guy around 60 years old appeared into view holding a pistol in both hands. With that, he heard the Voyager start up and with a cloud of dust, it disappeared back the way they came.

After a few seconds, another tall guy appeared and with little effort, picked Tyrone up from under his arms and bundled him into another waiting vehicle. A transit van. Darren threw him into the back and fed him a pill, with water. Miguel and Darren climbed into the cab and drove further up the hill. Within ten minutes, Tyrone was unconscious, laying awkwardly in the back of the transit. Miguel climbed through to the back and strapped up Tyrone's leg, or what was left of it, and climbed back into the cab. 'Not time to die yet Mr. O'Mally,' he said with a pursed grin.

Lucy had viewed the villa and to her amazement it was perfect. She suddenly had an air of excitement again, just as she did when she first arrived. It was fast approaching 6 pm so she headed for the agreed bar to meet Tyrone, in case he had arrived that day. She ordered a large chardonnay and checked her mobile phone for messages. She was sat in a prominent table where she was able to see both ways down the street to look out for him.

The transit pulled up at an old looking villa which was surrounded by trees and shrubs. The dirt track leading to an open area where a BMW 5 Series was parked. The front door of the BMW swung open as the transit pulled in next to it, and Shelley climbed out from the passenger seat on the right. She walked over to the villa and as she approached, the door opened and two Spanish men emerged, both dressed in black. They walked over to the rear of the transit and opened the doors. Miguel and Darren climbed out of the cab and assisted with lifting Tyrone, who was unresponsive, and carrying him into the villa. They placed Tyrone onto a bed in the back room of the single storey house and stood waiting for Shelley to return from the bathroom.

Shelley appeared and took one look at Tyrone before marching over to him and punching him hard in the face. She saw red and was thinking of all the shit he had caused. The punch loosened one of Tyrone's front teeth, and he groaned slightly as his head fell to one side.

Lucy was losing hope of seeing Tyrone that night and settled the bill at 7:30. She had eaten a pizza and three large glasses of wine, so was feeling relaxed. Then she noticed a familiar figure. She ran across the bar and out onto the promenade. 'Ann!' she shouted.

Ann heard Lucy in the distance and walked faster. She would not know what to say to her so thought it best to get back into the private mooring quickly and pretend she had not heard Lucy call out. She walked briskly towards the vessel, and as she boarded, opened the hatch door and went straight down into the cabin, leaving the hatch open. She walked to the far side of the cabin and dropped the shopping on the floor. Sure enough, a pair of feet appeared, and Lucy climbed down into the cabin backwards. She turned around and as she saw Ann, she smiled and breathed in, just about to say something. As she opened her mouth, Mike's arm appeared and placed a rag over her mouth which stopped her voice and held her nose tightly. Within ten seconds she passed out and Mike placed her on the couch. He wasted no time and zip tied her hands behind her back, her ankles together and a gag around her head, across her open mouth. Then Ann placed a black hood over her head and a bed sheet over her whilst Mike was closing the cabin curtains. Mike climbed the steps and Ann followed him closing and locking the hatch behind her. They left the vessel and walked briskly up the pontoon and towards the town centre, Mike making a phone call on the way, informing Shelley of the capture.

Tyrone started to come around, and immediately the pain returned. His face was white and his eyes dark. Raising his head from the bed he could only see a faint light coming through a gap in the curtains and just make out the outline of the door frame opposite. He tried to move and as he did, the pain in his left leg was so great he let out a child-like scream, a tear running from each eye. He then realised his hands were tied to the bed posts and were numb. And his right leg was also tied to the bed frame, tightly. The bed was cold and wet where he had urinated in his sleep and the stench of flesh and urine was intense enough to make him feel nauseous. He tried to break the zip ties around his wrists, but they just dug in, almost cutting into his skin.

Ten minutes after Tyrone came around, he heard someone turn a key in the door and his heart jumped. The door handle went down, and bright light filled the room as the door swung open with a gentle screech. The light above the bed came on and Shelley entered the room looking straight at Tyrone, with a disgusted look on her face, as the stench hit her nostrils.

'Remember me?' she asked, as she walked around to Tyrone's side, with a confident swagger.

Tyrone paused for a couple of seconds, recognising her but trying to recall where from. 'Yes, but… I… What have I ever done to you?' he asked with a look of despair on his face.

'Well, how long have you got? I'm in no hurry, I'll tell you everything you've done to me and my friends and family. Let's start with that slapper you were engaged to. She slept with my brother telling him she was single. You then beat fuck out of her, and your best mate nearly killed him with a barstool.' She stopped talking, produced a baseball bat from her side, and hit his already unrecognisable left knee hard.

Tyrone screamed for a minute or two before calming

down, hyper ventilating. 'I'm sorry, I'm sorry, please stop, I'm begging you!'

'Ok, calm down.' Shelley said gently. 'Cast your mind back to Barnstaple. A man in a JCB who died in a fire in his cab on the roadside. Do you know anything about that?'

'No! I don't know what you are talking about! I… They tried to kill me by burying me alive! I didn't kill anyone I swear I don't know what…'

Shelley hit him hard in the leg again. Tyrone was screaming loud, his head thrashing from side to side and his eyes streaming. 'Miguel, go and get Lucy. See what she has to say.' Miguel gave a nod and left in the BMW.

'How about a nice evening down the pub in Barnstaple? Did you go for a piss down a side street and bump into another friend of mine by any chance? You know, the one where you poked his eye out before stabbing him, a bit like this.' Shelley stuck a sharp middle finger- nail into Tyrone's right eye, not quite hard enough to do too much damage, but enough to hurt, badly. She then pulled a small paring knife from her pocket and stabbed him in the stomach, just deep enough to hurt badly, but not enough to cause too much damage.

Tyrone was crying like a baby. He knew at this point that he was going to die, and it was going to be painful. 'Just end it now! Kill me now!' he said loudly.

'How about the farmhouse? Lucy's auntie was in bed at the time, but you knew that didn't you? She didn't stand a chance, did she? Was it all part of the plan? Chris dead, Theresa dead, the inheritance going to their favourite niece? Now here you both are starting over in Barcelona. How convenient.'

Tyrone looked at her through his tear-filled eyes. 'What inheritance? I don't know anything about it!'

Shelley's face trembled with anger, and she raised the bat and hovered it over Tyrone's knee, gently raising it.

'NO! I SWEAR I DON'T KNOW ABOUT THE MONEY!' he shouted, with a look of sheer terror across his face, eyes bulging, with his right eye swollen and red. 'Alright, I did cause the explosion, but I thought the house was empty,' he said, eye-brows raised, trying his best to convince Shelley, who was looking at him menacingly, with the baseball bat raised ready to strike. 'What do you want? If you want the money, get hold of Lucy and she will pay up! She wanted us to be together, she wouldn't care about the money.'

Shelley hit both knees with all her strength.

Lucy started to come around. It was dark and the yacht was gently bobbing on the water. She knew immediately that she had been restrained as she couldn't move without the plastic digging into her wrists and ankles. She was breathing heavily through her nose and her mouth was drooling over the cotton gag which she was trying to bite, hoping it would break. No chance. She felt the edge strip of the couch behind her and went to work on the zip ties around her wrists, and bit by bit, tearing at the plastic. By then, Mike and Ann were at the airport, checking in for a flight back to East Midlands airport. Their work was done, and payment had been made.

After an hour Lucy had broken the zip tie binding her wrists together and she struggled but managed to untie the gag before working on her ankle tie. She reached into the kitchen drawer hoping to find a sharp knife but there were only blunt ones, but better than nothing. Ten minutes later she was free. She escaped the cabin and walked briskly off the pontoon and onto the street, trying not to attract too much attention. Thinking what to do next. They must have Tyrone. He might be hurt, or worse. She began to panic and sat on a bench holding her head. 'The baby!' she said out loud, then glanced around hoping no one heard, or understood.

She remembered the exact apartment block where Shelley's friend had taken her, and it was about a five-minute walk. She set off and dodged through the crowds of tourists and street sales-persons and got to the apartment block at 10:20 pm. The entry door was locked, and the trade button was deactivated at this time of night, so she waited. Shure enough, a guy came past and used his key to open the entrance door, and Lucy followed him in, heading for the lift. The guy pressed floor 7, and Lucy reached over and pressed 5. As the lift doors opened, Lucy cautiously walked down the corridor, checking that the lift had gone before knocking on 517.

'Hola?' the voice behind the door said gently.

'It's Shelley. Hi,' Lucy said loudly.

The chain was removed from the door, and it swung open. As soon as Lucy saw Isabel, she kicked the door hard, and punched her in the face, sending her backwards onto the sofa. Lucy slammed the door closed and could not resist but to punch her victim another four times, hard in the face, making her nose and lips bleed as she lay there delirious and barely conscious. Lucy sat her up and slapped her across the face. 'Where have they taken Tyrone, you fucking bitch?'

'I don't know! I'm just the babysitter!' she answered, crying.

Lucy laid into her, punching her in the face and ribs repeatedly. Then stood up and walked into the second bedroom, picking India from her cot. 'She gets it if you don't tell me!' she said, grabbing a kitchen knife from the drawer.

'NO!' Isabel screamed. 'They have a villa in the hills, past the Olympic village and it's called Villa Barras.' She gave detailed directions and pointed to the set of car keys on the shelf.

Lucy grabbed the keys, Isabel's mobile phone and left with India still asleep on her arm.

She walked down the street pressing the unlock button until a red SEAT Ibiza's hazard lights flashed, and the doors unlocked. There was a baby seat in the back, which was complicated, but she sorted it out eventually. She drove up through the town centre trying not to break the speed limit which was difficult because of how anxious she was feeling. Twenty minutes later she slowly drove past the villa and carried on another 50 metres to a lay by. She took India and slowly walked to the villa, which appeared at first to be empty until she got close. There was talking inside and music playing. She banged on the door and ran back towards the wall, stood on it which was a sheer drop behind of over 30 metres. The door swung open and Darren peered out, one hand concealing a pistol behind him. As he saw Lucy, he raised his head in surprise, then he saw she was holding a baby, which worried him.

'Where's Tyrone?' she asked loudly. 'I want to see him!'

'Shelley, come here!' Darren shouted, over his shoulder. As he did, he walked out holding the pistol up. But not pointing directly at Lucy.

'What's up Dar?' Shelley said as she appeared through the door, and immediately froze. 'India! You fucking lay one finger on her you fucking bitch!'

'Give me Tyrone or I will kill her. I swear!'

Shelley was scared. Her baby was in danger, and she had limited options. Her worst nightmare was unfolding in front of her. 'OK, just come down from the wall, then we can talk.' She said, her voice cracking.

'You take one more step bitch!' Lucy shouted, waking India who started crying and moving her arms.

Shelley held her face. After a few seconds, she turned to Darren and said, 'Get Tyrone.'

Darren disappeared into the villa and a minute later returned with Tyrone in a fireman's lift over his right shoulder. He had redressed his leg and tidied him up after injecting him with ketamine to sedate him before round 2 of Shelley's torture. Darren eased Tyrone onto the floor and placed him into the recovery position and then standing back.

'There you go, have him. Now just give me my baby!'

'No, not yet. I have some questions. First what happened to his leg?' Lucy said, rocking gently from side-to-side. 'What's up with him? Is he dead?'

'No, he's sedated to control the pain. He fell over and smashed his knee on the journey. Give me my baby!' Shelley yelled, stepping forward.

'Stop or I'll jump!' Lucy screamed. Why are you doing this? Why can't you just leave us alone to start over? I've done nothing to you!'

'We know what you did, Chris and Theresa were good people who did everything for you. Why did you want to do that to them? Just for money?' Shelley said desperately. 'It's a mob thing. I'm working for someone who Chris was involved with, and they want Tyrone taken out for the killings.'

Lucy was shaking her head in disbelief. 'No. Tyrone didn't kill them. Chris died of a heart attack working late on the farm. Theresa…' She paused.

'Yes. The gas explosion. It was Tyrone who killed Theresa. Knowing you were going to be the benefactor to the estate. Did you really think you'd get away with it? We have assets worldwide Lucy. You can't outrun us. Give me my baby!'

Lucy's legs were weakening, and she was looking unsteady on the wall. This made Shelley even more worried. She was sobbing loudly with tears running down her face, looking straight at Shelley. 'Get away from me!' she shouted, as Shelley too another two steps forward. She looked across to Darren who was holding a pistol with both hands, pointing it downwards, with an alert look on his face.

Darren's mobile rang, and he reached into his back pocket to answer it.

'Leave it!' Lucy shouted, over India's crying. Thinking about what to do next.

'What are you going to do, harm an innocent baby?' Darren said gently. 'That baby has done nothing to harm anyone. She has her whole life ahead of her. DO you really want to hurt her?'

Lucy was visibly distraught and could not cope with the situation. Her knees were becoming increasingly weaker, and she was feeling weak and unbalanced. The wall she was standing on was over two feet thick, but there was a sheer drop behind her into woodland. If she fell it would be difficult to get to her, or the baby. Shelley was breathing heavily, her heart racing with stress and she was trembling from head- to- toe. 'Come down Lucy, Come down from the wall. We will let you go, both of you. I promise. Just come down. You don't want to fall backwards it will be the most painful way to go love.' She said calmly.

Lucy's legs buckled, and she regained her balance. Shelley screamed, and lurched forward, then back. She held her arms out as if to hold them and sobbed loudly.

'Put the gun down,' Lucy said with a shaky voice.

Darren reached in front of him and placed the pistol on the ground and stepped back. Knowing that the safety catch was off, and it was ready to go if needed. As he stepped back, Tyrone let out a groan and moved his head to the side, his eyes closed and mouth open.

Hearing Tyrone's voice assures Lucy that he was alive, but not sure how badly hurt he was. 'Go into the villa and put the key in the outside of the lock. When you're both in there, stand in the kitchen window where I can see you both. Any fucking about and I will throw your precious baby over the wall!' I'm staying on this wall until I know

you're all in and the door is closed. Kick the gun over here!'
she shouted over India's screaming.

Darren did what he was told, being careful as he knew
that if he kicked it a certain way, he would discharge a
bullet. Then he and Shelley backed into the villa and put the
key in the outside of the lock and closed the door, heading
straight to the kitchen window where they could see Lucy
and Tyrone.

Lucy stayed on the wall for a minute, observing and
ensuring that they were still in sight and not playing games.
She slowly and gently lowered herself off the wall and walked
over to the pistol, pointing it at India's head as she walked
towards Tyrone, glancing at the window where she could
see Shelley in floods of tears, and Darren staring outside
with his arm around her. Lucy crouched down with India
still on her right arm, pistol in her left hand over Tyrone's
face and shook his head to wake him up, dropping the pistol
as she did it. BANG!

Chapter 32

'NO!' Shelley yelled, as she ran out of the kitchen and burst through the front door of the villa. It was silent outside, and the fear had gripped her. She ran over to find Lucy collapsed onto Tyrone and India. She grabbed Lucy's hair but as she pulled her hand slipped away and was instantly covered in blood. She grabbed her by the head and pulled her away finding India underneath and stared in horror. Then India let out a whimper and smiled at Shelley.

Darren appeared at their side and Miguel walked across the courtyard with a pistol in his right hand. Darren looked down and noticed his pistol still on Tyrone's chest, so he removed it quickly. As he did, he looked at Lucy and saw the bullet wound in the side of her skull just above her right ear.

Shelley was sat on the floor clutching India, crying her heart out as Miguel patted her on the shoulder. She pulled herself together, looked up and said, 'Thank you Miguel.'

Darren turned to Shelley. 'Do you want to finish the job, Shell?'

'With pleasure Dar!' She said with a frown, swapping the gun for India. She pointed it at Tyrone's forehead and without hesitation pulled the trigger twice.

She didn't look back as she took India back who was

not bothered by the gunshot noise, and disappeared back into the villa to clean up, as Miguel and Darren carried the bodies to the ditch, they had prepared the day before.

After 30 minutes, the bodies were fully buried, and the grass seed spread with hoses ready for their daily irrigation. Shelley was cleaned up and India was fast asleep. Darren drove them out of the courtyard and back to Barcelona. They arrived at the apartment at 1:30 and Shelley entered to find Isabel covered in blood and asleep on the sofa. She quietly put India to bed, closed her bedroom door and knelt next to Isabel gently waking her up. Isabel breathed in deeply as she opened her eyes. As soon as she saw Shelley she burst into tears. Shelley held her in her arms and said 'It's OK. Everything's OK,' as Isabel was hysterically trying to explain.

Shelley bathed Isabel's swollen bloodied lips and nose and showed her India asleep in bed, to put her mind at rest. 'I'm sorry that you had to go through that.' She said, hugging her again. 'Why don't you stay here tonight. That must have been a shock.'

The morning came and Shelley woke early and checked on India. She was still asleep and looked more beautiful than ever. The sense of relief was incredible, knowing that she had completed all the nasty work with the firm. There was just one more thing. Confessing to Jack. She felt it would be important that they had no secrets, and that it really was all over with the mob now. She opened her laptop and logged in to her work emails, not paying any attention to the inbox, but straight to compose. 'Andrew, I have finished my work so if OK with you, taking the day off.' This was the mission accomplished code, which was likely to be seen by others in the company.

A reply came back within seconds. 'Well done, Shelley, yes that's fine.'

A few minutes later her mobile rang. 'Hi Andrew.'

'Hi Shelley, I hear things almost went to shit? Are you OK love?' Andrew asked, with genuine concern.

'Yes, it was intense, but we got there in the end. The main thing is we're all OK and the job is done. Just a couple of transactions to finish off then We can talk about the finances.'

'Yes, definitely. You know that we'll look after you, don't you Shelley?'

'Yes, I know you will, Thanks Andrew,' Shelley said before ending the call.

Isabel woke up and walked into the kitchen where Shelley was filling a cafetiere with boiling water, the smell of fresh coffee filling the air. They greeted each other with a smile and Isabel brushed her hair back with her hands. 'What are you doing today? I was not expecting you back for another two days so I could look after India for you.'

'Let's all go out together. I need to go to the bank and sort something out, then shall we go to the beach for the day and catch some sun?'

'OK, that sounds lovely' Isabel said, pleasantly surprised.

They headed out towards the town centre and Shelley entered the bank and came out 20 minutes later whilst Isabel and India sat in the park opposite in the shade. Shelley looked content and pleased with herself but did not talk about why. As they walked towards the beach, her phone rang and she answered it, leaving Isabel to push the buggy about ten metres ahead of her so she could take the call privately.

'Hi Andrew, Is everything OK?'

'Yes Shelley, everything is in order thanks to you. Listen, on behalf of the company, we'd like to offer you a bonus. Having paid Miguel, Darren, Mike, Ann and some of the other security staff, informers and legal eagles, you will be paid £850,000. Is that OK?'

Shelley stopped walking and stood stunned on the pavement. 'Thank you, Andrew. That's more than OK, that's amazing.'

'We owed you for previous jobs as well so we decided that this figure would cover it all. Enjoy your break love, see you soon. Take a break from the office Shelley, you need to have some family time. I want you to take as long as you want, you deserve it. You tell me if, and when you want to come back. There will always be a job here waiting for you if you want it. We will all miss you in the company, but we will get by. Do what is right for you, Jack and India love.' Andrew ended the call.

The day at the beach was lovely, and all three of them had a great time. Shelley slipped into day-dreams occasionally and Isabel couldn't work out why but chose not to ask. Shelley asked Isabel to apply sun cream to her back as she lay on a sun lounger and Isabel did so but enjoyed it more than Shelley knew. Especially around her bikini line which seemed to take ages. Her hands seemed to be spreading sun cream all over her bum for ages, until Shelley raised her head and looked over her shoulder. Isabel stopped immediately and felt instantly awkward.

'That was nice.' Shelley said, to make her feel better, although she actually felt slightly awkward herself. The rest of the afternoon was slightly different, but Shelley managed to keep the friendly atmosphere going, albeit slightly quiet.

As they entered the apartment Shelley jolted backwards in shock, then her face lit up.

'Surprise!' Jack said, with a bunch of flowers in one hand, and a bottle of prosecco in the other.

'Jack!' she screamed, as she threw herself at him. 'Oh my god! What a lovely surprise!' as she said it, she was thinking how lucky she was with the timing.

'Oh, hi. I don't think we've met.' Jack said, smiling at Isabel.

'This is Isabel, the nanny. I hired her in as I had some work to finish off yesterday.'

Isabel looked gutted but sucked it in and politely nodded at Jack before disappearing into the bedroom to pack her bag, holding back the tears. She reappeared with her bag over her shoulder a couple of minutes later and kissed India on the forehead before saying goodbye to Shelley and waving politely to Jack.

'I'm just going to see Isabel to her cab. Give me a minute love.' Shelley said and followed Isabel out of the apartment and into the lift. As the lift door closed, Shelley grabbed her and kissed her on the lips for a whole minute before the lift doors opened at the ground floor. They walked holding hands to the main door and Shelley handed her an envelope containing 1000 Euro's. 'You'll get the rest directly into your bank account, including a new car. You were fantastic, please stay in touch.'

Shelley watched as Isabel walked down the street, wiping her eyes. As she disappeared, she returned to the lift and as the doors closed took a deep breath and closed her eyes. Entering the apartment, she closed the door and Jack was dancing around the lounge with India elevated in his hands, giggling.

'Jack, there's something I need to tell you,' Shelley said, nervously.

'I know. I have always known.' Jack interrupted. 'My managing director, Kurt. He tells me everything. I also know that it's all over and that you have promised that there are no more jobs,' Jack said, still dancing, not wanting to look at her. 'I have something to tell you.'

Shelley's blood went cold. 'What is it?' she asked, worried.

'The company has fallen into trouble. One of the other directors took on a major project with an aerospace company and lost a fortune. They have called in the administrators. I might not be going back.'

Shelley was silent for a minute. 'Let's stay here for a while longer. Think things through.'

Kurt was sat at home considering retirement now that the company was liquidated. He was in the lounge watching something uninteresting on the TV and an email came up on his phone. It was Joe from another engineering company with good contacts. 'Hi Kurt, can we meet for a drink? I have a proposal for you.'

They arranged for the Thursday night in a pub called the trout in Keynsham, which meant that Kurt would need to drive from his home in Emerson's Green, around the ring road. He arrived at 7:30 as planned and Joe was already there, and had a job offer for a senior project manager for him, which they discussed until 10:30. Kurt was interested, as he had already become bored being at home for the last three weeks.

They said their goodbyes and Kurt drove his Mercedes E-class through Keynsham, past the rugby club, and onto the ring road. The weather was good, and although dark, quite warm, being mid-July. He stopped at the roundabout traffic lights at Warmley and when they turned green, he accelerated and carried on, not noticing the scaffold truck behind him. Keeping to the speed limit, he reached some road works before the next roundabout which caused all the traffic to come to a stop. The scaffold truck behind him came very close, and there was an excavator in the cordoned-off road works to his right. There was a concrete wagon in front of him which was blocking the way forward, and a lay by to the left. There was a tap on the window, and a man with a high vis and hard hat said, 'Excuse me mate, can I have a word?'

Kurt pressed the button, and the window came down. In a split second, the barrel of a silenced pistol was produced, and the bullet went through his brain. Two other men appeared, opening the driver's door and carried the body into the boot. The assassin took off the high vis and hard hat and climbed into the passenger seat of a waiting black land rover discovery sport. Andrew looked across. 'Good work Chris, welcome back.'

Chris looked straight ahead with the pistol resting on his lap.

'You can put the gun away now Chris,' Andrew said, looking concerned.

Chris turned and looked at Andrew with a stone-cold expression.

The end.